PRAISE FOR NIC

A WALKER IN 1

◇◇◇◇◇◇◇◇◇◇◇◇◇◇◇

"Nick Owchar gives us an absorbing novel about how we struggle to come to terms with past mistakes and often don't. This is a well-told tale combining an English gothic story with glimpses of life in a Ukrainian village that is worth the time of all readers who enjoy such stories."
 – **Philippa Gregory**, author of *The Other Boleyn Girl*, *The White Queen*, and other novels

"A tale of supernatural menace and mysterious destiny set in 19th-century London and Eastern Europe and featuring a cast of darkly sinister and memorable characters... Nick Owchar's clever narration is captivating and often surprising, and his tale is certain to raise a chill in the reader now and again!"
 —**Richard Zimler**, author of *The Last Kabbalist of Lisbon* and *The Incandescent Threads*

"Here is a wide-ranging tale, deploying both the present tense and the reconstructed past. Moving from mediaeval Galicia—now absorbed into the struggling nation of Ukraine—it focuses on 19th century London and the pre-Raphaelite circle of Dante Gabriel Rossetti and Algernon Charles Swinburne. Nick Owchar makes us privy to the inner esoteric workings of the 'Supramundane'; there are imps and spirits and beneficent totems at work and dangerous play throughout this adventure. Which is, finally, the haunting account of a son's hunt for his father. As Owchar's narrator suggests, 'The word "extraordinary" risks becoming meaningless in my story, but that's the best way to describe our meeting.' And the novel too."
 —**Nicholas Delbanco**, author, most recently, of *Why Writing Matters* and *Still Life at Eighty: A Memoir*

"A Walker in the Evening is a novel about a return. As such, it is an uncommon book about a character going back to the land left behind by his father. Nick Owchar reverses the traditional progression from the Old World to the New, that of the exiles who fled the horrors of the first half of the 20th century in Europe for America. He takes us back to the eye of the storm as the black clouds were gathering over Ukraine and the rest of the world. So vivid is the writing that you accompany Owchar as he is giving life to his world and the characters that populate it, with such a faithful immediacy that you almost sense he is fashioning them out of the earth and the world he so lovingly describes, the same muddy terrain — the rasputitsa or bezdorizhzhia — where Russian tanks stalled as they invaded Ukraine in 2022. The grand history and micro-history seamlessly woven into this plot convey a keen sense of urgency about the gathering storm that would soon befall that part of the world in the decades ahead."

—**Avedis Hadjian**, journalist, critic, and author of *Secret Nation: The Hidden Armenians of Turkey*

"With A Walker in the Evening, Nick Owchar gives us a novel rich in history, suspense and psychological complexity. Against a backdrop that mixes the occult and folklore with a richly evoked historical background, the protagonist, caught between faith and mystery, struggles with identity, redemption and the search for belonging. A wonderful read that makes us reflect on the choices we make and the paths we take toward finding our true selves."

—**Ross King**, historian and author of *The Bookseller of Florence, Brunelleschi's Dome, Ex-Libris,* and other books

About the Author

Nick Owchar is former deputy editor of books coverage and a columnist ("The Siren's Call") for the *Los Angeles Times.* His writing has appeared in numerous publications and publishing outlets, including the *Los Angeles Review of Books, Kirkus Reviews,* and Chronicle Books.

I hope you enjoy walking in my village (be careful!).
Best wishes,

A WALKER
in the EVENING

A NOVEL

NICK OWCHAR

Nick Owchar
6/2025

RUBY VIOLET
PUBLISHERS

RUBY VIOLET - PUBLISHERS
GREEN BAY ~ LOS ANGELES ~ CHICAGO

RUBY VIOLET
PUBLISHERS

www.rubyviolet-publishers.com
An imprint of Samson Strong, LLC
32 N Gould St, Ste. R
Sheridan, WY 82801

Illustration: "Evening in Ukraine" (1901) by Konstantin Kryzhitsky.
https://www.wikiart.org/en/konstantin-kryzhitsky/evening-in-ukraine

Cover art and design, and map of Prehovinka
by Jay Toffoli Design Co.
www.jaytoffoli.com

ISBN: 979-8-9917863-0-0

Text set in Baskerville

MADE IN THE USA
8 7 6 5 4 3 2 1 0

For Coco

◇◇◇◇◇◇◇◇

moye sertse

Light up the torch of the pale moon in the sky,
illuminate the darkness of the night with stars,
let hearts that are sick with loneliness take comfort
when they see thousands of Your worlds.

  – Bohdan Ihor Antonych (1932)
   (Translated by Michael M. Naydan)

Contents

◇◇◇◇◇◇◇◇

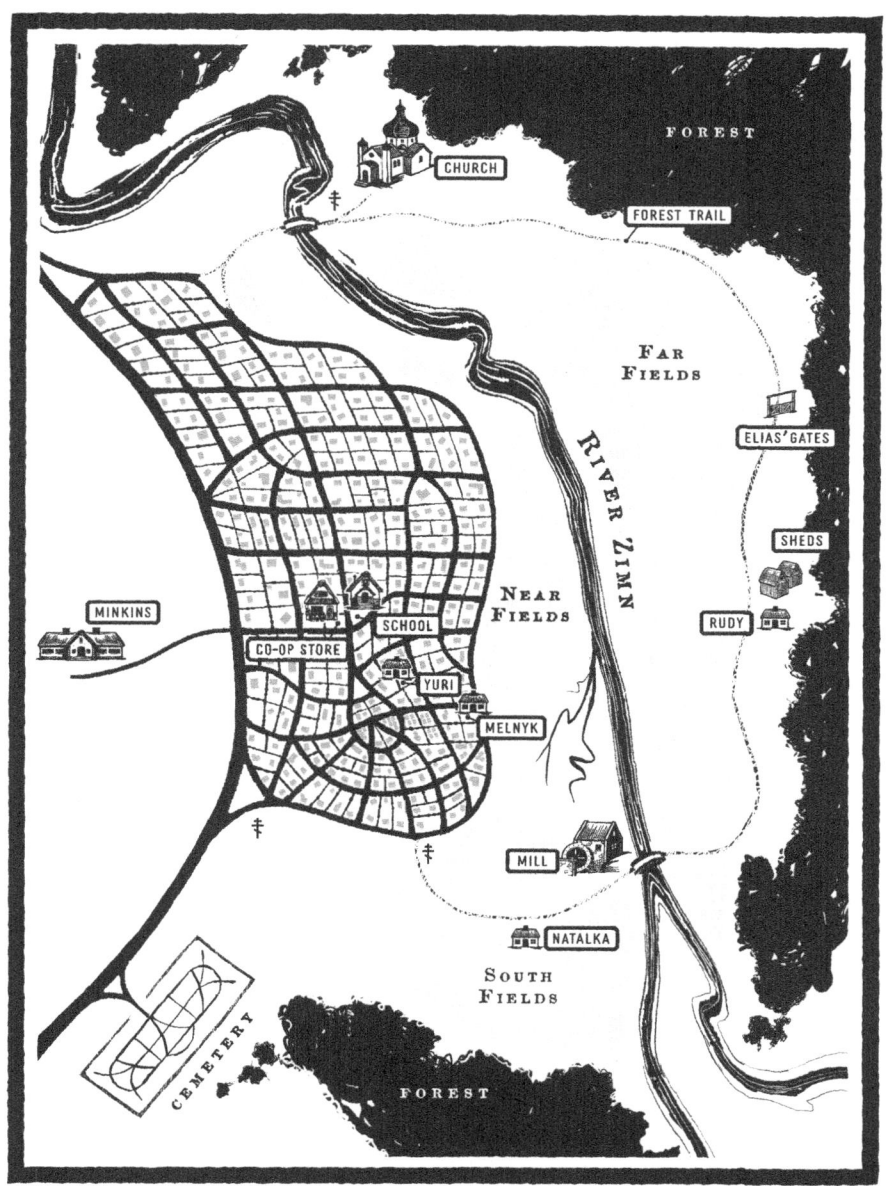

PREHOVINKA

GALICIA ~ 1909

1

◇◇◇◇◇◇◇

Setting out

Galicia
Austro-Hungarian Empire
1909

8:00 p.m.

IT ISN'T THE WIND THAT WAKES ME. I'm dozing on the rug by the fire, dreaming of falling leaves, when I hear a thudding sound. It's right outside our kitchen door. I get up and walk over to the window.

I'm just in time to see Ivan Sturanka leaving our yard. I recognize his large silhouette as he's slinking away in the gloom. He walks up the gravel path to the front and crosses into his own yard through a break in the fence. He's limping. Probably because of his new boots. I told him not to wear them, but he's stubborn. He'd rather do things his own way than take my advice.

As he disappears into his house, I rub my back and look at the porch. There's something huddling in the corner. *Hello there. It's time again, isn't it? Haven't seen you in a while.* Eugenie comes up behind me. She clears her throat.

"Here," she says. "You should go before it gets late. Unless you've changed your mind. You know you still can."

I turn. She's already holding our small oil lamp in one hand, my greatcoat in the other. The coat's two pockets belly out; she's stuffed them with fresh cherries and good black bread, an old flask I've had for years, and some other useful things. She wishes one of the boys would take my place.

"I know, but I want to, *diwchata*," I tell her. "Listen, this is something I have to do. I said before, I need—"

"I know what you said. You don't have to tell me again," she says, frowning. "You need your time *to think*."

I ignore her tone.

"Don't worry about me. I'll be fine." I want to kiss her before I go, but when I bend toward her, she doesn't offer me her cheek. She looks away. I don't want to start off the night this way.

"Listen, I want you to know I'm sorry. I didn't mean it. Any of it. I'm sorry for upsetting you. Can we talk about this tomorrow?"

She shrugs.

"We can talk whenever you like." Her tone isn't very encouraging. "See you in the morning." She hands me my things and goes into the kitchen.

YEARS AGO, I performed the night walk several times a year. I was young, and I liked it. It was new to me, and it's easy to like something when it's new. I found the whole practice interesting and useful. It was a good way to get to know the village. I took along a pencil and some paper and scratched out a crude little map. I noted everything that seemed important: the co-op store, the schoolhouse, the cobbler, the bridges by the church and mill, the best ways in and out of the fields, the locations of several wells, the part of the cemetery where my family is buried. I never threw the map away. It's somewhere in my books and papers. It didn't take long to become well acquainted with the village because I was walking on many nights. We all were. We didn't have a choice. A bad wave of typhus had come through, and too many people were sick. The rest of us had to make it up.

Everything's different now. The village has recovered to its former size—we have about three hundred families, a thousand souls, living in four square miles, including the fields—and my family's obligation happens once or twice a year. It's hard to complain about something that infrequent. Our turn usually comes in the late spring anyway. The rains of April are over, the alders are greening, and the evenings are cool but not cold. The nights are perfect. This is the best weather that we have all year.

I stand in the doorway and put on my coat. I smell the air and look up. The sky's dark. Dusted with stars. Thousands of them. More than I could ever count. Our turn's come later this time, in June. I can't say why it's later, but it's all right. Sometimes this just happens. Leo's up in the sky now; Regulus winks in his chest. "The stars are lanterns held by our loved ones," Eugenie once told me. "Your mother and father are up there. Mine are, too."

I go on the porch and pick up the totem. He stares at me with a devilish grin. I'm careful not to poke myself in the eye with one of his horns. When this little fellow lands at your door, it's your family's turn for the walk. But it's more than just a simple reminder. If it were only used for that, we wouldn't need it. A flag or a scarf passed from house to house would be enough. The first time Sturanka left it for me, I didn't see it and walked right past it out of the yard. I was well down the main road by the time Eugenie caught up to me. "Wait," she called out, breathless. I didn't even hear her running; she was barefoot. Didn't bother to slip on her shoes. She moved as stealthily as a cat. I shined the lamp on her. "Here," she said, handing the totem to me. "This needs to go with you. You're not supposed to walk without it."

WHEN I LEAVE the yard, clouds are crowding on the horizon like penned sheep, and the wind's picking up. The breeze feels warm on my face. Warm and damp. A summer storm is coming. *Well, don't come too soon.*

While the two outer pockets of my greatcoat are stuffed with food and drink, a pouch Eugenie sewed on the inside (which I'm sure would horrify the clothiers at Baker's, where my mother bought it years ago for my father) carries several other things I might need tonight: a handful of garlic cloves large and smooth as river stones and some clipped pieces of wormwood tied with string in tight little bundles. I'm also bringing some old letters and papers with me. They're from my former life. They might help with the thinking Eugenie doesn't understand.

I make the sign of the cross as I pass one of the little sheltered cruci-fixes standing at every crossroad in Prehovinka. I forget and make it the Catholic way, from left to right shoulder. It's done the opposite way here. Sometimes I still forget during the Sunday liturgy. Roman doesn't care, but some still give me dirty looks.

I turn right, taking the road west out of the village. It runs white between two fields like a part in someone's hair. After about a mile, it joins up with the main road, which is where I turn right again—turn left, and you'll be headed in the direction of Stanislau, the nearest city. I start walking up the main road next to the village. Long broken sections of fencing lean along the roadside, and the houses sit right up against them. The fencing is sorry-looking; it wouldn't give anyone much trouble to slip through the gaps and sneak into one of the yards. But that's why I'm out tonight; that's the point of this duty. I'm here to discourage that sort of thing. And if I'm unsuccessful, if I'm not intimidating enough, there's something else that is—just about every yard here has a big unfriendly hound chained up outside. They bark and howl at the slightest provoca-tion. I don't think I'd ever get a good night's sleep if we lived over here.

All the houses are dark except for a few with candles shining on their windowsills. The little points of light mark the route ahead. I know this way well. From a distance, with the night sky above them, the candle flames look like stars low on the horizon. Each time the wind blows, my lamp flickers, and the leaves of the beech trees tinkle overhead like tiny bells.

On the other side of the road is a big empty field. Nothing's been planted there in a long time. Beyond it shine the tiny yellow lights of the manor house. The whole house is lit up. From here, it looks like a distant ship. The Minkins live there. They act like gentry, though they're just ten-ants themselves. Count Gradwolski uses them to manage village business.

I'm hardly twenty paces up the road when a voice calls out of the darkness. My heart skips a beat. I can't see who it is.

"You there. Stop where you're going. Stop right now."

It's one of the Minkin boys. It sounds like Jacob, the oldest.

"Hello? Jacob? Is that you?"

He comes up onto the road on his horse. When he reaches me, I can feel the heat coming off the horse's flanks. He's been riding around after dark. That's fine if you stay on the main roads but not if you go in the fields. You can ruin a good horse that way.

"Who's speaking? Identify yourself. Now."

I hold the lamp up to my face.

"Oh, it's you," he says. His tone changes, softens a little. "Yuri. So you've got the watch tonight?"

"Yes."

Jacob's in his early twenties. He has a thick black beard. He wears it to make himself look older, but it doesn't work. He's got soft pink cheeks and mild blue eyes. A baby's face, even with a beard. I've found that he's the kindest member of their family when it comes to the villagers. He's talkative and curious; sometimes he seems almost empathetic about our lives. He speaks Polish to me, and I answer him in Ruthenian; they're cousin languages, close enough that we can understand each other.

"That means you have that . . . thing with you, too, right?"

I shine the lamp on it.

"Yes, of course. Anyone with the night duty has to, Jacob," I say. "You should know that by now."

His horse takes a sudden step back.

"That's enough," he says. "Put it away. You're scaring Asher. For God's sake."

"I'm sorry." I put the lamp down and hide the totem in the folds of my coat. "I didn't mean to. You did ask me if I had it."

It takes him a moment to settle Asher down. The horse snorts and nervously shifts its hooves in the dirt. I hear him mutter to himself, "Damn superstitions."

"What's that, Jacob? I didn't hear what you said."

"Nothing. Never mind."

I always like talking to him. I never have to use any flattery. No special words or courtesy. Just plain talk like I use with my sons. It's the same with his brothers. I treat them all the same whenever they ride out to check on us in the fields. If I'm busy digging and see one of their shadows come up, I'll ignore it and keep digging. If I'm talking to someone and one of them tries to interrupt, I'll hold up my hand and make them wait. No one else in Prehovinka would dare, not even Father Roman. But it's my special status as an Englishman and the fact that Gradwolski likes having me in the village that permits me to be impertinent. I'm as exotic to the count as a white leopard. The Minkins know that. But tonight, Jacob seems irritated. He's too on edge to mind himself with me. I can hear it in his voice. It makes me wary.

"I'm surprised to see a man your age out here tonight," he says.

"Really? Why is that?" A man my age. The nerve.

"You've got grown sons, don't you? They should be doing this for you. Like David, Bram, and me. You don't see our old man ever dealing with the village, do you?"

It's true. I never do. One rarely ever sees the Minkin father or mother, but the three sons are a constant presence in Prehovinka.

"And how are your parents, Jacob? I haven't seen them in a long time. I think the last time was in Stanislau. Are they well?"

He ignores my question and asks his own.

"Listen, Yuri, have you run into anyone tonight?"

"Tonight? I've only just started. You're the first person I've seen. Why?"

"Someone's been throwing rocks at our house again. Someone did earlier and broke a window. I heard laughing. It sounded like children."

"No, Jacob, I haven't seen anyone."

"You'd tell me if you did, wouldn't you?"

His question doesn't offend me. It's reasonable, considering his family's situation. I try to answer him sincerely.

"Of course I would, Jacob. I hope you know that. Listen, if I see anyone tonight who seems suspicious, I'll let you know. Right away. Then you can investigate. Would that help?" But I have no intention of actually helping him.

My answer seems sufficient. He says good night and rides back in the direction of his house. I listen to the sound of the hooves until they fade. I'm worried for the horse.

I think Jacob's right. Some child probably did it. It wouldn't be the first time. The Minkins have always experienced some form of harassment, and if I'm being honest, children aren't always the culprits. The family that lived here and managed us before them was treated the same way. But what does he expect? His family does the dirty work for Gradwolski—restrict our access to the forests, pursue delinquent mortgages, manage the harvest, dicker over fees for using the mill—so they're bound to get blamed for anything that makes our lives harder. It's always been that way. I'm sure the count pays them well for their trouble, though; they do get to live in that nice big manor house. I'm sure they can afford a new window. Easily. It's a shrewd strategy to use them as managers. The count isn't the only one who does it, either. That's the situation I'm referring to. It would be better, I think, if the Minkins and other Jewish families didn't keep separate but lived with us in Prehovinka the way they do in other parts of Galicia. If more of them did, it might help. Fewer broken windows. Only the ones who work at the mill live here; their families all have houses on the northwest side of the village. They keep to themselves; you only see them sometimes in the co-op store (never in the tavern) or in their wagons on the way to the synagogue. There's one in the shtetl up the road. If we saw them more often, I'm sure they would seem less strange, less mysterious.

But even then, if they all moved in tomorrow and mingled with us, nothing would change. Not right away. Fear and suspicions would still be there. Acceptance takes time. I've been here twenty-five years, and I still don't feel completely accepted. Everyone still regards me as different, which is sometimes an advantage—sometimes it isn't—and I haven't caused any offenses like the Minkins.

So it's not hard to understand why someone broke their window tonight. A few months ago, the Minkins started taking a higher percentage of our flour in exchange for grinding wheat at the mill. Everyone's upset about it. It's cutting deeper into what we need to survive. If I was a child and saw how upset my parents were about it, I'd want to break one of their windows, too.

AS I MAKE my way up the road, the sounds of the Zimn's rushing waters get louder. I can't hear my feet crunching on the gravel. The Zimn is a big, healthy branch of the Dniester; it cuts down through our fields like a jagged bolt of lightning. The land on either side of it is rich and dark. The land closer to us we call the near fields, and the land that's on the other side—here's a shocking revelation—we call the far fields. It is no wonder someone decided to stop here and start a village. The river's name is well deserved—icy cold, *zimno*, in all seasons. The first time I ever dropped my pants and dove into its waters, I squealed like a baby. It was wonderful.

Farther south, the Zimn divides. The right fork turns the wheel of our mill; the left breaks off sharply back into the trees, vanishing for many miles before emerging near the town of Striy. The left fork is full of fallen trunks and boughs, and it froths and steams as it rushes over these, throwing great twirling clouds of mist into the air. The mist, which never dissipates, which is continually fed by the churning waters, makes this part of the forest seem enchanted and mysterious.

I'm nearing the place on the main road where the village ends and where the highway turns northeast and eventually passes the shtetl on its way to Partisilatsia, a Polish settlement. At this bend, there's a place where I can enter the village through a gap between two houses where a small shed burned down years ago. It's very easy to miss, especially at night, but I haven't made that mistake in a long time.

When I reach the gap, I step over a fallen fence post and walk through some very tall grass. A dog barks at me—it's an inquisitive bark, not a growl. The dogs all know me. Over the years, I've befriended them with a few bones and a handful of gristle. It doesn't take much to win a hound's gratitude. It helps keep them quiet even though walkers here should be as natural and familiar to them as the rising of the moon. I dig my fingers into the pocket carrying my flask and feel around for a few broken, marrowy pieces of bone that Eugenie used in our stew. I throw one of these into the yard and move on.

The lane I'm on splinters off into many smaller ones running between and behind each of the yards. I'll spend most of the night on these. I check my pocket watch. It's just after eight. Still a bit of a glow on the horizon despite the clouds.

I love summer evenings. I love the moist, cool smells of the earth after a hot day. I love the way the coolness creeps up the back of your neck. It's a good coolness, and it always seems to bring with it other things. Other smells. I'm nearing one of the garlic bushes that are planted all over the village. You find them in the yards and back gardens, by the river, along fences—they're as ubiquitous as hawthorn bushes or carp in the Zimn. Their tiny white florets give off a sharp, pungent scent. It always reminds me of my mother's cooking. Suddenly I'm back in her kitchen again, and there's a big pot of tomato sauce bubbling on the stove. Chopped up cloves sizzling in oil in the skillet. The smell makes me long for those days again, but I don't feel sad about it. There are some memories that make you feel regret and some you're just grateful for. I'm grateful for that one.

As I move farther along the main road, I hear sounds—soft laughter from an open window, someone's loud belch. A baby's cry from one of the houses to my right. Then another cry coming from the next row. I know I'll probably hear more later, especially around feeding time. We welcome many babies this time of year. We have a special name for them. Winter's children. *Zimovi deeteh.* I was born in August, and my father used to call me that, too. Winter's child. I never understood what a summer birth had to do with the winter, but if I asked him, he wouldn't answer; he'd just look at my mother and smile.

Above me there's a whooshing sound in the air followed by an owl's screech. It must've spotted a mouse in one of the yards. They have incredible eyes. I wish I had them tonight.

Everyone's settling in now. Soon I'll be one of the few awake around here. Some old ladies might be up a while, mending ripped shirts and trousers, but that's it. The quiet here at night is complete the way it never was—the way it couldn't be—back in London. Early Sunday mornings there sometimes came close to what I experience now, but even then, there was always some human activity going on.

Jacob's right. The night duty's better handled by younger men. If I get into real trouble out here—let's say I encounter thieves or something worse—what will I be able to do? Stop them? My back hurts all the time. The rheumatism in my right leg is acting up. So's my gout. I'm the poorest sort of sentry imaginable. I'll get my throat cut before I can run or cry for help. I agree with him; it would be better if I stayed home and let my sons do this.

But then I think about Eugenie's chilly goodbye. I can't. The reason I'm out here is because of her.

2

◇◇◇◇◇◇◇

Natalka

EUGENIE HAS BEEN HAVING TROUBLED DREAMS LATELY.
It's not unusual. Not in a place like this. A hard life creates many fears,
and they always come out in your dreams. It's easy enough to avoid them
in the daylight. There's too much to do then. But when the night comes,
they hound you. They're relentless. As you're drifting off, the questions
start: *Will we grow enough this year? What if we don't get any rain? What if her fever
won't break? Where will I find the money we need? Should I ask the Minkins?* Then
the wolves come, too. Sometimes all you can see are their flashing eyes
and snapping teeth. There's nothing to stop them . . . unless you drink a
lot. Drink enough horilka, and it just might get you past the wolves and
push you straight into oblivion. That's probably why many have tried over
the years to get the tavern to stay open during the week. "Tavern" is what
we call our co-op store and supply building on Saturday afternoons and
evenings. Tables and chairs are set up in the main room, and the counter
where we buy seeds, equipment, and other things is cleared off and used
for selling ale, whiskey, horilka, and a horrible concoction of distilled
plum juice that will have you running to the outhouse at all hours of the
night. A stop there after a long day's work might keep those wolves at bay.

But Roman won't hear of it. His opposition's been so fierce no one will challenge him.

I said Eugenie's been having bad dreams, but that's wrong. It's not several. She's been having the same one every night since the summer began.

When I ask her about it, she says there isn't much to say. She says that when she closes her eyes and goes to sleep, she sees me. I look the way I do now. My hair's thin as a hummingbird's nest. A long gray beard. A little fat around the middle. I'm wearing my deacon's cassock. I look like any grizzly starets you see in these parts, not the young priest who arrived here years ago. In her dream, I'm standing in a forest clearing. Everything is dark around me, but there's a light coming from somewhere, and it is falling on me. It is a soft yellow light. I turn and look at Eugenie and smile, but I don't say anything. Then there's a sound off to my left, and suddenly a beautiful woman appears at my side. She steps into that strange spotlight. She is tall and young and very beautiful. She doesn't look at Eugenie; she doesn't seem to be aware my wife is there. She keeps her eyes on me and reaches for one of my hands. Then, with my hand clasped in hers, she turns and walks into the dark again, gently pulling me after her. I look back at Eugenie before I disappear. She wants to cry out for me to come back, but she says she always wakes before she can.

"WHAT DO YOU think it means?"

My question was directed at a little old woman with stooped shoulders. I went to see her a few days ago. When I asked her, she did what she does to most questions. She shrugged.

"It's probably nothing, Yuri. Or it's something."

"Well, thank you, Natalka. That's very helpful."

She's our healer. She's descended from a long line of cunning folk who have served our village and surrounding ones a long time. She helps us with all kinds of ailments; she fills the gap left by the single district doctor assigned the impossible task of caring for everyone from here to Kalush. I lived with her when I first arrived here. I had to; she was the only one who could help me with my situation, which was difficult and terrifying and involved bad dreams, too. I realized her skills applied not just to physical problems but to metaphysical ones, too.

It's hard to tell Natalka's age. She looked old when I first came here; she looks the same now. My mother used to say some people are just born with an old face; they spend their whole lives growing into it. I think Natalka is one of them. She wears a single long braid of silvery hair down her back. It dangles almost to her ankles. Her feet are brown and tough. She stays barefoot throughout the year; she says it's important to stay in touch with the earth. Her toes are strong, simian-like. Plenty of times, I've watched her pick up a slice of apple or a fallen utensil without needing to bend down.

She lives at the village's southern end. She doesn't have any neighbors. Her house is all alone, like a sentry post in the middle of nowhere. After Eugenie told me about the dream, I went to see her.

The smell of herbs and wax hits you the moment she opens the door. Strings of drying flowers are always hanging from the ceiling in the front room. A large old dresser with chipped yellow paint contains jars and pouches of salves, balms, powders, and unguents that people come from miles around to buy. I went to see her because I didn't know what else to do. I needed advice. Ever since she started having the dream, Eugenie has been angry at me and barely says a thing. When I begged her to tell me what was wrong, all she said was that she couldn't believe I would go off with that young girl and not stay with her. I told her she was being ridiculous. I said it was unfair to get angry at me for something my dream self did. I told her that I once dreamed she threw a pan at my head (and missed). I didn't hold that against her, did I? But my reasoning doesn't matter to her. She says even the strangest dreams contain some kernel of truth.

Natalka chuckled.

"Oh, come now, what I think about the dream isn't important. Not yet. Yuri Volodymyrovich, what does she think it means?"

I took a swallow of tea.

"She thinks it's about London."

Natalka frowned.

"Say again?"

"London. The city of London. I think she thinks the woman *is* London."

"The place you're from?"

I nodded.

"She thinks I want to go back. She thinks I miss it. The woman, I guess, is taking me back there. Back to my old life."

"Do you?"

"Do I what?"

"Miss it. Your old life."

"No. Not at all, Natalka. You know I don't."

"Why would she ever think that, then? There must be something."

"It's because of her dream."

I told her I think Roman's to blame. And any other priest. They all speak the same way. I should know. Natalka laughed, but she stopped when she saw I was serious. I told her the way we're taught about life here, the way we're taught in church, is the problem. When he's up in the pulpit, Roman is always turning people and situations into things bigger than themselves. Take the tavern, for instance. The last time someone wanted to keep it open during the week, Roman spent several sermons railing against alcohol—even though he's no stranger to a good tipple himself—and talking about how alcohol is the Key to Evil and that the Devil uses that Unholy Key to unlock our hearts. He called the front door of the tavern the Doorway to Sin even though, I'll say again, he's spent plenty of Saturday nights there. But the way he talked reminded me of Bunyan. Big allegorical explanations. Capital letters for everything. And when Eugenie cried out in her sleep and I woke her and asked her to describe her dream, she sounded just like him. The lady didn't just reflect simple fears that I'd be tempted by a young maid like some old fool. No, she said the woman represented something more than that, my old life . . . the way in medieval stories, you have courtly ladies representing Chivalry, Honor, and other things. To her, the girl in her dream is Lady London. I tried making her see it was nothing to worry about, that I didn't care about my English life anymore, but she said I was being dismissive. She said I was insulting her intelligence. She said she's always trusted her dreams. Ever since she was a little girl. I told all of this to Natalka. She agreed.

"It's true. Eugenie does have a gift for them. There's a talent there I wish she'd have developed. I offered to help her a long time ago." She cleared her throat. "Still, it is quite a stretch for her to be worrying about London now, after all this time. How long have you been here?"

"Twenty-five years."

"Twenty-five! It seems like yesterday you stayed with me and Yevhen. Remember?" Yevhen was her old sheepdog.

"Yes." I smiled. "It's hard for me to believe, too."

"Still, something must have provoked this. Something recent. Listen, are you telling me everything? Is there any other reason why she'd be worrying about London all of a sudden?"

She pronounced it the way Eugenie does—*Lun-dahn*. I couldn't help smiling.

"What? Am I being funny now?"

"No, you're not. I'm sorry." I sipped my tea. "I didn't think of it before, Natalka, but something did happen recently. I met someone in Stanislau when we went to the market. Eugenie saw. It really upset her. I think it was right when she started having the dream."

"A pretty young woman? Tall? Long hair?"

"No. A young Englishman. A writer."

She gave me a puzzled look.

It happened about a month ago. Every few weeks we take our vegetables and other things to Stanislau to sell. It's one of the larger cities in Galicia, which is the northeastern province of the Austro-Hungarian Empire. It's located about fifteen miles from us, which means we have to leave very early to get there in time and find a good space. Nothing is reserved. Farmers from everywhere flood the square, bartering and arguing for hours under the gaze of a greening Habsburg eagle on one of the nearby ministry buildings. Stanislau is a beautiful imperial city. I like it more than Lemberg, which some of our friends don't understand. Lemberg is our Vienna, they say, so grand and cosmopolitan. So cultured. That may be true, but Lemberg is too big for me; it's easy to get lost in its mazy streets. No one ever gets lost in Stanislau—not even a traveler who doesn't know his way around. This one was as conspicuous as a sunflower sticking up in a wheat field. Seeing him reminded me of my own arrival years ago: the shouts of the peddlers, the hum of voices, the way people watched me weave between carts piled high with potatoes and cabbages, trying not to stumble.

It was too early in the season to have much to sell, but we decided to take some of our supplies that hadn't been used in the winter. Potatoes, corn, milk, some eggs. Business was brisk. I wanted to ignore the traveler, but it was impossible. He was standing near our cart, struggling to buy cheese and bread from an old woman. She kept shaking her head at the money in his hand and saying *za bohato, za bohato!*

"You're giving her too much money," I finally called out. I'm sure he didn't expect a fat, old deacon in dirty robes to come up and address him in perfect English.

"I am?" he said, his eyes widening as I reached out and picked the right number of coins from his upturned palm. Then I gave them to the old baba and waved her away. "And who might I be speaking to?"

I introduced myself in English as George Frost and told him I'd been living here a long time. He was astounded. He said he was a writer gathering material for a travel book. He was staying the night in Stanislau before taking the Nord Express down into Bukovina. When he told me his name was Fielding, I laughed.

"What is it?"

"It's just lovely to hear an English name for once. The ones I usually hear have a 'yuk' or a 'chuk' on the end like a kite's tail."

He smiled.

"I agree. It's wonderful to hear English after several weeks abroad. I must say, I certainly wasn't expecting to meet anyone like you! I would desperately love to learn more about you. Do you have time?"

"All the time in the world."

Eugenie was haggling with some customers. When she turned and saw Fielding, she made a quick assessment and glared at me. I pretended not to see. I thought she was mad because I wasn't helping her. Honestly, she's never needed my help. Anyone who's never bargained with Eugenie is in for a rude awakening if they think she's some country bumpkin. She's very shrewd. I'm not. I don't like haggling; I'd sooner give away anything than argue over a few extra cents. I could see she had everything under control. I turned back to the fellow. He explained that he'd enjoyed some success in the London papers as a chronicler of exotic places. With this trip, he hoped to gather enough material to leave journalism behind and enter the ranks of full-fledged authordom. We talked for the better part of the afternoon, and I learned much about the country I'd left, but we spent most of our time together talking about me. He wanted me to explain why I'd settled here, and I gave him partial answers—just enough to satisfy him, and he wrote it all down in a small notepad with a nubby bit of pencil. Eugenie looked over at us several times and gave me a worried look. I shrugged at her. *Everything is fine,* I signaled back.

By late afternoon the poor fellow looked absolutely worn out. He teetered on his heels. I finally pointed him in the direction of Lypova Street. Who knows how long since he'd slept in a decent bed? I told him he'd find plenty of nice accommodations there. I even offered to speak to the proprietors for him, but he said it wouldn't be necessary. As a gesture of thanks, he removed a small bottle from the bundle on his back and handed it to me. It was Irish whiskey. The bottle was half-empty, but he said he hoped what was left would give me as much pleasure as our conversation had given him. I didn't know what to say. I looked over at Eugenie, who had her back to me, and pulled the cork and quickly tipped the bottle to my lips. I hadn't tasted such wonderful stuff in years. When he saw my reaction, Fielding chuckled and readjusted his bundle. He shook my hand and said he was grateful for our meeting. I wished him a happy life and much future success, and he turned to go. I watched him move among the carts in the direction of Lypova and felt very good about myself. It had been a long time since I told someone about my experiences.

As I walked back to our cart, my feeling of satisfaction evaporated when I saw the frown on Eugenie's face. She didn't say anything to me then, but I could tell she was upset. I didn't try to ask her why; that would've been kicking the hornet's nest. I just kept my mouth shut.

Later, on the ride home, she turned to me.

"So what did you tell that man about yourself? What did you say?" Our sons were up front, driving the horse. We sat in the back, down in the wagon's bed. I told her he was stunned to find another Englishman living here. I said he wanted to know what brought me here. If the roles had been reversed, I'd have felt the same way. I decided to oblige him, and this made her angry. She interrupted me.

"You told him your name. I heard."

"No, I didn't. I said I'm George." That's who I am now, *Yuri,* but that wasn't the name my parents gave me. "What is it? What's wrong with that?"

"He's going to write about you in his book. Someone will find out you're here. They'll come for you."

I think she still has some grand idea about my past, about my importance, which is flattering but untrue.

"No one is looking for me, Eugenie. Not now. Not ever. No one cares." For the rest of our ride home, she kept insulting me. She called me a fool. I knew it was because she was scared, that she was just being protective of me. I was too tired to argue back. When she noticed my silence, she tried something else to draw me out.

"You should have been more careful, Yuri. But maybe you weren't careful on purpose. Maybe you want them to come and take you away. Like the woman in my dream."

This wasn't just unfair; it was ridiculous. But what I said next didn't help.

"It's not true, Eugenie. That young traveler just reminded me of myself. I enjoyed hearing about England. That's all. It's been a long time."

"You wish you were him."

"What? No, no. I don't wish I were him. He just reminded me of when I was young. I started thinking about the choices we make to create our lives, understand? That's all. How life could be different if we made different choices. That's all."

"You mean better, not different. Life could have been better for you. I knew it. I knew you weren't happy here anymore."

"*Diwchata*, that's not what I meant at all. Why do you keep saying that?"

"Because it's true."

"OK, well, it might have been better in some ways." She started to interrupt me, but I talked over her. "But not in the ways that matter most."

"See, I knew it."

"No, you don't. You're not understanding me. What I mean is, my life in London would never have been the way I really wanted because you wouldn't be in it. The boys wouldn't. Or our grandchildren, *znayesh*?"

She looked straight ahead. She didn't seem to be hearing me anymore. I was irritated for giving in and arguing. I said things I shouldn't have. If I hadn't been so tired, I would have been more careful. The whole time we argued, I noticed our sons trying to hold a separate conversation, but now everyone fell into silence. The entire ride home was quiet and uncomfortable. I wanted to make things better, but nothing I could say would help. I was annoyed with myself. Why did I have to say I thought it could have been better? I know how she is. Why did I try to explain? Soon, I lost her face in the gloom as the sun went down. I'd been so thrilled to meet Fielding; now I regretted helping him with that old lady. Why didn't I just mind my business? Why didn't I keep my thoughts to myself? Eugenie's a farmer's daughter. She's used to dealing in practicalities, not philosophy. "What might have been" doesn't have a place in her world. I should know that by now.

NATALKA SMIRKED WHEN I was done.

"That wasn't too smart," she said. "You *should* know that by now. Twenty-five years. Now I understand her interpretation of the dream. She's connected it in her mind with the traveler. And the way you acted with him. Sounds like you were too enthusiastic. Too excited. Maybe she's right."

"What? No, she's not right. That's not it. Natalka, I need to get her to stop making that connection. It's not right. I don't want to leave her. I love her. I don't know what to do. Maybe you could talk to her."

"Why would I do that?"

"She'll listen to you. Everybody does. You know how I was when I came here. You helped me with my problems. With what followed me here. Remember?"

She looked at me but didn't say anything. She sipped her tea and stared at her feet.

"Natalka, I'd never want to go back. Never. Too many bad things happened to me in London. More than even what you know about."

"There's your answer, then. That's what you need to tell your wife. You need to tell her something about London. Make her understand why you'd never go back."

"Tell her all of it?"

"I don't know. Maybe. It's for you to decide. You have to do it, not me. I can't do it for you. You didn't tell me everything about your past, but I'm a little surprised Eugenie doesn't know all of it. There are plenty of husbands here who keep secrets. I didn't think you were one of them."

"I'm not. I'm not like them. I'm not trying to hurt her. I just did some terrible things. And I'm ashamed. That's why I've never wanted to talk about any of it."

"Well, that's silly. That's no reason not to tell her. She can handle your stories, whatever they are. You've lived here long enough, Yuri, and still you don't understand one simple rule about us. We like simplicity. Honesty. That's it. That's all you have to do with her. Be honest. And simple. Don't make it fancy."

"But that's just it, Natalka. I don't think I can. My past isn't simple. I don't know how to talk about it. I don't know if I can find the right words."

The old woman's eyebrows arched.

"Is the totem almost to your house?"

"Yes. It's a few houses up. It will be our turn later this week."

"That's good. When it comes to your house, do the walk, Yuri. Don't make your sons."

I'd been looking forward to having one of them take my place. Natalka shook her head.

"You just said you were having trouble finding the right words to talk about your past, didn't you?"

"Yes."

"The walk will give you plenty of time to find them."

3

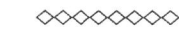

Encounter

9:30 p.m.

PREHOVINKA SITS ON A FLAT EXPANSE of farmland with a ridge of hills in the north and west. Dense humid forests of pine, oak, aspen, and linden border and enclose us in the north and east. The forests make our village easy to overlook, which is probably where we get our name (*preho-vannay* means hidden). Whoever started this village made a good decision about the location. After heavy rains the Zimn floods and spreads its rich soil all over our fields. That has meant successful harvests year after year. The flooding's never been severe enough to threaten our houses except for one time right before I arrived. It rained so hard that everyone had to climb up on their roofs and wait until the water receded. It took several days.

The moon's rising now. Its gibbous face, crisp and golden, hangs above the forest. The white plaster walls of our homes and barns glow.

I reach in my coat pocket for a few cherries and a piece of black bread. Time for a little sustenance.

I spit the cherry stones in the dirt. Then I wash it down with a swig from a flask that contains tea, not Fielding's whiskey. That's in another flask.

Natalka's right. I've never told Eugenie why I left England. I didn't think I had to. I know the mystery of my past makes her feel uncomfortable. I suppose it's like living with someone who's a secret agent. You never know what they're concealing. You never know for sure if you're truly seeing who they really are. Even when we met, Eugenie pointed out I was too different to ever fit in with village life. She was wearing her pretty yellow dress that day, the one that matched the color of her hair. I still remember. She smiled and told me she expected I'd be leaving soon.

"Leaving? But I only just arrived. Why?"

"Country life is boring, especially for a city boy."

"It doesn't seem boring to me. Everything is so beautiful here." Starting with you, I wanted to say.

She shook her head.

"Yes, it's beautiful. At first. But once you get used to it you won't even notice it anymore. You won't find any adventure here."

"I don't want adventures anymore. I've had enough."

I'm making it sound like we had a very easy back-and-forth conversation, but we didn't. I didn't know the language. My father never taught me. When I met Eugenie, our communication relied mostly on pantomime. It was very awkward. But I'm glad for it. Because I was so completely helpless, she felt sorry for me and decided to help me learn the language. She took me around the village and introduced me to their way of life. She taught me the names of things. Basic things. I felt like a child, but it wasn't humiliating. I needed to start over. I was ready to start over.

"*Sonse,*" she said, pointing at the sun. The sweat glistened on her forehead. She wiped it with the back of her hand. "*Sonse hrie.*" She smiled. It was a lovely smile.

When an apple fell from a tree, she picked it up in her small hands and showed me.

"*Yabluko,*" she said. Then she made a downward gesture. "*Yabluko padaye.*"

Looking in her eyes, I wanted to tell her my heart *padaye* along with that apple. But I think she knew.

Communicating with her was difficult, and it went on for several weeks like that. Later, once I started to understand, I pretended that I didn't. I didn't want our lessons to end. I liked spending time with her. She knew I was up to something.

"Yuri, *sloo-kai do mene!*"

"I am. I am listening to you. I just don't understand everything you're saying."

"Yes, you do. You're lying. I can tell."

"How?"

"By the dumb look on your face. You're staring at me like a fool. Stop it."

"I am not! It's hard to explain, Eugenie. Listen, have you ever been on that one hill on the north side of the fields to watch the sun rise?"

"Of course. Everyone has."

"I haven't. Tell me what it's like."

"The sun shines down on the fields. The wind blows. That's all. I'm not sure what you want me to say. If the fields are planted with wheat, the morning sun turns it all to pure gold. It is very beautiful."

I took a big risk with what I said next.

"That is how I feel when I look at you."

She rolled her eyes and looked away from me. I couldn't see her face, but I could tell she was smiling.

She agreed to continue with our lessons.

I'VE STOPPED BY the two main buildings located at the center of the village: the co-op store and the schoolhouse. It's not Saturday, so the tavern's not open; the co-op is all dark. So is the schoolhouse. That's the place where our children learn just enough writing and arithmetic to one day sign their names to unfair loans or agree to new terms on their family's mortgages.

It's getting hot in my greatcoat. I wish Eugenie hadn't given it to me. She said it looked like it's going to rain later and insisted on me wearing it. Last year I was very sick; she doesn't want to take any chances. It does look like it might rain later, and I know I'll be grateful if it does . . . but right now I'm hot. The back of my neck is getting sweaty. But if I take it off, I'm going to have to carry the coat, the lamp, and the totem. It's too much.

As I'm trying to figure out what to do, two small figures round the schoolhouse corner and crash into me. I don't fall, but the collision causes me to cry out and drop the totem.

"What in God's name?"

It's the Kindras' little boys. Victor and Volodya. Victor is ten, and Volodya is seven. They're both barefoot. Volodya hunches a little to one side like he's expecting someone to strike him. It's because he was born with a spinal deformity.

"What are you two doing out at this hour?"

Victor speaks first. He says they are looking for a chicken that escaped from their yard. I highly doubt it. The Kindras are very careful with their animals, and I doubt Marko would send his two little boys out in the dark to find it. Volodya giggles. Victor tells him to shut his mouth.

"I know where you're really coming from, boys. Don't lie to me," I tell them. The gap between the houses I used earlier when I left the main road is not far. "I think you're coming from the main road. And the Minkins' place. You broke one of their windows tonight, didn't you?"

Victor gasps.

"No, Deacon, it wasn't us! We didn't do it. We swear to you!"

The fact that he knows about it all but confirms it for me.

"Don't swear to me. Swear to God." I point at the faint silvery church cupolas that are floating above the rooftops a few lanes over. Then I hold up the totem. "Swear to him, too."

They look at each other. It doesn't take more than that. The boys blurt out a confession, and I chide them for it—even though I understand. Marko, their father, has had a bad year with his crops and had to take another loan; I'm sure the terms weren't good. I'm sure the boys heard him complaining at the dinner table. But I can't show them any sympathy, or they'll do it again. I don't want them to get caught. I sternly tell them to go home. I tell them the Minkins are out looking for them and might catch them. Worse still, they might fall into the clutches of the Devil or one of his minions tonight if they're not careful.

As I watch the little boys walk up the road, I realize they already have. Most children never leave Prehovinka. If they do, it's only because their father's luck hasn't improved, and they have to go live with cousins somewhere. That's the order of things here. Everyone is locked in a difficult cycle of life that travelers like Fielding overlook—all they notice are the colorful clothes and rustic customs, not the poverty—and I think that's another reason why Eugenie couldn't believe that I'd ever permanently give up my life in London for this place. And her. But I've told her many times my family's situation there was no better. My parents and I belonged to that vast class of people Mayhew calls the working poor. Similar restraints and class limitations determined our lives. No way out. But my parents did manage to find one for me; they pushed me into the priesthood. I certainly didn't enter it because of any special calling or interest in the vows (especially chastity). I was just good with words and had a nice voice, and the church needed people like me.

My parents thought it would give me a good life.

4

◇◇◇◇◇◇◇◇

Showing Off

MY VERY FIRST CLERICAL ASSIGNMENT out of the seminary at Hammersmith was in London. That was unusual. While other new priests were being sent off to obscure parts of the country, I stayed in the city. I was sent to Saint Martha's in Chelsea. It was one of the shining jewels in the Westminster crown. The church was experiencing some problems and the diocese believed I could fix them. I was foolish enough to think so, too.

In the seminary, we all dreamed about going to a place like Saint Martha's. That's what you do when you're young. You don't think about life's limitations, only its possibilities. But Saint Martha's was a reward, the kind of assignment you received after serving a long, exhausting career somewhere else. Hoping for a post like that straight off was ridiculous; it was blind to the facts, to the needs of the One True Catholic and Apostolic Church in the years I'm speaking of. I was born in the late 1850s and studied at Saint Thomas in the 1870s. My early life spanned a period of expansion and consolidation for the Church after many years of persecution and hiding. It was a time of liberation and a dispersal of everything—all her resources—to the farthest edges of the isle. When I say "resources," I am not referring to candles or cakes of incense. I mean us, her new priests. We were her flesh-and-blood capital. The odds were thoroughly set against any of us starting off in one of the diocese's best churches, and that's why it was a waste of time to dream of such a thing. It was pure fantasy. That's what every class of seminarians was told by Father John Cremins, our rector at Saint Thomas.

"Lads, when you become priests, you'll be sent off to the hinterlands," he'd say. He was a kindly old man with a carbuncled nose. "That's where God needs you most. Try not to be disappointed. Think of the Baptizer; you're following in his footsteps! He went out into the wilderness to prepare Our Lord's way, didn't he? He wasn't sitting on some regal throne; he wore horsehair and ate grasshoppers and wild honey! If he was able to accept such an existence, so can you. Don't expect to be posted in London or anywhere like it. That's an assignment that won't happen for a long time. Maybe it will never happen. But you must remember one thing no matter what. Whatever it is, wherever it is, you must accept the assignment you're given with grace and gratitude. Because that's God's will."

God's will or not, most of us still dreamed about being sent to a gorgeous cathedral even though a poor village was our probable destination. I tried to do what Fr. Cremins asked us to do; I tried not to wish for something so grand, but it was hard. I prayed to God every night to at least give me something better than a chapel barn for my first post. I never expected it would be that domed wonder in Chelsea, for that's truly what it was, a wonder—so stately and elegant amid the grubby brown lodging houses of Cadogan Street. It had angel statues at the roof's four corners and towers designed by the great Pugin himself, all of it built on a fine pile of Anglo-Saxon stones.

At the time of my ordination, Saint Martha's was struggling; the church stood half-empty on Sundays. The older parishioners were shuffling off their mortal coils, and no one was taking their places. That wasn't true of the sects around her; they all seemed to be thriving. Turn a corner, and you'd stumble into a large crowd of them, spilling into the streets with flushed faces and trembling voices.

If Saint Martha's had been some poorhouse church like the ones in the East End, she would have been ignored. But the church was too important—second only to Saint Mary Moorfields, which was the closest thing we had to a cathedral until the one in Kensington was built. The neighborhoods surrounding her were associated with artists, with glorious names—Ruskin, Pater, Carlyle, the Brownings, and the painter-poet Dante Gabriel Rossetti, whom I met in the last year of his life. My involvement with him is one of the reasons why I left London and came to Prehovinka—but not yet, it's still too soon. I'd rather stay with my beginning for now. Beginnings are easier.

To let Saint Martha's congregation shrink was something the diocese, and Henry Manning, our cardinal archbishop, wouldn't allow.

That would've been too embarrassing, especially considering the construction boom that followed the restoration of our hierarchy in 1850. Everyone was expecting England's conversion to Catholicism at any minute, and more churches were being built in anticipation. It seemed deserved; in that first decade of new freedom, the English Catholic Church received some spectacular Anglican defections—Manning among them—and many took it as a sign that change was just around the corner. But two decades on, everyone was still waiting; allowing a church like Saint Martha's to shrink and dwindle would've been an admission that Manning, the English hierarchy, and even the Holy Father had been wrong.

What Saint Martha's needed on Sundays was a good speaker, someone who could shift between being a poet and a circus barker—someone, in other words, like me. I've always enjoyed speaking in front of crowds. My enthusiasm for it came from my mother; she instilled in me a fierce love of books. After dinner she would read to us, my father and I, from the Lambs' Shakespeare or a yellowed Latin primer. It's one of the few cherished memories I still have of her . . . she died of typhus when I was little. The memories I have are few, and her reading to us is one of them. I can see her seated on the ottoman next to the fireplace, the light dancing on her face, her body swaying, her eyes half-shut because she knew the stories already and didn't need to read them word for word. She seemed like a sorceress at those moments. Bending over the book in her lap like she was casting a spell.

A book, if it was a good one, should affect you this way. That was the measure of its worth, not what anyone else said about it. That's what she taught me. I remembered her every mannerism, her wonderfully dramatic gestures when she read . . . they were sunk so deeply in the folds of my brain I could summon them whenever I wanted. In school I tried to do the same. I recited from Propertius, Virgil, Cicero, and other Latin writers with dramatic performances that impressed my teachers—and put off the other boys. They stayed away from me, and that hurt, but the praise of my superiors mattered more than the rejection of my classmates.

I attended the Mortimer Academy in East London, one of the schools set up in those years by the Poor School Committees for Catholic children. It was a day school located just east of the city's center and run by the Dominican Brothers. The student body consisted of boys from the surrounding working-class neighborhoods, and it had some very good teachers from several elite institutions who'd been forced out by the usual politics and needed somewhere else to ply their trade.

The Mortimer Academy taught the same things most English schools did, but with conspicuous differences. There might be nothing unusual about the school's approach to mathematics or grammar, but English history? While Protestant schoolboys stuck pins in the eyes of Mary Tudor in their textbooks, Mortimer students learned her reign was bright and tragically brief (but not bloody). We were taught that the Reformation and Protestantism, not surprisingly, were disasters even as our instructors struggled to explain away the prosperity of the Pax Elizabethiana.

Though my mother was gone by the time I finished and moved on to the brand-new Catholic University, my future had already been determined. She and my father had decided on the priesthood. I said before they just wanted a good life for me, a very safe straightforward one, and for a poor family, nothing seemed straighter or safer than a priest's.

My father didn't get a chance to enjoy the completion of this plan. He died just a few weeks after my ordination. For years he'd been suffering from a consumptive condition, and it suddenly became very bad. I didn't realize how bad when I kissed him goodbye one afternoon and returned to Hammersmith. He looked so tired when I said goodbye, more than usual, but he brushed away my concerns. "It's been a hard week. All I need is a little sleep is all, Mikhaylo," he said. "Don't worry."

A few days later, on a warm morning in late summer, my father's friend Ivan Luzak, who came to England with him, went to the house and knocked. No one answered. He went home and returned with a spare key. Inside, he found my father still in bed, staring at the ceiling. He was about to give him a hard time, but then he realized something was wrong. My father's eyes didn't blink. He wasn't moving. Ivan said he'd looked so normal at first, but then he tried to rouse him and noticed the stiffness. He saw something like dried tomato pulp at the corner of his mouth.

In the eastern end of the Pancras churchyard, which is buried with so many Catholics it's called Catholic Pancras, several of my instructors were there among the mourners. I didn't expect this, and I was deeply touched. Among them was Monsignor Ambrose Leheny, a short, curly-haired Irishman with muscular arms—a real terror on the cricket field. He also happened to be the personal secretary to Cardinal Manning, and that made him a terror everywhere else. Before the burial, he walked up to me, grabbed my hand, and squeezed it so hard it went numb. I had been a very good batsman at Saint Thomas, and Leheny used to come and watch our games. Sometimes he stepped in and coached us if he saw someone doing something wrong. He expressed his condolences and urged me to bear up and put my trust in the Lord. He said he didn't know why a bright seminary career had to go hand in hand with such a tragedy. That, he said, was beyond his wisdom.

"But not his," he said, casting a da Vinci finger at the sky. "Dark and bright are sometimes two sides of the same coin, lad. All I can say is to trust in God's will. You'll get through."

In addition to Leheny and my instructors, there were several people from the furnishings shop where my father worked as a carver. They included Giuseppe Montini, the owner, who loved my father deeply and kept sobbing and loudly blowing his nose in a frilly lace handkerchief. I was moved by everyone's affection and respect for my father (and for me), and I was especially moved that the monsignor had even bothered to attend the funeral of a new priest's parent. But Leheny was a compassionate man, even if he hid his feelings behind a crusty exterior. I think he lost his own parents at roughly my age. I wanted to do something special to impress him at the funeral. As my father's coffin was lowered into the grave, I wanted to show him why I had been one of the brightest seminarians at Saint Thomas. So I stepped forward and performed the necessary blessings, scattered holy water across the casket, and then recited some poetry. I think it was something from Donne or Shakespeare, or maybe it was Gray's famous elegy—I can't remember which—but I do remember reaching down and taking a handful of dirt from the pile that would soon cover the coffin. I held it out and let it spill dramatically through my fingers. I muttered something about the transient nature of life as I looked around me. I think I honestly expected applause for that. It was idiotic.

The monsignor didn't think so. I learned later he'd been struck by my poise, my stoicism in the face of a personal tragedy, and my eloquence. I'd demonstrated to him, at a moment of great pain, that I possessed everything Saint Martha's needed—youth, energy, vigor, strength, and above all, a taste for theatricality.

To this day I still recall the wonder of looking up at the list of parish assignments and finding my name. A few weeks after my father's funeral, the listing was posted on a board in the refectory, and there were about a dozen of us, fresh and ready, waiting, preparing for wherever God was going to send us. I spent several long moments staring up at the list as if it had been written in another language—*Fr. Michael Frost, Saint Martha's, Chelsea*—before I let myself really believe what it said.

Then I heard someone whisper behind me, "They gave him Saint Martha's!" It was followed by excited whispers of congratulations and stifled protests. Some of my snobbier classmates couldn't believe it, and I was like them—I couldn't believe it, either. But I think it was the murmurs of shock and outrage that finally convinced me I wasn't dreaming. I didn't come from a privileged old Catholic family like many of them—some with ancestral homes surrounded by vast stubbly fields—but now I possessed something their status couldn't get them.

5

◇◇◇◇◇◇◇

Dmitro's House

10:30 p.m.

MY RIGHT FOOT IS THROBBING. My gout's acting up. Sometimes my foot swells so much it feels like it's going to burst. The only thing that ever helps is sticking it in a bucket of cold water. This is what getting old is. Everything starts failing you. Earlier, when Victor was spinning his lie about the lost chicken, I kept watching his little brother. Volodya was nervous. I could tell. He couldn't stand still. He kept twirling back and forth on the balls of his feet, and I thought, I can't move like that anymore. I'm too old. If I tried, it would hurt too much.

On the next lane there's a good place to stop. Dmitro Melnyk is a successful cobbler who sells some of the best honey in the area. There's always a crowd around his wagon at the market. In his front yard, under the apple trees, there are several large blue wood boxes. That's where he keeps his bees, and the honey they make after walking around inside the blossoms is unlike anything you've ever tasted. Pure heaven.

There are two chairs right outside his gate. A large lantern hangs from one of the gateposts. It casts a lovely amber light. It's a perfect place to sit and rest. You'll usually find Dmitro there on most afternoons, chatting with his neighbors. He leaves the chairs out for anyone on the night walk. Very thoughtful.

I reach his house and sit down. I lean the totem against the gate and take off my coat. What a relief. My shirt's moist under the arms. I unbutton my collar and let the night air cool me. There's a mellow droning coming from the blue boxes behind me. Like a thousand Lhasan monks at their prayers. It's pleasant. Soothing. So is the smell of the apple blossoms. I inhale the fragrance and close my eyes. If I'm not careful I could fall asleep.

WHEN I WAS first told about the night walk, I thought it was strange that we were expected to do this. "What about the authorities? Where's the militia?" I asked several times. I never received an answer that made sense. But I came to see that the walk's a vital necessity, a very old practice I'm sure Fielding would love to include in his book of travels. Our families live on lots that are wide and very deep, deeper than any cricket field, and big enough to support the gardens sustaining us throughout the year. The gardens are for personal use, and the fields that belong to each family are where we grow what gets sold in the markets, sent to the mill, or given to the Minkins and Gradwolski's other collecting agents. This is good soil, very rich, and we've always had good harvests. Prehovinka is a thriving, active community. But that doesn't matter to the regional authority. They still don't offer us any special protections or benefits . . . The militia never sets foot in our village. It's been this way for a long time—long before the Potocki business soured our relationship with the Poles. Potocki was a Polish aristocrat and the governor of Galicia. He was murdered last year in Lemberg. He was shot point-blank as he was giving an audience. The assassin, a young Ruthenian nationalist, was killed by the guards, who kept putting bullets into him long after it was obvious he was dead. But even before this happened, patrolling villages like ours was regarded as a waste of time to the authorities, even though landholders like Gradwolski demand protection for their interests. To appease them, a few soldiers go out, usually in pairs . . . but they never come any closer to the village than the main entrance. You can't see them, but sometimes the glowing ends of their cigarettes are visible. They look like fireflies. For a few minutes they glow and dance in little circles, and then the fireflies are gone—the soldiers have moved on.

That's why we've always needed the night walk. It fills the void; it serves as an important part of our daily security. Without it, there would be no one to look out for accidents or other emergencies in the middle of the night. Over the years, several small barn fires have been stopped thanks to the vigilance of our watch. Any fire left unchecked, so close to neighbors who can't afford to trade their hay roofs for tin, would be nothing less than apocalyptic.

To be honest, I'm surprised Prehovinka hasn't burned down already.

But we don't carry the imp, which is what I call the wood totem, for this reason alone. It's important to our security in another way. It has to do with its unusual face. It isn't ugly, even though I'm sure one could draw that conclusion from a first impression. I did. But I've learned it's always possible to find beauty in unusual things, and that's certainly true of the imp . . . even though it scared me the first time I encountered it down in the cellar of Saint Martha's. I think I flinched worse than Asher.

THAT ENCOUNTER TOOK place not long after my father's burial. I said my father made his living as a carver, but that word doesn't seem to adequately describe him. I don't mean to be rude to anyone in any of the trades; a tradesman's life is honorable, but my father was more than that. He was an artist. In fact, I have no qualms mentioning him in the same breath as Dante Rossetti, even though their arts were different. He didn't paint voluptuous maidens the way Rossetti did; he didn't transform someone's seamstress or chambermaid into a figure from classical myth. But he did make inanimate things seem animate. I'm reminded of a story I heard about Jesus when I was in the seminary—how, when he was a child, he made doves from clay and blew into their beaks so that they started moving and flew away to roost in the trees. It was like that for my father. He did something similar with wood. He made his creations come alive—seem to, I mean.

A FORTNIGHT AFTER his burial, a driver pulled up to the rectory door with a delivery for me. He'd come straight from Giuseppe Montini's shop on Regent Street and had all my father's work things in the back of his cart. I saw two large crates covered by a length of canvas.

I burned with curiosity to open them right away, but I couldn't. I had a full day's work ahead of me. Several bedridden parishioners had requested Eucharist, and it would take most of the morning to travel between their homes; in the afternoon, there were confessions to hear and a rosary that would likely fill up the rest of the day. Then, after that, I still wasn't done. I had to lead the benediction, which was better attended than Sunday Mass. So I instructed the driver to take the crates and store them down in the cellar, and it wasn't until late in the evening, after dinner, that I finally had a chance to open them. I stopped in the kitchen for a lighted candle and then hurried to the cellar door faster than a child on Christmas morning.

I touched the cellar doorknob and heard a voice behind me.

"Off on a little adventure, Frost? My, those two crates must be full of surprises!"

I turned. It was Felix Veach, the church's associate pastor. He was standing in the gloom of the stairwell's upper landing, watching me.

"No, Father, we just need more coal tablets for tomorrow's funerals, and I'm going to see how many we have," I said, irritated. "What we have in the sacristy won't be enough." My voice trembled a little as I looked up at him, a thin, slight man with a smug expression on his pale, ghostly face. It shouldn't have mattered what I was doing, but I didn't like the curious, unfriendly tone of his voice. He responded with an "mmm" and picked his teeth with the nail of his pinky finger. He seemed to be trying to decide if he believed me or not. I didn't wait for an answer. I opened the door and hurried down the stairs before he could say anything.

The driver had put the crates in a corner next to some broken statuary. One of them opened easily. The lid slid right off. I found two heavy leather pouches holding bulky linen rolls of my father's carving tools: chisels, hooks, gouges, rasps. Several of these had handles made of ash—he had the original wood replaced because of an old craftsman's superstition about the magical properties of ash.

I found an old corncob pipe and a rag holding some dried tobacco cured with honey (the honey didn't help; it still smelled like Beelzebub entered the room whenever he smoked it); *A Treatise on Wood Engravings, Historical and Practical*, second edition, by William Andrew Chatto, published in London in 1861, an absolute necessity for any craftsman; a skullcap of faded brown cloth he wore on cold days to cover a bald area that, over the years, had slowly spread to the size of a Spanish medallion; and two smocks stained with varnish.

The crate also contained several broken portrait frames and what looked like two tree branches, but I wouldn't understand what these were until later. I searched the bottom of the crate with my hands and didn't find anything else. I turned to the other crate. Its lid wasn't easy to remove; I felt along the edges with my fingertips and realized it was sealed up with more nails than a coffin maker uses.

Why? The first crate didn't have any nails. I thought the lid might loosen up if I pulled hard enough, but nothing happened. I strained until the tips of my fingers turned white. I needed something to pry off the lid. Not one of my father's tools—they'd never work. They were sturdy implements, but the blunt force I needed would bend and ruin them. On one of the cellar shelves, I found a holy water dispenser made of solid bronze. I wedged the end of the handle into a shallow groove between the crate and lid. After some persistent tugging and pulling, the nails whimpered, and the lid slowly began to lift. A few more vigorous pulls, and it came right off.

The box was filled to the top with old sheets, sofa stuffing, ripped pieces of fabric, and thick and matted fragments of upholstery. I couldn't understand it. All that effort for this? A boxful of rubbish? It couldn't be. I plunged my hands in like I'd done with the other one and found something bundled up.

I should have opened the crate upstairs in better light. The shock might have been less. But I was too impatient. I didn't want to wait. And Veach was probably still up there. I didn't want him to see.

The sheets and fabric pieces fell away as I lifted the bundle out of the crate, and its heaviness reminded me of the weight of a small child. It was an odd thought, I know, but the crate did seem a little like a miniature coffin. I shivered—was it because of that morbid thought, or was it because I knew, deep down, my life was about to change? I peeled back the blankets to see what was so delicate that it needed this kind of protection. I wasn't prepared for what I saw.

A lethal little face, smiling, leering at me. It was like something you see in the depths of fever dreams and nightmares.

6

◇◇◇◇◇◇◇◇

"God Help Me!"

I BLAMED MY FIRST IMPRESSION of the imp on the poor lighting in the cellar. I thought it was an effect of the shadows, or my eyes straining too hard . . . my mind playing a mean little trick on itself. I wanted to take it up to my room for a closer look, but I couldn't—not with Fr. Veach lurking in the kitchen. He was still there, drinking an after-supper cup of tea, when I emerged from the cellar. It was obvious he was waiting for me, and when he saw I was empty-handed, he put his cup down. He said he was very tired and couldn't keep his eyes open much longer.

Later, near midnight, I crept out of bed and down the stairs. Even though that horrid little face scared me, I couldn't leave it in the cellar. Veach was too curious, too distrustful of me. He and William Bramble, the church's pastor, would never leave those crates alone. I'd gotten off to a very poor start with them because of a sealed letter I had carried from the diocese when I first arrived. I wished I had withheld it for a few days before they'd read it. Maybe everything would have turned out better if I'd waited, if I'd given them time to see me as a new colleague, not a threat.

"How do you like that, Felix? We've been demoted!" the pastor said, looking at Veach and waving the letter in his hand.

Bramble was a tall old fellow with big hands and a deep voice. He scratched the back of his bald head in exasperation as he reread the letter, and when I pled ignorance about it, he glared at me and thrust it in my face. "Read for yourself," he said, "and be ignorant no longer." The letter was short, tersely written, expressing Cardinal Manning's deep disappointment with the falling attendance and the Sunday sermons and placing that duty solely in my hands—the hands of a very junior associate. The letter was written by Monsignor Leheny on behalf of Manning. Both priests must have felt relieved to surrender this regular duty to me—it's a very heavy chore, and neither was any good at it. But it was humiliating to have it taken away like this.

"Gentlemen, please, we should discuss this. It must be a mistake. There must be some way—"

"There's nothing to discuss. It's been decided," the pastor said, tossing the letter on the dining room table. "It says what you're required to do. What we're required to let you do. Our efforts have been deemed unsatisfactory. But it seems you're very gifted. The monsignor says you're incapable of making mistakes." He glared at me. "I highly doubt it." When I tried to protest, he straightened up to his full height and loomed over me like a bear on its hind legs.

"Save what you would say for your first sermon, Fr. Frost. You only have a few days to prepare. Your time is running out."

Bitter old man. It wasn't my fault, but he blamed me anyways. They both did; they blamed me for whatever dissatisfactions they were feeling and, honestly, what could those be? How bad were they? They lived and worked at Saint Martha's, an excellent post in a beautiful part of the city . . . and I was carrying the Sunday duties for them, duties they'd never liked anyway! They were free—free to minister to the people, free to help the poor, to spend as much time as they liked pondering scripture or kneeling in prayer before the monstrance in the side chapel. They were living lives we dreamed about at Saint Thomas.

From the moment that diocesan letter was read, they watched me, noting my every mistake, every misstep, even the little things I said to parishioners that were awkward because I didn't know them well. I had no doubt they'd eventually make a case for my dismissal. That's why I didn't like Veach's obvious interest in my father's crates. I needed to get the imp out of there before they found it and used it against me.

The cellar stairs creaked horribly. I panicked and stopped several times to listen. All was quiet. I could hear the muffled snores of my associates two floors above me. I continued down the stairs as my candle threw wild, contorted shadows on the spars and oddments the church had accumulated over the years. Reaching the bottom, I nearly jumped out of my skin as my light fell on a gargoylish face next to the stair railings. The demonic face was almost as shocking as the imp's; it belonged to a statue once hanging above the church's main doors.

"God help me!" I said, stepping back.

The gargoyle's face receded into the shadows.

I removed the bundle from the crate and hurried up the stairs. In my haste, I was clumsy, and the wrappings came undone. I was halfway up the stairs when I found myself eye to eye with that terrible visage again. The candlelight added something to the awful effect: shadows played across the imp's face in the flickering light. The eyes seemed to widen and the mouth gape, as if I'd startled it, as if it was a living thing, and I completely lost my head. I dropped it. And the candle. The lighting went topsy-turvy as the imp tumbled down the stairs. It made a terrific thudding sound when it landed on the flagstones at the bottom. It sounded like it was being driven into the ground.

I stumbled back down the stairs after it. It was resting on its side, next to my sputtering candle. *Fool!* I said to myself. I was furious. *Get a hold of yourself! Look, he's laughing at you!* It was true—the imp *was* smirking, as it always does.

Up in my room, I peeled away the sheets and leaned the imp against the wall under my brightest lamp.

The imp had the width and thickness of a fence post, and it stood as high as my waist. It looked heavy, like it was carved from oak, but I lifted it easily . . . too easily for oak, I thought. Was it beech, then? No, the deep-brown color and dark veining suggested another wood. Rosewood, probably. My father had regularly used it in Montini's shop. That's what it had to be, rosewood, or else I'd never have manipulated the imp so easily in my arms. Leave it to a woodcarver's son to know the differences.

There was something else about the imp that was interesting: over its natural coloring, my father had applied a lacquer that deepened its reddish-brown appearance. The imp possessed a ruby-red glow in the lamplight. It was unexpected . . . and beautiful . . . and unlike anything I'd ever seen before. I slowly rotated the imp and studied its body. Its entire length was decorated with an intricate series of lines and patterns like a spider's web. None of these were on its head, though, which was polished smooth. I studied its face. I couldn't help shivering again despite the bright lamplight. There was no mistaking it. It was a devil's face. The features were appropriate to some goblin huddling in a dark corner of hell.

There were hollows where the eyes should have been—like a skull—and a small protuberance, like a button, for its nose. Decorative curls were inscribed along the chin. Its diabolical expression, however, was achieved most by its twisted mouth. It was an ugly expression, frozen between a laugh and a grimace, between mirth and despair—certainly terrifying to me but, I later discovered, it was intended to frighten the things that frighten us.

7

◇◇◇◇◇◇◇◇

The near fields

10:45 p.m.

THERE'S ALWAYS A GREAT DEAL OF SADNESS in our village, and not all of it comes from the pressures of Gradwolski's proxies. Life is cruel here. Beautiful but cruel. I recognized it as soon as I arrived. A farmer might leave his house in the morning and never return. He might stumble over something in the fields and fall in front of the oxen pulling the plow. Or slip on the mossy steps by the mill and tumble into its turning wheel. Or faint under the hot sun and never wake up. Sometimes Father Roman or I get to them in time, but not always.

There's a sadness hovering over the Melnyk house now. The cause of their sadness is different from the examples I've just given. Recently, they lost one of their grandsons, Paul. He was a big, handsome teenager. He went for a swim in the Zimn after working in the fields all day. It was supposed to be a quick dip, only to cool off, but he never returned. The next day, half the village was out looking for him. We searched everywhere, but there was no sign of him, not even down at the mill bridge. Paul had disappeared. Somebody suggested he'd run away. But why? There was no reason for it. As I said, it's a hard life here, and most children never leave, but Paul and his siblings' situation was better than most. Their parents both died, and they'd been living with their grandparents since they were little. Dmitro was training him as a cobbler; he wanted him to take over the business, and Paul was excited about it. He had a very promising future. It wouldn't take long for him to earn enough to build his own house. Dmitro's property is one of the largest in Prehovinka, and he was planning to divide it up and give half to his grandson. The village girls all knew about that; you could see them already sizing Paul up in church when he came to the front to receive the Eucharist. But he's never been seen since that late afternoon. It's a mystery, and it doesn't make any sense. Everyone's unsettled by it.

As a deacon, I'm supposed to offer consolations. Paul's disappearance troubles me, too, and it's been hard hiding this from Dmitro and Anna. Or Paul's two little sisters. I've tried. I've tried to help them. So has Roman. It is so hard to look in their sad faces and try to be encouraging. How do you say there's meaning in a loss that makes no sense?

Dmitro's bees are droning even louder now as I take out my flask of tea again. I tilt it to my lips, and as I'm tasting its earthy, loamy coolness, I hear, over the din of the bees, someone calling my name. I can't believe it. I look at my pocket watch. It's getting late. Who could be calling me now?

I see old Joseph Okrusko coming from his outhouse just across the way. He waves as he hobbles up to his front gate and crosses the lane.

"Evening, Joseph."

"Evening to you, Deacon," he says as he comes up, and then, eyeing the imp, "evening to you *both*." From a pocket he pulls a small leather pouch of tobacco and his pipe, which has an enormous bowl and a long white stem. He packs the bowl without looking up at me.

"How's the walk been?"

"Good," I say. "All's quiet."

He nods. "That's good . . . Of course, it's still early." He strikes a match on the heel of his boot. When the light flares up, I can see his smile. "The bogies are probably still asleep. Or maybe they're just hiding from you."

"Well, if I happen to find any tonight, I'll be sure to send them your way. Leave your door unlocked, won't you?"

He chuckles.

It's difficult to tell Joseph's age. Sixty? Seventy? Joseph has a good head of thick white hair, dark skin, and bright eyes like a lemur's. He squints in the direction of the woods just beyond his house. They say he came out of the womb frowning like that. But that flinty look is just a deception—he has a very good sense of humor once you get to know him. Whenever I tell him a silly joke, his eyes glow like blown-on coals. I like his company.

He exhales a puff of smoke and offers me the pipe.

"I did hear something out there while I was doing my business just now," he says as I take the bit between my teeth. He points at the small patch of woods. "It might be a wolf. I don't know. You could take the little fellow out there for a look if you want."

"Out there?" I say, exhaling and handing the pipe back. "A wolf?"

He shrugs.

"The Lemkos say they saw one the other night."

"They did?"

He nods. The concern on his face surprises me. He's not the sort who scares easily.

"But maybe it wasn't that, Joseph. It was probably someone gathering firewood. You know now's the best time for it. The Minkins aren't usually around."

The old farmer exhales another cloud of smoke.

"Maybe so, but it seems late for doing that, doesn't it? Who'd be building a fire now?"

He hands the pipe back to me.

"If you want me to go and look, I will. But you know this"—I indicate the imp against the fence—"won't do any good if there's a wolf out there."

"No, I know that. Listen, forget it, Yuri. Don't go. I was just thinking, it being a midsummer night and all, it could be one of the *voyiny* stirring things up." He looks back over his shoulder at the Melnyks' house. His voice lowers. "It's such a shame, isn't it?" He sucks on the pipe again, and the bowl flares.

"Yes. Poor family."

"How are they? I haven't had the courage to ask."

"Everyone's denying what's happened." I try to whisper. "They think he ran away, which doesn't make any sense."

"Dmitro, too?"

"Yes. But I can tell he doesn't believe it. I think he knows Paul's gone. He just doesn't want to upset the girls."

"How horrible."

"It really is."

The word he used, *voyiny*, refers to warriors. A long time ago, before there was ever a Galicia or an Austro-Hungary, a small band of Slavs was annihilated here by an overwhelming force of Tatars. It's chronicled in an old Slavonic history. The Tatars killed them right on the spot. Sliced off the tops of their skulls and used the curved skull pieces to drink a victory toast. They probably didn't even bother to clean out the brain matter. Or bury them. Gruesome, but not uncommon. And the spirits of those poor Slavs, local lore insists, have been rooted to the woods ever since.

It doesn't take long for Joseph and me to finish our smoke. When we're done, he smacks the bowl against his knee and lets the burned to-bacco fall in the dirt. He stands and says good night. He says he doesn't want to keep me any longer. I tell him I'm in no hurry if he wants to smoke another.

"Oh, no, Yuri, I should get back. The wife worries if I'm gone too long. I just figured you'd like some company a minute. Good to see you. Be safe," he says and starts to limp back to his yard.

As I'm watching him, I hear another sound coming up the lane. It's a horse galloping hard. Joseph hears it, too, and he hobbles to the other side just in time.

The rider flies by us, and I can see it's not Jacob. This time it's Bram, his younger brother. He gallops by without slowing or noticing us. He's on the search for the window breakers, too. I'm sure he won't hesitate to drive his horse into the fields if he thinks they're out there. He won't care if it twists an ankle. He'll just get another one. He's shorter than his brothers, stronger than both, and not very nice. His body's square and compact, and he has big shoulders. And a bad temper. I've seen him pull a full sack of flour off a farmer's wagon without the slightest exertion. I've also watched him beat his horses mercilessly if they didn't do what he wanted them to do.

Thank God Victor and Volodya are home now.

Joseph turns to wave one last time before he goes inside. I wave back as I walk along the side of his yard and head toward the woods. I'm not far from it when I hear movements inside the tree line. Twigs snapping. Scuttling paws. I hold up the imp so that he can get a better look.

Other villages use different practices to scare the ghosts away—bright bonfires built in the corners of their villages, young men running out into the fields and beating sticks or shaking bells. I've heard some Slovenes and Bulgars, and the Russians around Novgorod, use devil's masks. Their village elders walk around wearing them for the same reason I'm carrying the imp. Their creations are so crude and ugly next to our imp. I saw a Novgorodian mask in Lemberg once—it was made of thick, uneven strips of leather, and it had eyeholes and a jagged mouth so rudimentary I thought it had been made by a child.

We stop at the field's edge. Another fifteen paces or so, and we'll be inside the tree line. We're close enough. I set down my lamp, hold the imp with one arm, and take a clove of garlic from my coat pocket. Whatever's out there won't like the smell and should go away. I hope. Could it be one of the *voyiny*?

"Away from this place," I say in a loud hiss. "Away, in God's name!"

I throw the clove into the darkness. More branches snap, and then something thuds to the ground. I hear a murmur of voices, and suddenly two small figures emerge from the elderberry bushes at the edge of the woods. They stare at me, and it's all I can do not to howl in rage at them.

"Victor and Volodya! I told you to go home, didn't I? What are you doing? Come here this instant!"

As before, they don't have a good excuse for me. In fact, they use the same one. They say they're still looking for their lost chicken.

"There really is one, Deacon," Victor says. "His name is Henryk."

Henryk is apparently the family's pet. When I ask where their father is, they say he's out looking for Henryk, too.

"I don't believe this. Any of it. I know you're lying to me like you lied about the Minkins, and lying is a sin! A terrible sin!" I decide to do what always made me behave when I was a child: I'm going to scare them. "Listen, do you know what happened to Paul Melnyk? Do you?" I point at the house across the way. "Something got him when he was swimming. He was in the river, and it gobbled him up." I can see their earnest faces in the moonlight. "The monster's still out there somewhere. It climbed out of the water and is walking around tonight, looking for little boys. Did you know that?" I point at the moon. "It's a good night for hunting. Do you want it to find you? It got another boy up in Studinka a few months ago, too. Did you know that? Did your parents not tell you? It's true. Do you want it to gobble you up? No? All right, then. Get going. Now."

I don't leave anything to chance this time. I march them straight over to their house, which isn't far from Dmitro's. I walk them right up to the side door. I stand and wait until they're inside and I hear Marko's sleepy voice.

What I said about the boy from the other village isn't a lie. He was swimming, too. I don't think he was ever found.

I leave the Kindras' yard. I walk past several houses when a horse suddenly comes out of the shadows and blocks my way. I know who it is, but I shine my lamp up at him anyway.

"Oh. It's you. Hello, Bram. I wasn't expecting anyone. What are you doing out at this hour?"

I wonder how long he's been watching me. He must have come back around when he saw me and Joseph.

"What were you doing just now, Yuri?"

"What do you mean? I wasn't doing anything."

"Yes, you were. I saw. You're coming from the Okruskos' and Kindras'."

I think of the boys. His question makes me nervous, but I manage to keep my voice steady.

"Oh, yes, you're right. I was. I was doing something for Joseph. I saw him a little while ago."

Bram is impatient.

"What were you doing?"

I tell him about the wolf. I keep it simple. I tell him I went out to the little patch of woods by the field to look. If he's been spying on me, he probably saw me with the boys and knows I'm lying. But I'm not going to admit anything. He's going to have to show his hand first.

"It might have been a wolf, Bram. I don't know. Joseph wasn't sure. I just went to check."

He doesn't say anything. He keeps looking at me. Studying me. Waiting. Then he mutters like he's talking to himself.

"Going out there with that thing." He indicates the imp. "Ridiculous. You should be carrying a rifle. That's not going to protect you from a wolf. Or anything."

"It does offer protection," I say, adjusting my foot. It's starting to ache again. "It just doesn't offer what you're talking about."

"Nonsense. Pure nonsense. Somebody's going to get killed one day doing what you're doing."

"No one has yet."

"Was the wolf in Kindra's yard?"

"What?"

"It looked like you were coming from his yard just now."

"I wasn't. You're mistaken. I was taking the path between his yard and Joseph's."

He looks up at the moon. He's clearly irritated, but I don't think it has to do with me. If I were talking to Jacob now, I'd risk asking him what's bothering him.

"You'll have to excuse me now, Bram. I have to get back to my work. It's important."

I can't see his face, but I know I've amused him. I hear him chuckle.

"Oh yes, by all means. Please get back to your work," he says. "Your very important work."

I turn and walk by Dmitro's again. Bram and his horse go in the opposite direction. The lantern on the gatepost shines on the imp's face.

"Can you believe that?" I say to him. "That was a close one."

The imp smiles at me. He can't believe what happened, either. His expression might be fixed, but somehow it always seems to fit every situation. It doesn't scare me anymore. I don't know how my father managed to give its unchanging expression an ability to change. It's a mystery. The skill it took is beyond my understanding. He also gave it something else I should probably mention now. The imp looks almost black in the light of Dmitro's lantern, and the reason is simple. The lacquer that produces its peculiar glow—the substance that puzzled me at first and that I couldn't identify—was so common I didn't even consider it. More common than the beeswax and linseed oil my father used in Giuseppe Montini's shop. Blood. My father made the imp out of a piece of wood soaked in animal blood.

8

Blood

MY FATHER'S WORK ETHIC HAD BEEN EXCEPTIONAL. If he wasn't working on a project, he was helping someone. After applying paraffin to the oak (to make it less tasty to the woodworms), he might sweep up in the front shop, help carry lumber in the back, or show Giuseppe's wheelwright how to make a nice, smooth cut in a piece of wych elm to make a cartwheel. No chore was beneath him, not even scrap gathering. He'd venture out into the streets to collect bits of wood for the shop—you never knew when you might come across something interesting—and few of his coworkers were willing because it made them feel like rag-and-bone men. But it didn't bother my father; when you've lost your home and country, when you've been kicked around Europe by everybody, you don't care what people think. And besides that, his collecting work earned us extra money, including the halfpennies he sometimes gave me to buy warm pieces of caramel. He went anywhere in search of discarded pieces of wood that might be valuable, and he knew the London streets better than Cruchley and Davis or any other city mapmaker.

Giuseppe wrote to me at Saint Martha's and asked me to come and see him. He was missing my father and wanted to talk about him. He'd been too emotional, too overcome, to say much at the funeral. When I visited him at his shop, our conversation turned into a eulogy of sorts. He praised my father in countless ways. He praised his dedication and willingness to do anything necessary, which also sometimes revealed his eccentric behavior. Once, Giuseppe recalled, my father returned to the shop with a cartload of floorboards and broken tables he found south of London Bridge by the tanneries and slaughterhouses. They had been abandoned behind several large vats of offal. But Giuseppe couldn't use them; he said they were disgusting—too slick with the agonies of a thousand animals to ever be cleaned.

"Michael, I would never have used that wood for my furniture," he said, and the memory of how it looked and smelled made him spit in the dirt. We were standing in a small yard behind the shop where workers were sawing fresh lumber. Sawdust floated in the air and tickled my nose. "It was impossible that I could ever use that wood for anything. Too much badness, too much . . . *cattiveria* in it, you understand? But that was your father. He didn't understand my hesitation." He chuckled. "He never wanted to waste a thing. I had to explain to him why I couldn't."

Giuseppe asked my father to throw the wood away. He did, but not all of it. He'd kept one piece.

The imp had been troubling enough before, but the blood made it worse. I was suddenly terrified for my father's soul. I knew too much about the horrible punishments reserved for idolaters in hell; they'd been drummed into us in the seminary. I never dreamed my father could ever be one, that he could ever deserve eternal torment. Why did he make this thing? What did he need it for? Why would he risk his soul for this? And why did he seal it up in the crate? I had so many questions—and no answers. I was terrified and confused. The blood was a bad sign. Even before I made any progress in my occult studies, I knew the blood meant something terrible. I remembered a story from the *Odyssey*. When he wanted to speak to the dead, Odysseus filled up trenches with sheep blood, and the spirits swarmed over him like bees. One of my instructors at the Mortimer Academy acted out that moment so convincingly, it gave me nightmares for several weeks. My father had to know about the power of blood. It's something most people seem to understand regardless of their experiences or education.

Dear God, I thought, was he trying to summon the dead like Odysseus? Maybe he missed my mother. Was he trying to contact her?

In the 1870s and 1880s, séances were wildly fashionable in the city; spiritualist establishments and bookshops were popping up all over London like mushrooms after a heavy rain. You could find tarot cards or rune stones as easily as a tin of valerian in your local apothecary's shop. Mediums enjoyed vast reputations and incomes, and it didn't matter that Browning had pilloried one of them, the Scotsman Home, in his Sludge poem. The public was in such a frenzy over the occult that *Punch* even complained that if the "spirit-moving mania be carried on much further, it will be necessary for persons who are about to marry to take steps to secure themselves from buying haunted furniture!"

My search for answers was aligned with popular tastes at the time. It was the silver lining in an otherwise desperate situation.

My research sent me all over the city, from the bookstalls of Paternoster Row to the spirit libraries of Marylebone Street, and I decided my study of totems and talismans, runes and rituals could feed my sermons. It was a shame to waste it, so I'd put it to use with my congregation, and that was why I became a very successful preacher.

If people wondered why a mandrake root screams when you pull it from the ground or how to make a Hand of Glory after a criminal's execution, let them hear it from me. Let me use their curiosity about the demonic world to swell Saint Martha's dwindling ranks. That's why I'd been put there, wasn't it? What was the worst that could happen to me? If my stories failed to attract crowds or offended someone, the diocese could always send me off to that chapel barn assignment that I'd been dreading.

But I didn't fail. My sermons succeeded in halting the church's decline. I witnessed a sharp reversal in attendance (and the collections) in a short amount of time.

The pews started filling up with all those spirit-moving maniacs *Punch* complained about as word spread of my unusual sermons—including the costlier seats, the shilling ones, near the front. I even attracted attention from the London press.

I take a yellowed strip of paper from my coat pocket:

A Captivating Dose of
Devilry in Chelsea

Sunday morning found the Sketchist not happily
under his bedcovers, recuperating from the previ-

ous night's tedious premiere of *The Tempest* at the Garden, but at Saint Martha's Catholic Church, Cadogan Street, Chelsea—in the very back pew (of course). What brought him there? Was it a sudden impulse to repent his loathsome treatment of all the horrid actors he has endured through the years? My heavens, no!

I'd been hearing about Father Michael Frost, the church's new young cleric, for several weeks, and quite frankly, I'd had enough of this! I decided to see for myself why tongues have been wagging so excitedly about a man of the cloth. It turns out that on a succession of Sundays, Fr. Frost has been packing them in with tales of supernatural mischief. What, the Sketchist conjectured, could be better than to start off one's Sunday with a little dose of devilry?

This appeared in the *Daily Telegraph* early in the fall of 1881 in the theatrical reviews section. It wasn't unusual for newspapers to publish the sermons of some of the city's most notable preachers. Whole pages were devoted to these, usually right alongside advertisements for products promising exceptional hygiene and wellness. But a review in the theater section by one of London's most popular columnists? Unthinkable! The Sketchist's column brought many newcomers to Saint Martha's the next Sunday.

The primary lesson of the sermon that day, a meditation upon the First Letter of Paul to the Corinthians, was that our world teems with demons. Our world is as crowded with this malevolent crew as a Friday evening in Piccadilly, although we do not know it. Fascinating!

And what's more, Fr. Frost tells his congregation, God is under siege and needs our help. He is not strong enough to stop them on his own. Daring!

The effect upon his listeners is readily apparent. Worry on the faces of the old, rapture on the young! I would hope that Fr. Frost will continue in this vein in future sermons. My only recommendation is that the church offer a much later service: then they will surely have even more attendees . . . and see me again!

I remain, faithfully yours,

THE SKETCHIST

The Sketchist refers to a sermon I delivered on the famous lines of Saint Paul asking us to wear "the armor of light." Instead of taking the apostle's words in a metaphorical sense, I treated them literally. What if he really meant that we need to wear armor? What if he really meant that we are at war? I thought about all the possible angles. That morning, I climbed into the pulpit, looked out on a sea of faces, and began:

Brothers and sisters, why would the Apostle want us to wear armor if the war in heaven, the war that ejected the rebel angels, was over? God's omnipotence settled that matter, didn't it? Our God is omnipotent, isn't he?

I must confess something to you: I don't think he is.

If you knew the literature of demonology, then you would realize that there is no other way to explain why there are so many demonic manifestations taking place in our world today. The first war, between God and Lucifer, isn't over. Our God is locked in a terrible struggle.

This is why you must be careful. Demons are all around us. They aren't only to be found in remote places in distant lands. They are outside these very doors, at the periphery of this space that has been consecrated for God's purpose.

They are on the streets, in public buildings, in shops . . . and in your homes.

Catholic sermons at Saint Martha's had been a dismal affair before me. As I mentioned before, Bramble and Veach didn't have it in them to deliver a good story. The structure of the Sunday Mass is meant to erase the

individuality of the priest—one is no different from another. We speak
the same prayers, perform the same meticulous series of movements with
our backs to the people most of the time—except for the occasional *Do-
minus vobiscum* when we turn on our heels and move from one side of the
altar to the other. Priests are indistinguishable gears and levers in the vast
Tridentine machinery of the Mass. But the sermon is the one place in
that machine where a priest can shine. Most didn't; most just muttered
some platitudes before hurrying out of the pulpit, and it's understandable.
English Catholicism had been very plain and quiet for many years out
of respect for (fear of, actually) our Protestant cousins. For much of the
English penal years, there was a prayer book, *Garden of the Soul*, that was
prevalent in English Catholic homes. It encouraged the faithful to embrace modesty and reticence. This way of thinking lingered on long after
the restoration of the 1850s, and I can't entirely blame Saint Martha's
dwindling attendance on the incompetence of Bramble and Veach. The
art of the sermon hadn't been taught to them. There were guidelines and
some technical suggestions given in seminary, but you either have a taste
for it or you don't. *Brothers and sisters,* I said near the end,

> *. . . when you say your prayers tonight, make them heartfelt. Say
> not only the words of the Lord's Prayer. Fall to your knees, like Shake-
> speare's Prince Hal on the eve of Agincourt, and tell the Lord that you
> are ready to help him win this war! That you are ready to put on Paul's
> armor and fight with him! Pray to him with these words:*
>
> *O great God of battles, steel our hearts!
> Take from us any sense of reckoning, if th' opposed numbers
> pluck our hearts from us!*
>
> *Not today, O Lord, not today!*

Then I fell to my knees. A loud gasp went up. Two men near the front
darted forward to help me, but I waved them away. I closed my eyes. My
God, I thought, how perfect. Just what I wanted. The Sketchist included
a sketch of me with his review. His drawing did a wonderful job of cap-
turing the regal, throne-like beauty of the altar—and he was very kind in

regard to my physical appearance, too. That may explain why, the next Sunday, the proportion of women to men at Mass did seem higher.

After a few moments, I rose to my feet, adjusted my stole, and looked at the congregation. Everyone was quiet. They were all watching me, waiting. Near the back, where we kept a small table with the bread and wine before their transformations, I saw a movement in the shadows. Someone was standing there. It was Father Bramble.

Even from a distance, even with a glare in my eyes because of the bright morning sunlight, I could see his face. He was furious.

9

◇◇◇◇◇◇◇◇

The church

12:50 a.m.

LIGHTNING SHIVERS UP THE CHURCH WALLS and flashes inside the dome.

Our church is relatively new. It was built in the past ten years. When I first arrived, the village had been using a barn for a long time . . . and the irony wasn't lost on me. I looked at it and thought, *Well, here's the chapel barn none of us ever wanted in the seminary!* The villagers didn't want a barn for a church, either, but they didn't have a choice. The barn had to be used because the old church—which was a simple box-shaped structure with three cupolas in honor of the Father, Son, and Holy Ghost—had burned down. Some said it was an accident; others insisted the fire had been started by Russian Orthodox believers because they consider Uniates traitors (or maybe it was the Poles for the same reason). The Uniate arrangement with Rome, in my opinion, is a sensible compromise, and everyone seems to hate it. The culprits in the church's destruction were never found, but the villagers nonetheless appealed to Gradwolski and the magistrate in Stanislau for help, which was what they were supposed to do. They asked

for restitution to help us rebuild and received just what they expected—
nothing. Neither did anything about it. No kronen, no help of any kind.

It's taken a long time for construction to get this far.

It started raining when I reached the northern side of the village.
At first it didn't seem to be a heavy rain, so I stood under a cherry tree
in front of the Semeluk house and thought I could wait it out there. But
large drops started slipping through the leaves and falling on my bald spot.
I hurried up the lane, trying not to slip in the quickly forming puddles as
I searched for better shelter. I needed more than a tree. The wind picked
up, and I shivered. Suddenly I was grateful for my coat. I could hear
Eugenie's voice, "There, see? Why would you ever doubt me?" In the
flashes of lightning, I saw the new church's silver domes glistening ahead.
It sits on the other side of the Zimn, separated from us by a long bridge.
I rushed across the bridge and fumbled for the key Roman keeps hidden
behind a loose piece of mortar by the church's front door. I found it just
as the downpour intensified, and I hurried inside.

There's another flash of lightning, and the image of the Pantocrator
up in the dome appears for a moment. The Lord Jesus as dreadful judge.
It's a terrifying sight, especially because of the effect of the lightning—and
it's supposed to be. The ones who painted it for us were two Ruthenian
boys who once lived somewhere east of Brody, which is under the Russian
czar. They managed to escape their village and come west for a better
life, and they needed money to keep going. They were willing to paint this
image for much less than what the iconographers in Lemberg were asking.

Jesus clasps an enormous book in his hand. He grips it like he's going
to swat us with it. I think the painters intended a little private joke in his
features. Something about the scowl, the angry eyes, the chestnut color
and shape of the beard reminds me of a painting I once saw of Nicholas
II. I wonder if it was intentional. I should've asked about it, but I didn't
notice until they were gone.

That angry face reminds me of someone else, too—Fr. Bramble, on
the day I decided to play Henry V for my surprised parishioners. I saw
that old priest stiffen up and clench his jaw as he watched me from the
back of the church. Later, when the Mass was done, and I was in the sacristy changing my clothes, he burst into the room.

"Goddamn *you!*" he boomed. The acolyte assisting me shrank back.
"Fallen angels? A weak Heavenly Father? How dare you!"

My sermon was vile, he roared. A blasphemous display of theatrics and a misuse of my authority.

The sacristy door opened again. Veach floated in.

"You can't trust these young ones," he said, pointing a bony finger at me. "They're spiteful and arrogant. They don't know what respect means."

I turned to look at him.

"What are you talking about? The diocese said I'm in charge of the Sunday Masses, including the homilies. Don't you remember the letter? Do you want to read it again? How I'm supposed to conduct myself and my sermons is my decision, not yours."

I was about to say something else, but Bramble shouted over me. He ordered me back to the rectory. He shook his fist. His behavior was so shocking and unexpected that I did what he said. I went back to the rectory. I should have stood my ground. But he was my superior, and I felt helpless to do anything except obey him. As I climbed the stairs to my rooms, I thought, *What are you doing, Michael? Where are you going? You're not a child anymore, are you? You didn't do anything wrong.* I turned back and went down the stairs.

A few minutes later, I heard my associates enter the rectory. They looked in the kitchen for something to eat and found me sitting at the dining room table, reading earlier drafts of my sermon. I pretended to lazily flip through the pages even though I was tense and angry inside.

"Who said you could come down here?" Bramble growled.

I ignored him. I kept my eyes on the papers. I didn't want either of them to see I was upset. I heard Veach whisper to Bramble, "Go on. Tell him. Like we've agreed." Then the other priest cleared his throat and announced that until he had a chance to discuss my behavior with Westminster, I wouldn't be allowed to give another sermon. That took me completely by surprise. I pushed back my chair and stood up.

"You cannot do that! You have no right! *No right!*"

Veach stepped forward.

"Oh, but we have every right," he said, adding that I would participate at the Sunday Masses only in the capacity of a server.

I was incensed. I shouted back at them.

"That's what you want? To turn me into an acolyte? To embarrass me? I'm sorry, but no, I will not do that. *I will not!*"

"No? You think you can talk to us like that, little whelp?" Bramble said threateningly. "Get upstairs! Now!"

I gathered up the papers I had just finished straightening and threw them in the air. As the pages scattered at their feet, I stormed out of the rectory with no idea what to do next. But I did feel certain of one thing: I'd given those two fools just what they wanted—a good reason to have me removed from Saint Martha's and their lives.

I SPENT TWO WEEKS away from Saint Martha's thanks to the hospitality of a friend. I will get to him later. For now, the important part is that a letter from Father Bramble found me there and ordered me back to the church to resume the Sunday Masses. I learned that Cardinal Manning had been delighted by the attention I'd received in the Sketchist's column—apparently, he was a reader of the column, too—and he sent Monsignor Leheny to attend Mass at Saint Martha's on the following Sunday and convey his thanks. When Leheny reported what he found, that Bramble was back in the pulpit and I was nowhere to be seen, His Eminence was furious. This was just the sort of opportunity Saint Martha's needed, and Leheny demanded to know my whereabouts. Bramble told him what happened—his version—and must have expected Leheny would share his sense of outrage. Instead—I learned all of this from Nessie, our housekeeper, who was cooking in the kitchen and had very good ears—the Monsignor waved a copy of the Sketchist's article at Bramble and told him that I was to have complete freedom (Nessie said he put a fierce inflection in the word) to pursue whatever I deemed necessary. Bramble started to object, but then everything went quiet and was soon followed by the slamming of the front door. Veach came downstairs and found Bramble in the kitchen, red-faced and sullen, drinking a glass of water. When he asked what happened, Bramble said the two of them would find themselves in a prison chaplaincy if I wasn't back in the pulpit by next Sunday.

On my return, as my carriage pulled up to the rectory, the first thing I noticed was a large banner, the sort used in political campaigns. It was festooned across the church building on its street-facing side. I couldn't believe it:

THIS SUNDAY!
Father Michael Frost holds forth on
intriguing aspects of the Bible!
ALL ARE WELCOME!
9:00 a.m. and Noon

The sign had only recently been painted. I could see rivulets of paint running down from the letters in thin, spiky streaks. Inside, I found Father Bramble in the common room. He welcomed me with few words and a tired look. He said he was retiring early, and when he turned to go, I noticed his hands. There was black paint on them.

That wasn't the only surprise waiting for me. In the kitchen, Nessie greeted me with a warm smile and a letter. I thought it might be from the monsignor, but it wasn't. In fact, it wasn't an official letter at all—it was something far more wonderful and unexpected.

My dearest Reverend,

Upon hearing one of your exquisite sermons, I realized you might highly enjoy an opportunity to mingle with some of London's interesting and artistic minds. An evening has been organized to honor one of their own, the esteemed Dante Gabriel Rossetti, and I would be delighted to have you as my guest.

If this is agreeable, I must risk causing insult here by adding that among the personalities one finds in artistic circles, the appearance of a clerical collar may have, how can I put this, a certain freezing effect on the convivial mood. I hope you won't misunderstand. I don't wish to suggest you are boorish by any means! Not from where I sat on Sunday. Not from what the Sketchist wrote about you. It is so clear to me, and not only to me, that had the Roman Church not claimed you, the artists of London would have welcomed you with open arms. Yet, you surely understand, some people form opinions based on little more than the clothes we wear.

If I do not receive your regrets by the day of the party, I shall take the liberty of calling upon you at the rectory at 8 upon

the evening of the 8th. I do hope you'll join me. Until then,
I remain

Most sincerely yours,

Lionel Ashburnham
Mayfair

Occasionally I received a kind note from a parishioner, but nothing
like this. Never mind that this stranger, in just a few sentences, managed to
charm and offend me at the same time—please don't dress like a priest!—I
was too overcome by his flattering words. I didn't know then, couldn't
know, that Lionel Ashburnham had other reasons for engaging me. He
didn't attend my sermon on a lark and invite me to this party purely for
my personal enjoyment. When he entered Saint Martha's that Sunday
morning, he needed my help. He needed someone with a certain kind of
arcane knowledge and expertise, and word had spread about the exotic
nature of my sermons. If I'd known that from the onset, if I'd known what
to expect, I might have been better prepared for the oddness of the party.
But Lionel was the sort of person who kept his motives hidden unless he
saw an advantage in sharing them.

All of these "if I had knowns" and "might haves" wouldn't make any
sense to Eugenie. Would she understand? Does she need to? She'd probably tell me I should have ignored the letter and stayed focused on my work.
I'd agree with her now, but I couldn't help it then. I was young. Too young.
I didn't know any better. I was basking in the glow of the Sketchist's column and thrilled at the thought of meeting artists and spending time with
someone who seemed eager to be my friend. Life, I felt, was compensating
me for losing my mother and my father, for the classmates who hated me
and never wanted my friendship, for the meanness of my two associates,
for the lonely path I'd taken as a priest.

I had no reason to be cautious. I should have been.

10

◇◇◇◇◇◇◇◇

16 Cheyne Walk

SOME PEOPLE LEAVE A LASTING IMPRESSION on you from the moment you see them; Lionel Ashburnham was one. I still remember seeing him on the day of the sermon celebrated by the Sketchist. I had no idea who he was or what he would mean to me. He sat off to one side, next to a bank of votive candles in a small alcove—it was a place where late-comers hid with the young mothers and their infants. If that had been his plan, to hide, he failed miserably. He wore light plaid slacks on his slender legs; a stark white shirt carefully and precisely pressed; a yellow frock coat with a precious green lapel stone gleaming like the morning star; and his hair, that thick, ridiculous red hair, had been teased to a frothy, spectacular height. I felt sorry for the people behind him.

As I said, he failed miserably at being inconspicuous. Everything about him, the cut of his clothes, his handsome face, his broody air of worldliness, all of it forced itself on your senses. But on the night of Rossetti's party, when his cab pulled up in front of the rectory, that dashing figure was nowhere to be seen. Gone was the vivid apparel he'd worn: he dressed in a plain brown suit instead. His thick, red hair was plastered down with macassar oil, and the flatness of his hairstyle made his nose seem larger, like a bloodhound's snout. Restraint may have marked his clothing, but there was still a jaunty air about him. He laughed when he saw me and grabbed my hand, pulling me into the cab, which reeked of cologne.

"I am so glad to have your company tonight, Father!" he said, pulling me up into the carriage.

I was usually reserved with strangers, but I wasn't with Lionel. His personality—his good humor and attentiveness, his charm and friendliness—drew me out. I lapped up his interest in me like a starving dog. I told him about my early life, my father's recent death, how my parish associates hated me, and anything else I could think of: I'd neatly summarized my entire life before we'd traveled very far. When I was done, he leaned forward.

"The one thing you haven't mentioned is your devotion to art, Frost. Your sermon showed that. You're as much of a slave to it as I am. I suspect your absence from the Sunday services won't continue because of that auspicious showing in the Sketchist's column, right?"

I told him that he was correct. I said I'd be back in the pulpit the next Sunday. He grinned and patted my knee.

"My heartiest congratulations. You know, I'm acquainted with the person who wrote that column about you. He's a jolly fat fellow who always wears a straw hat. Did you not see him? He was sitting near me in the alcove. No? Well, that's quite all right. There are another ten like him. The *Telegraph* uses a small army under the moniker of the Sketchist to cover the city's theater news. How do you like that, Father? You're considered news! I caught up with him after your service. He said he thought you were positively impressive. 'Revelatory,' I think, was a word he used. I told him he had impeccable taste."

Lionel smiled warmly and explained the reason for the night's celebration. Dante Rossetti was sick and in low spirits. A small party had been planned to cheer him. When I told Lionel that I admired Rossetti's paintings and poetry, he said that Gabriel—I didn't know that was what the artist liked his intimates to call him—would be delighted to meet me. I added that I only knew what most people did about his work—some of the paintings, *Lilith* and *The Girlhood of Mary Virgin*, and a few of the more famous poems, "The Blessed Damozel" and the Willowwood sonnets. I hoped Rossetti wouldn't expect too much of me.

"Don't worry, friend," Lionel said with a soft chuckle. "I'm sure you know more than most of the people we'll see tonight."

The carriage turned a corner, and I saw the Thames beyond a screen of trees. We were near Cheyne Walk. It was obvious to which house we were headed. The windows on all the floors of Number 16 were ablaze, and there was a steady stream of guests entering and leaving by the front doors. It was hardly the small party Lionel had described.

The home's entrance hall was extraordinary. Figures of daydreaming ethereal maidens with mirrors and archaic-looking musical instruments gazed at us from the walls. My eyes passed over them, over their dreamy, seductive faces. Down their long white arms. I was mesmerized . . . more than mesmerized . . . and embarrassed at how quickly a painting—a painting, for God's sake—could unlock one's desires.

The rooms were very crowded. Lionel was surprised to see so many people invited to what was supposed to be an intimate affair. Dishes were being removed from the dining room by hired servants. They picked the best remaining parts of each course and rearranged them on a small table for latecomers like Lionel and me. He looked disappointed . . . and annoyed.

Another source of aggravation was soon apparent: a young man named Lawrence Klein. He was handsome and well-dressed, rich, and something of a poet and scholar. Lionel learned from another guest that Klein had taken part in an earlier meal with Rossetti and a much smaller group of people—a meal he didn't know about. That angered him; I could see it on his face, but when he saw me watching, he shrugged and forced a smile, saying, "Well, what can we do now? Are you hungry? Let's hope the other crows haven't picked the carcasses clean already." I followed him into the drawing room, and Lionel spotted Klein in a doorway. He groaned and turned away, but it was too late. Klein saw him.

"Ah, Christ," Lionel muttered.

"Ashburnham, there you are," Klein said loudly as he approached. "And where is your uncle?"

The glass of burgundy in his hand matched the dazzling color of his dinner jacket and the gemstone in his lapel. Lionel's humble brown suit didn't stand a chance against it. He glared back at him.

"Good to see you, too, Klein." He grabbed a glass of claret from a passing servant. "Why don't *you* tell me where he is? You probably have a better idea than I do." He took a swig.

"I haven't seen him," Klein said innocently. Then he gave me a side-long glance as though I'd just coalesced out of thin air. Lionel introduced me as an old friend.

"Michael's an idler, like us," he said, struggling to be cordial.

"A pleasure to meet you," I said.

Klein's response was a faint smile. Then he drifted off without saying another word. We watched him move to the stairs where more people were arriving—probably to see if Lionel's uncle was among them.

"Apologies for that," Lionel said.

I asked who he was. Lionel sniffed.

"Just a Jew who wishes he was Italian. His family has slightly less money than Jehovah." Then, as if something occurred to him, he added, "I do suppose I shouldn't treat him so harshly. He has suffered more than most."

"Suffered how?"

"He and his wife lost their child. A little girl. She died of scarlet fever a year ago, I believe. Or maybe two. Better not to mention it if you're ever in conversation with him. Klein's a scholar of Italian art. I think losing the child has made him plunge deeper into his work. It's understandable. It's his way of coping. Books instead of the opium den. But scholarship's always been his obsession, aside from managing the family's name and reputation." He said the Klein family's wealth came from a combination of banks, collieries, and maritime ventures.

"His situation must be like yours," I said.

"Oh, we both have family names to uphold, but having a name and having wealth aren't the same thing, Frost," he said with a pained smile. "At least in my case. Not for Klein." He stopped a passing servant and asked if his uncle had arrived. He hadn't, she said. When he turned back, I asked why his uncle's attendance was so important to Klein.

"Because he might recite something for us tonight, and Lawrence wants to be sure," he said. "My uncle's Algernon Swinburne."

"My God . . . Lionel," I said, aghast. "The poet? He is your uncle?"

"The one and only," he said with a flourish of his hands.

They were cousins, he explained, but the older man's age and affection always made him seem like an uncle. Ashburnham was the maternal side of the family; Lionel said he was grateful for the distance his surname gave him, especially as he pursued a career in journalism and criticism. He didn't want the help that a clear association might have given him; he wanted to earn his rightful place on his own, though it was obvious he savored their connection (and who wouldn't?). I recalled seeing Lionel in the church. His style had reminded me of the flashiness of Swinburne's younger days. He hadn't been trying to hide the association then. By the time I met Lionel, though, much had changed for his cousin; he was a far healthier version of his younger dissipated self. He dressed and behaved more like a banker; in fact, there was a greater chance they'd resemble each other now than if Lionel had dressed in a more bohemian style. Swinburne, he explained, had taken the cure years ago and saved his life.

"Some say it's cost him his best lyrical powers," he added. "They wish he stayed drunk."

Years ago, Lionel had aspired to climb high in artistic circles alongside Swinburne. He had hoped that being his guardian would guarantee his admittance to these circles. But he didn't have the temperament for being a caretaker—he couldn't really handle the daily responsibilities that his "uncle's" demons required. The family briefly allowed him to try, but when it was clear Lionel was unsuited for it, Lionel watched as another, a man named Theodore Watts-Dunton, insinuated himself so tenaciously into Swinburne's life that he couldn't be removed. Lionel and much of the family had their access to the poet severely limited by this fierce custodian. It was no wonder, then, that Lionel studied the crowd so eagerly—more eagerly than Klein—because the party afforded a chance to see his beloved, avuncular cousin again.

As he studied the crowd, Lionel spotted a tall, red-haired man crossing the room. His name was Hall Caine. He was a novelist and journalist remembered less for his own writing and more for his association with Rossetti and others, like Bram Stoker, who dedicated a vampire book to him. Lionel called him over.

"Caine, why on earth was Klein at the earlier meal and not I? Why wasn't I invited?" he demanded.

The man gave him an impatient look. He said the seating had been too small at dinner to include everyone because Gabriel also invited some old friends he hadn't seen in a long time.

"And besides," the man said as he was about to turn away, "Klein paid for it all. He couldn't possibly be excluded, could he?"

11

◇◇◇◇◇◇◇◇

Guests

A THOUSAND BAUBLES, A THOUSAND PIECES of antique flotsam and jetsam, were strewn throughout Rossetti's home—much of it perilously in our way. Rossetti was an indiscriminate collector of the highest order . . . and a poorly organized one, too. In the sitting rooms, I might have tripped over an exquisite marble chess set carelessly abandoned on the floor if Lionel hadn't been there. I'd have been utterly lost without him—and probably injured, too. He grabbed my arm and gently navigated me past shelves loaded with porcelain figurines and placid-looking gargoyles made of soapstone (the imp would've been in good company there), thick wall hangings and ivory crucifixes, and ill-arranged stacks of blue china that the artist kept proudly on display. He guided me down gloomy passageways choked with dark-paneled cabinets. I realized, early in my relationship with him, that he liked to be flattered about his usefulness. I told him he reminded me of Theseus in the labyrinth.

"Well, let's hope we don't run into any minotaurs." He laughed. "I won't know what to do then."

In the dining room, we helped ourselves to what was left of some boiled fish and mutton as we watched the ebb and flow of guests. I was happy to eat my little plate of leftovers with Lionel; like the other guests, I was eager to see Rossetti and Swinburne together.

Lionel pointed at several older gentlemen studying Rossetti's paintings and sketches. These had been set up on easels and tables throughout the house. Lionel said Rossetti's brother hoped to get a sale or two. A few of these men, I thought, seemed familiar to me, as if I'd seen them in my pews. Others, dressed in worn coats and scuffed boots resembling half-dead crocodiles, seemed more like the beggars you saw outside the church on Sundays asking for money and meal tickets; they looked desperate, more interested in a free meal than the reunion of two great artists.

Where female guests were concerned, some had served as models for the bone-white, pensive faces I saw in the entrance hall. It didn't require much mental energy to see that—other women, though, seemed present for other reasons. I watched as they approached certain men and flirted with them, engaging in another kind of commerce that didn't involve the purchase of a painting or a sketch. That night several arguments and scuffles broke out between men you'd never expect—quiet types, the sort who'd probably never used their fists before. You could tell from the way they swung at each other—like they were shooing away butterflies. That night, Rossetti also lost a precious piece of chinoiserie when one guest threw it at another; a few more items disappeared into the pockets of departing guests, and the servants caught some before they left (though not all). I couldn't understand why Rossetti would tolerate all these bad hats, but Lionel explained they were entertaining and engaging enough that Rossetti liked having them around.

It was easy to expect tensions and fights because of too much drink and the crowded rooms. But as I look back now, I know it wasn't just drink or too many people that created the odd atmosphere in the house. There was something else there, an entity of some kind, winding its way through the rooms, supping on our selfishness, nudging us toward shameful behavior. It was only later, much later, that I recognized the signs of its presence.

We moved into the drawing room, which stretched across the entire first floor of the house, with large bay windows looking out on the Thames.

"There," Lionel said. "Do you see that man on the sofa over there?" I looked in the direction he indicated. "That is tonight's guest of honor."

Settled back on billowy cushions was the artist himself. I had noticed a self-portrait of Rossetti in one of the rooms: a gallant young man with wavy black hair; dark beard; and a bold, yearning stare. The man I saw before us now, though certainly the same, was pallid, puffy, more of a government clerk than a daring aesthete. He still wore a beard, but it was gray and faded, and the hair on his head was very thin. He continually raised a silk handkerchief to dab the sweat from his cheeks and forehead. A group of young men had dropped anchor a few paces to the left of his sofa; even though they cast anxious glances at him that he undoubtedly felt, none had the courage to leave their mooring and engage him.

Maybe they were maintaining a respectful distance, like everyone else, because Rossetti looked so unwell. The poor man seemed like he'd been drained by a vampire, and maybe he had. I'd said in one of my sermons that nothing pleases evil spirits more than the pain of a degraded soul, and Rossetti was certainly that. He'd experienced plenty of pain and corruption in his life. There had been that awful business with his wife, Elizabeth Siddal, that still found its way into conversations, that still floated into any room where he happened to be. I'm sure I wasn't the only one thinking of it as I looked at him. At the time of the party, it had been at least ten or twelve years since it happened, and still, the story exerted a fascination over people as much as anything in my sermons. Rossetti had made a bold gesture at the funeral of his young wife, who died while grieving the loss of their stillborn child. He slipped the sole manuscript of his poems into the coffin, and later, when the poetic success of his friends gnawed at him, he had the poems retrieved from her grave. Some whispered that Rossetti hadn't been waiting at home while the grave was being exhumed. He'd been there at the cemetery, Highgate, and that he'd been the one who reached into the coffin and found the book, caked with the waxy remains of his beloved. It was scandalous gossip, and yet there certainly had to be some kernel of horrible truth to it. There weren't trenches of sheep blood at 16 Cheyne Walk, but the artist was carrying enough psychical wounds to attract any spirit.

Lionel poked a finger in the direction of the young men near Rossetti and mocked them for being too timid to approach the artist. He grabbed my arm and he said we wouldn't make their foolish mistake. He pulled me in the direction of Rossetti's sofa.

12

◇◇◇◇◇◇◇◇

Propertius

"GABRIEL, HERE'S THE FELLOW I mentioned before."

Rossetti looked up at me and smiled.

"Oh yes. You're the young scholar of classics Lionel told me about. I'm so glad you were able to join us. Welcome to my home."

A servant approached and whispered something in Lionel's ear. He turned to us.

"It seems my other guest has arrived, though my uncle's whereabouts remain unknown. Please excuse me a moment." He walked off to the stairwell.

Another guest? I thought. But wasn't I his guest, his *only* guest?

I turned back to Rossetti. He asked me to sit by him. It wasn't easy: the sofa was small, and he'd planted himself right in the middle. I managed to balance at one of the ends and shot a proud glance at the group of young fools watching us.

Rossetti was very kind to me, considering I held no status in his world. It wasn't entirely true, of course; there had been my appearance in the Sketchist's column, but that was a secret; I couldn't mention it. I looked at him and desperately wanted to show that I was more than just some ordinary admirer of his work. I struggled for something interesting to say, and I think he sensed my distress. He asked what scholarly work I was currently engaged in. I thought of the imp.

"I'm studying archaeology," I said. His face brightened.

"Oh really? If you're a scholar of the classics, your work must involve the Greeks or Romans?"

"Neither, I'm afraid. It's something more primitive than that. Slavic. Or Norse. I'm unsure. My research is still very new."

That seemed to please him. He described several artifacts given to him by friends traveling in the Far East—travels he might have joined if he hadn't so many projects and commissions to complete. A shadow fell on us as we talked, and we both looked up. I thought Lionel had returned, but it was Caine, his tall, strained-looking associate whom Lionel accosted earlier.

"Algernon's here, Gabriel. He's in the entrance hall."

Rossetti nodded.

"Wonderful. William was sure he would join us. I'm not in the spirit to read tonight. I'm sorry. But I'm certain Algernon will be. I'm sure he'll give everyone a pleasant evening."

Caine said he hoped so. He also asked for Rossetti's permission to make some remarks about his new Dante work, but the artist was against it. He dabbed his brow and said he wasn't sure it was the right time to embark on a new project. Caine sighed, and Rossetti gently scolded him.

"Haven't I done enough about Dante already?" he said. "My grand painting has found a home! Isn't that enough of a success? I don't wish to be perceived as incapable of finding new inspirations. Isn't that what people will think if they hear I'm returning to that old subject again?"

"No, Gabriel, I don't think they will. You're worrying for no reason."

"Am I? How can you be sure? You've never experienced criticism like I have. Everyone smiles and applauds you, but they can just as quickly cut you with their knives." He looked at me. "And what about you? What do you think of my situation? If I take on any new commissions about Dante, will I be judged poorly for it, *Mister* Frost?"

I was shocked he wanted my opinion.

"I would have to agree with this gentleman," I said slowly. "Such a judgment would be conferred only on a lesser artist. Not you."

"That's right, Gabriel, a lesser artist," Caine said. He gave me a grateful look.

STILL IN HIS TRAVEL DRESS, Swinburne was standing in the drawing room.

He was a small man, slight and thin, but there was a striking air of intensity about him. He hardly acknowledged any of us even though there were more eyes trained on him than Argus had. He had a waxed mustache and beard and the smartest of hats, a black cattlemen's hat, which he handed with his coat to a servant. He looked over at Gabriel and nodded. Lionel told me they hadn't been on good terms for a long time; the only reason he'd come that night was as a favor to Gabriel's brother. The discord between them stemmed back, as everything in Rossetti's life seemed to, to the burial of his wife and the retrieval of his poetry.

"Ah, Uncle! Just in time!" Lionel said, striding over to him. Lionel's sullen attitude from earlier was gone. He laughed and spoke loudly. He clasped one of Swinburne's hands. "Come now, give the good people some verse! They've been waiting for you!"

The poet laughed and pulled his hand away.

"No, not yet, not yet!" he said. "Can't you see I've just arrived? Give me some air, cousin! Let me breathe a moment! Besides, I'm waiting for Watts. He's outside settling our fare. If I start without him, he'll get very cross, and we wouldn't want that."

Swinburne walked over to the sofa and greeted Rossetti. He sat down next to him, and they spoke in quiet voices that the rest of us couldn't hear. Someone else cleared his throat loudly, and we turned in the direction of the sound. It was Lawrence Klein. He was standing by the fireplace.

"Well, everyone, while we await Algernon, I have a special announcement. My book is finally completed and about to be published."

Rossetti sat forward.

"Wonderful news! What did you finally decide to write about?" His tone was kind; he seemed truly interested.

"Well," Klein said. "I know we've been over this before—"

Rossetti interrupted him.

"Oh dear, not that old business again!" It was a surprise to see Rossetti so animated.

"Yes, Gabriel, *that old business*, I'm afraid. I've studied Dante's *Comedy* a great deal, and there's no doubt in my mind anymore. There's a significant change in the quality of 'Paradiso'. It is less interesting and less dramatic than what you find in the epic's first two canticles. I wanted to understand why. I realized it was worthy of a scholarly endeavor."

Swinburne smirked.

"It's obvious why there's a change in the last canticle. Heaven is boring," he said. "It's always more pleasurable writing about sinners. You didn't need to waste time writing an entire book about that."

There was soft laughter from the guests; everyone was listening intently. Someone handed Swinburne a tumbler of brandy. Klein cleared his throat again.

"No, no, please, it's not just that, Algernon. To anyone as fluent in Italian as I am, the change is about more than simple boredom. There's a falling off in the poet's voice that's impossible to ignore, and I think it's because Dante didn't finish the poem. Someone else did." He said this with a sudden dramatic rise in his voice.

Rossetti shifted on the cushions.

"It sounds like your book is about what we've discussed already. That the poet's sons finished the *Comedy*, is that right? I'm sure everyone here would be interested in your theory."

I heard groans around me. I understood that everyone wanted to see Swinburne, but my interest was piqued. I wanted to hear—even if he'd treated me dismissively—what Klein had to say about Dante. He explained that the poet's enthusiasm for his epic ended with the second canticle, which concludes after the poet encounters his adored Beatrice at the top of the mountain in purgatory. Klein said Dante's readers felt the same way. They'd been eager for this meeting ever since he'd first described Beatrice in the *Vita Nuova*. After they meet in purgatory, the poem continues on with "Paradiso," and the language in that third part is much drier and more abstract than the rest. Boccaccio's life of the poet says there were unusual circumstances surrounding the completion of "Paradiso." He wrote that the final thirteen cantos of that canticle mysteriously disappeared after Dante's death. They were only recovered after the poet's ghost appeared to one of his sons and told him where they were hidden. Why they had been hidden in the first place didn't make any sense to Klein. He told us that what really happened, according to his new book, was that Gemma Donati, Dante's wife, had destroyed the final thirteen cantos in a fit of jealous rage. The story Boccaccio tells about their disappearance is a fairy tale—something created to hide what really happened.

"Compare the ghostly appearance of Dante with anything in *The Decameron*, and you'll see it's handled very differently," Klein said. "That's because Boccaccio was up to something different. I think Alighieri's sons needed his help. They asked him to concoct that story. They wanted to protect their mother."

Rossetti interrupted him again. The remark about Boccaccio annoyed him.

"Boccaccio was *not* an accomplice to a fraud," he said. (Strange that he was more upset about this than about what Klein alleged against Dante's wife.)

"Oh, I wouldn't accuse him of dishonesty, Gabriel. He was only trying to help the family," Klein said. "If the world had learned what Gemma Donati did, it wouldn't just have humiliated her; it would've devalued Dante's work. So the sons announced the cantos were missing, and it took them nine months to work up a suitable replacement for the lost thirteen. They knew their father's work well; they were his first commentators. And they were poets. Not like their father, of course. That's why the final cantos are so dull. But Boccaccio's story helped them avoid any suspicion."

Klein rested back against the fireplace and crossed his arms. He looked at all of us. He seemed very satisfied with himself. Swinburne leaned forward on the sofa.

"I'll tell you," he called out, "what's common in *The Decameron*. It isn't the ghosts."

He held his empty glass up to the light, squinting at its patterns as if it were a rare gem.

"And what is that?" Klein asked. He was delighted with Swinburne's interest. "What do you find that's so common?'"

"The fucking. There's just so much of it."

The room erupted in laughter. His lilting tone, the playful way he upended Klein's innocent question—how could we not? I felt sorry for Klein, but not sorry enough not to laugh. I never expected Swinburne to be so funny. He reached for the brandy bottle and refilled his tumbler. Then he stood and walked over to the fireplace. Now, finally, he seemed ready to give us what we wanted. Poetry, he announced in a loud voice, cannot be treated like a game of intrigue.

"Am I not right about this, Gabriel?" he said. "Because the tone of a poem changes, does one suppose another writer has taken over? What nonsense. The theory of a jackass scholar." He looked at Klein and shrugged. "Tone changes all the time. Just as the strings of a violin or a cello may go flat. It doesn't mean the player has changed."

Lionel appeared at my side. There was a man next to him I didn't recognize. It turned out to be Watts-Dunton, Swinburne's keeper. As he watched Swinburne fill his glass again, his eyes narrowed and his jaw clenched. I could understand his anger: the poor man was watching all his best efforts to keep the poet sober fall apart.

"Honestly, enough lectures! I don't wish to bore all of you!" Swinburne said merrily. "What do you say, Gabriel? Shall we give them some poetry now?"

There was loud applause. But Rossetti shook his head.

"I won't, not tonight. I'm not up to it," he said, "but I'm certain everyone would enjoy listening to you."

Swinburne read to us that night, but as a courtesy, he invited others to read first. I remember wishing I'd written some poetry. I wanted to take part so badly, but all I'd written thus far were my sermons. I hated standing there like the rest and staring at him with the blank expression one sees on a haddock in the fish market.

Klein stepped forward again. Hadn't Swinburne's put-down been enough? He took several folded sheets from his pocket. Another groan arose from the audience. He recited his poetry to us for nearly an hour, and I thought I'd die. It was an eternity. Thinking of Dante, I imagined there must be a place in hell where sinners were forced to listen to terrible poetry. Klein's was so bad I can still remember some of it:

Go from me, my love, but unlock the gate,
Let me rest here a while in the grass, so warm,
Leave me before the hour is late,
While caterpillars leave trails upon my arms.

In sleep I hear your sighs,
In sleep I await the sweet press
of lips upon my lidded eyes
recalling me to wakefulness.
In sleep I hear your soft rebuke,
"Awake now from your laziness!"

Go from me . . . let me . . . leave me . . . it was unbearable. When he was done—when we were sure he was really done—there was faint applause. Everyone watched Swinburne, who was still sitting next to Gabriel, balancing his glass on his knee. He snorted—I don't know how many glasses he'd had by then—and was about to say something that I think would have offended Klein. Rossetti spoke first.

"Very lovely images, Lawrence, truly," he said. "I sense the faintest reference to something Roman in that last one, don't I?" He tapped his chin thoughtfully. "Let me think. It isn't Horace or Catullus, is it? No. Too gentle to be either. What is it? I'm not mistaken, am I?"

Klein was delighted with the poet's interest. He said the poem had been wholly his own invention, and that enraged me. I knew he was lying. Any classicist worth his salt would have known that—Algernon probably did, too, but he was too muddled by the brandy to say something. Instead, I found myself stepping forward and challenging him.

"I think it's Propertius," I called out. "He's done a good job of hiding it, but it's there, Mr. Rossetti. The allusion you detected is to Sextus Propertius. I'm sure of it." I glared at Klein. "Quite sure."

Everyone looked at me.

"It can be found in Book Two of his elegies, I believe."

"Ah, we have a classicist among us!" Swinburne said, sitting forward. He looked pleased. He turned to Rossetti. "I believe he's right about that, Gabriel. The sublime Sextus. Yes, I heard it, too!"

"How do the lines go?" Rossetti said, smiling. "I'm certain I have his volume somewhere in the house, but if you have the faculty to recall it . . ."

"I do," I said. "It would be my honor."

Knowing something about Klein's private disappointments and losses, knowing he needed Rossetti's kindness probably more than any person in the room, I should have been more generous. I should have kept my mouth shut and let him have his moment, even if it wasn't entirely deserved. But I craved attention as much as he did. I was too young and stupid to control myself. I didn't think I had to.

"*O me felicem!*" I began, "*Nox o mihi candida! Et o tu lectule deliciis facte beate meis!*" (Envy me, Propertius says, for there's no greater happiness in life than being in bed with my Cynthia!)

Then, after reciting the entire section, I gave a translation that revealed Klein's theft:

With kisses pressed upon my eyelids,
she called me back to wakefulness.
"How dare you doze now, lazy one!" she said.

When I finished, there was loud applause. I looked at Rossetti again before returning to my place. Klein was nowhere to be seen. Swinburne was next. He recited from an unfinished poem based on Irish legends, and he looked at me several times for my reaction. It was incredibly flattering . . . and noticed by many in the room.

At the end, there was thunderous applause. Then Hall Caine stepped forward to give some remarks.

"Now, after so much poetry by our worthy guests, it seems appropriate to speak of what brings us together tonight. I don't need to remind you, but I shall, that it is our own Gabriel who single-handedly has done so much on behalf of his glorious namesake, Dante Alighieri. His translations and paintings have introduced that glorious Tuscan to so many new audiences. And I am happy to announce that he has agreed to return to his great subject for a new series of paintings, sponsored by his illustrious patron, Mr. Edward Dabney."

Caine gestured toward a small, stern-looking man with spectacles in a corner of the room. There was more applause. Mr. Dabney, Caine announced, was also the fortunate new owner of the magnificent canvas *Dante's Dream*. The man obviously wasn't used to so much attention. He nodded his head at Caine and coughed nervously. Rossetti stood and smiled.

"I suppose this series is a good thing," he said, giving us all a wistful look, "and to Mr. Dabney, I am grateful. And I am grateful to all of you for your continued faith in me."

13

◇◇◇◇◇◇◇

The painting

WHEN SWINBURNE WAS DONE, many of the guests rushed up to meet him. Several others, however, and this was stunning, rushed up to me. They lavished me with praise, and I didn't know what to do. I'd never experienced anything like it before. It wasn't just Lionel, who'd leaned in and whispered in my ear, "Well done, Frost, well done!" Several men slapped me on the back, offered me fresh glasses of wine, and toasted my triumph. I couldn't help noticing several attractive young women watching me, too. I was so overwhelmed by their attention that I had to break away and retreat to the back of the house. I needed a moment to myself— to compose myself, to calm my nerves. I sought out the quietest place I could find. At first, I considered going into the garden behind the house, but it was too cold outside. I went into the little anteroom of Rossetti's studio, which the previous owner had used as a dining room. The anteroom was separated from the studio by a thick portiere hanging in the doorway. The little room had a large, deep chair in front of a fireplace. A dozen or so paintings hung on the walls. It was a perfect place to hide.

I'd scarcely settled in the chair when I heard light footsteps behind me. Annoyed, I looked up.

It was a woman. At first, I thought she was one of my new admirers, but she wasn't. She introduced herself as Antonia Cox, a friend of Lionel's. So, I thought, this is the other guest he went searching for. She was very attractive, with soft, doe-like features and a round, delicate face; her eyes were bright, attentive, encircled by thick lashes, giving them the look of strange flowers. She wore an elegant dress of simple black. Unlike the flowing hair of the other female guests, hers was worn short—blonde, crimped and curled in the French manner. Her appearance was marred only by a toothy grin and the breathy cackle she made at just about everything I said . . . even when I wasn't trying to be funny.

I told her Lionel had invited me, too. She chuckled.

"Yes, I know. I thought I should seek you out since we're both here for the same reason."

That startled me.

"We are? What reason is that? Lionel didn't say anything about a reason," I said.

There was a loud commotion out in the hall, and several people entered the room before she could answer. Lionel was in the lead, with Rossetti and Caine just behind him. They were followed by Swinburne, Klein, and a few of Rossetti's other associates. There must have been at least ten people in all. Lionel flung back the portiere. There was a long table surrounded by chairs, several easels on tripods against the walls, and an immense canvas nearly spanning the entire room (it was the painting that Dabney had purchased). I watched as everyone sat down. I turned to leave, but Lionel called me back.

"Wait. Where are you going? Did you have a chance to meet Antonia? She is a supremely gifted reader of the tarot," he said. "We're about to have a private reading, and I need you. Come and join us. You'll enjoy it!"

I told him I couldn't, that I wasn't feeling well. I'd drunk too much and I was starting to feel it. I told him I'd wait in the anteroom until they were done. I could see he was disappointed; I was, too. He hadn't invited me to this party in the name of art or friendship; he wanted something from me. He hadn't even bothered to tell me what it was. But Antonia Cox seemed to know, and that irritated me even more.

I watched the portiere swing back into place and sat down again. I looked up at the walls and studied the paintings. They were lovely; they offered better views than any window would have. I looked at them while I waited for Cox to finish her reading.

Facing me was a work based on the life of Dante, *Beata Beatrix*, an evocation of the Tuscan's young muse at the hour of her death. A sundial floats in the murk to her left, the dial's shadow falling on that tragic hour. A dove sits next to her with poppy flowers in its beak—to help make the passage from life into death easier. Beatrice's eyes are closed; she seems lost in a mood of indescribable ecstasy.

As I marveled at its beauty and heard Cox's muffled voice explain something about the cards, this painting suddenly slid along its wire until it hung by a corner, swaying back and forth like a clock pendulum. Its sudden movement made me jump. It didn't help my stomach, either. I stood and inspected the painting, the wire, and the pegs, and everything looked intact. I couldn't understand what happened. I readjusted the painting and sat back down, and as soon as I did, the painting moved again.

Next to my chair was an ottoman. I pushed it against the wall, right under the painting, and climbed on it to inspect the wire and wall pegs. If anyone had come in at that moment, I'm sure I would've looked like I was trying to make off with one of Gabriel's possessions. I pulled on the wire running along the back of the picture frame, and it was taut and firm. So were the wall pegs. Everything seemed fine. I couldn't understand what happened. I kept testing the wire and pegs with my fingers, just to be sure, and that's when the painting moved again and trapped my poor fingers between the frame's edge and the wall. It felt like a knife was slicing off my fingertips, and the pain was so sharp and intense I jumped back and forgot I was standing on the ottoman. For a moment, I felt empty air under my feet, and then I fell to the floor with a loud crash.

The portiere whipped back. Lionel rushed to my side. Gabriel and Cox's faces appeared in the doorway.

"The painting," I said, embarrassed. "It moved. I . . . I was only trying to fix it."

"Fix it? Why? What happened?"

"Nothing. It was an accident." My fingers were throbbing, and my side ached. "It happened suddenly. It seemed about to fall. I was attempting to straighten it, and it pressed against my fingers. It moved."

Lionel frowned. He was about to ask me something else when Rossetti stepped forward.

"There, don't you see? It's another sign. It's her," he said. He pointed at the painting. "She's back! Don't you see? That painting! She wants me to know she's here! She's returned!"

Then he started to cry—a deep, shuddering cry that shook his shoulders and flushed his skin, causing the pate of his head to turn bright pink. A stern-looking man appeared in the doorway. It was his brother William. The artist looked over at him.

"William, don't frown so!" he said, wiping his eyes. "This is a happy, happy sign!" It was the most animated I'd seen Rossetti all evening. His brother gave him a worried look.

"I shouldn't have allowed this reception. I shouldn't have listened to Caine and Klein. A sign, Gabriel? This reception has been too much for your nerves. That's the only sign I see," he said. Then he turned to us. "My brother needs his rest. It's getting late." He addressed a servant. "Inform the guests that this party is over. I think it's time everyone left."

Despite his stern demeanor, Rossetti's brother tenderly put an arm around him. Rossetti seemed to collapse against him. They walked together to the stairs right outside the studio and took them up to his bedroom.

As everyone moved to the ground floor, I lost Lionel in the crowded hallway. In everyone's haste to leave, they heaved and pushed us apart like we were swimmers caught in a riptide. Outside, I saw Swinburne's guardian, Watts-Dunton, helping the poet with his coat. He was saying in a low, scolding voice, "Never again." Swinburne looked tired and shrunken, his eyes fixed on the ground. I wanted to say something to him but didn't. I kept walking.

I did see Lionel again. I saw him leaving the house with Antonia Cox in a carriage. Several cabs were lined up in front, and I saw them at the far end of the queue. Even from a distance, I could see the familiar way he clasped her waist and helped her up into the cab, and it bothered me. I didn't know Lionel's wife yet, but I already felt protective of her. That little show of intimacy wasn't the only thing that vexed me, either. As I watched their carriage pull away, I realized Lionel had completely forgotten about me. I'd been left to find my own way home.

14

Horns

THE SHOP OF ALFRED DEWEY & SONS, TAILORS, established in London for nearly a century, was closing for the night. Two customers were leaving as my carriage pulled up. There was a light drizzle in the air of rain and soot. Ivan Luzak was sweeping up bits of thread and fabric cuttings in the shop's main room. I could see his stooped silhouette through the shop's frosted windows. When I opened the door, a little bell attached to the top rang out. His voice boomed when he saw me.

"Mikhaylo!"

We hadn't seen each other since my father's funeral. I usually visited him every week, and I was expecting a good scolding. When he saw me, he rushed up, still with the broom in his hand, grabbed my hand and threw his arms around me and the bundle I was carrying. He gave me a crushing hug. He squeezed so hard I groaned and couldn't help exhaling in his face. Then he laughed and pushed me back. He held me out at arm's length, his big paws on my shoulders, and studied the blackness of my cassock with a fierce, proud look. "I wish your papa and mama could see you," he said.

"I do, too," I said quietly.

I asked if we might go somewhere and speak privately. I put down my bundle and told him it was urgent. He gave me a puzzled look.

"But we are private here, Mikhaylo, unless you don't want *these* to hear," he said. He pointed at several headless torsos against the wall. They wore dresses at different stages of completion. "There is no one else in the shop. Everyone has gone home. What's the matter? What's wrong? There must be something wrong for you to come and see a poor old man."

It may have been delayed, but there it was. Ivan's annoyance. I deserved it. He and my father had been as close as brothers. They'd treated each other with that special affection and irritation you only see among siblings—and I could see Ivan was annoyed with me the way my father sometimes annoyed him. We weren't blood-related, but Ivan still treated me like his nephew ... and a nephew has obligations to family. I'd failed in mine. I hadn't checked on him since the funeral. Not once. I hadn't even bothered to send a note. I may have lost my father, but I wasn't the only one grieving for him. I knew how much my father had always meant to Ivan. He was right. I should've come sooner. I had no real excuse, and I asked him to forgive me.

Ivan never held a grudge for very long. It went against his cheerful nature. He accepted my apology at once and said he understood I was busy. He asked me about my new life at Saint Martha's, and I told him about my responsibilities. He listened with an interested, slightly dazed look in his eyes. I think he was taking in my words and mentally reassembling them into Ruthenian so they made more sense to him. I asked if he had seen the Sketchist's column about me, but he hadn't. He rarely read English newspapers. I promised to show him next time. The party at Rossetti's had taken place just a few nights before our visit, and I told him about that, too ... but not about the strange accident or the fact that it brought the party to an end. I wasn't in the mood to explain. I didn't think I could.

My fingers were still sore where the painting frame cut into them; they throbbed painfully when Ivan grabbed my hand and hugged me. At that point I clung to an ordinary explanation for the incident. To believe an invisible presence had been there, that it had slammed the painting against my hand—even though I'd felt the frame lift in my hands all on its own—defied all logic. What happened at Rossetti's had been an ordinary accident, I told myself, and anything that seemed unusual about it, well ... blame that on the wine. And not enough food to soak up the wine. And besides, there had been so many other, *better* things to think about: Klein's foolish poetry, his fascinating theory about Dante and Gemma Donati, my improvised translation of Propertius, the reactions of Rossetti and Swinburne. My mind moved to these memories instead, including my last glimpse of Rossetti as his brother helped him up the stairs. Seeing them had reminded me of my father and Ivan. That's when I realized I should go and see him. If anyone understood what the imp was, it would be him.

I'd often witnessed that same sweet brotherly affection between them, especially when a sad mood swept over my father like a gale on an otherwise clear day. It was a sadness he never tried to explain, and my mother never confronted him about it. Maybe it seemed obvious to her that he missed his village back in Galicia. She never pressed him about it, though—I think she worried she might push him into a deeper bout of melancholy if she did.

But the person who challenged this homesickness theory was Ivan. He never seemed gloomy or troubled even though they had come over together, made the same sacrifices, endured the same hardships. Maybe the difference was just a matter of temperament: Ivan was loud and funny; my father was reserved and thoughtful. But I always felt, though I couldn't properly explain it, that it wasn't that simple. My father's mysterious sadness came from somewhere else, and there was no way to cure it. All we could do, when one of these spells struck, was wait for him until it was over … until he emerged on the other side. It required a patience Ivan clearly did not have, and often he challenged my father whenever that shadow fell. I remember once, when Giuseppe Montini asked my father to order a cask of sherry for the shop—to celebrate the completion of a big commission—that Ivan and I accompanied him to the tobacconist's shop to place the order. It was a low-ceilinged, smoky room with yellow windows. When he signed the bill of receipt, my father wrote carefully and slowly *Walter Frost*. Ivan teased him about it on the walk home.

"Valter Phrosht, let me see," he said in his deep voice. "Who is this Valter Phrosht? Do I know him? It cannot be you, can it? You are *roo-tenn!* Whatever happened to Volodomyr Moroz?!"

Ivan and my father always called themselves Ruthenians, and our villagers still do. The word refers to the ancient homeland that existed once in this area and might again—if our people can ever be made whole.

Even though Ivan used a teasing tone, my father didn't laugh; he just looked down at his boots and sulked. I remember looking up at him and trying to understand why he became silent. He seemed to be pondering Ivan's question, and when he noticed I was watching him, he took my hand and squeezed it. But he didn't say anything. He just smiled—a sad smile. Ivan wrapped an arm around him then. It was a more forceful version of what I saw William Rossetti do to his brother. Ivan regretted teasing him; he said something to my father in a hushed tone, but I heard it despite the noise and commotion of the street around us.

"Your friend is big and stupid," he said. "He has a big and stupid mouth, Volodomyr. I meant no harm." He pulled him closer, as if he thought he could squeeze the sadness out of him. It worked a little, and they resumed their conversation, but Ivan did most of the talking.

Ivan's teasing about my father's name pointed to something I'd never considered before—something so obvious, and I'd missed it anyways. For all the years of my young life I'd never wondered, until that day outside the tobacconist, why my father changed his name. Ivan had stayed Ivan Luzak in England, but my father became Walter Frost. Why? My mother hadn't suggested it to him; she didn't care what he called himself as long as they were together. Why did he do it?

I didn't have my answer until the night I visited Ivan.

He took a large brass key from his apron pocket and locked the shop's front doors. While his back was turned, I quickly unwrapped the imp and held it up. I didn't say anything; I wanted to see what he did when he saw it.

Ivan turned and froze. He seemed absolutely bewildered by the little grinning devil.

"Where," he said softly, "where did you get this?"

I told him it belonged to my father. I said he'd kept it sealed in a box at Montini's and that I didn't discover it until after the funeral. I didn't think anyone knew about it, not even my mother. Judging by his initial reaction, Ivan didn't seem to know what it was, either. I spoke slowly and gave him plenty of chances to interrupt me. I hoped he'd blurt out something important, some revelation, but he didn't. He was completely silent, and Ivan was never quiet about anything. The sight of the imp stunned him into silence. That should have told me he knew something. I knelt and started gathering up the sheets I'd used to conceal it. Another waste of time, I thought. Ivan knelt down beside me.

"Wait, don't cover it, Mikhaylo," he said, staying my arm. "Let me see. But where are its horns? Did your father not make them?"

He reached out and stroked the top of the imp's head.

"They should go there and there," he said, indicating two discreet holes that I'd overlooked. There were tears in his eyes now.

A carriage stopped outside. We heard footsteps at the shop doors. Someone pulled on the locked handles. Ivan wiped his eyes and straightened up.

"We are closed," he barked in a loud voice. Then he turned back to me.

"Mikhaylo," he said, "there are many sorrows, many sadnesses that parents hide from their children. It is no secret why they do that. I am not a parent, but I understand. It is to keep their innocence for as long as possible. Children will learn the selfish ways of the world soon enough. There is no need to rush it. Parents also hide their sorrows if they don't know how to cure them. They don't know what to say. That was true for your father."

He took the imp from my arms.

"This object," he said, "shows me he was never cured of his. I thought he was. It was such a long time ago. He made a mistake, but it wasn't his fault. It wasn't. I thought he had made peace with it." His eyes looked sad again. "But if he had, he never would have made this."

THE IMP, HE TOLD ME, went by another name in our village, *varta*, which means "guard." He described the custom of the night watch and the practical reasons for it. We sat in the deserted workroom at the rear of the shop. I did my best to be patient as he rambled on, which he always did, over so many topics besides the varta. He explained how he and my father inaugurated their friendship with an act of teamwork (climbing a tall cherry tree next to Ivan's house to reach the fruit-laden branches), how he'd been a mischievous child who played tricks on every adult he met—once, he even hid up in that same cherry tree and waited for the varta-carrier to come along. He wanted to drop an egg on his head. Even though it was very late and very dark, the egg found its target, but the man didn't move on. He stayed right there, under the tree, cursing, waiting for the dawn so he could identify Ivan and report him to his parents.

But Ivan didn't care—his parents were already gone by then. They'd been taken by the typhus that habitually struck the village. Some Luzak cousins from Drohobych had moved in when that happened. They said they wanted to care for him, but what they really wanted was his parent's farmland. Like all selfish relatives, they used a selfless reason to hide the actual one. That is why, Ivan explained, he couldn't stand them and wanted to leave the village as soon as he was old enough.

My father's circumstances were the same even though typhus hadn't taken his parents. His mother died of consumption, and a few years later his father fell off the roof while fixing a leak. The same thing happened to him. Self-interested relatives from another village soon arrived to care of him—a bossy old woman and her greedy family—and my father moved into the summer kitchen behind the house to get away from them. He used the excuse that the main house was too crowded. The stove and some blankets kept him warm enough on cold nights, but on the coldest ones he had no choice and slept inside the main house. He took care of everything, tending the family gardens and the larger fields, feeding the animals, and managing the winter provisions, especially the potatoes piled high in a small ditch and covered with thick straw.

He grew tired of this life. He knew the situation would never change even once he married and had sons of his own. The cousins would never leave. He would have to share the house and land with them. It wasn't fair. As the years passed, my father's resentment grew, and Ivan said he noticed a difference in him. Whenever Ivan brought up leaving Prehovinka together, my father didn't flatly refuse anymore. Ivan thought it was just a matter of time before he agreed.

The night before Ivan left, a night in the early spring, my father spent a long day in the fields digging up tree roots and clearing rocks. The fields were being prepared for corn that would be ready by the fall. He was exhausted, and his hands were blistered and raw. His cousin's husband had been unable to help with the work because he said he suffered from "a delicate condition" of his back.

"What he needed," Ivan said, "was a good kick in his delicate condition."

That evening, as my father dragged himself onto his pallet bed in the summer kitchen, there was a loud thud on the porch. He looked outside just in time to see his cousin's husband returning to the main house. On the porch he'd left the little totem with the mocking grin of a devil.

"This is a remarkable imitation of our varta," Ivan said, turning the imp in his hands. He described how the horns of the village's totem were curled to resemble a ram's. The patterns etched in its body had been worn smooth by generations of hands. When I asked where it came from, Ivan didn't know.

"No one knows. It was always there. It's as old as our village, Mikhaylo. Older probably," he told me. He shrugged. "I remember my own father carrying it when I was small."

He said my father was angry that he would have to make the night walk. He'd hoped the cousins would appreciate how hard he worked and volunteer for him. My father hastily drank some tea, grabbed a coat, and carried the varta out past the lighted windows of the main house.

A few houses away, Ivan was in his barn. He was making final preparations to leave. He had a good horse and an old government buggy once used for delivering mail. He could always sell everything if he needed more money—which he did when they stopped in Ghent, before crossing the channel to England. Ivan planned to leave in the middle of the night while the air was still cool. Around midnight, while he was dozing in the buggy, he heard the barn door creak open. He looked up. It was my father. For a moment, Ivan thought he'd come to say goodbye again.

"Your father looked scared, Mikhaylo. I'll never forget his face. I asked him what happened, and he told me there had been an accident. The varta had been lost."

Ivan sighed heavily.

"Then he said to me, 'Ivan, let me go with you.' I wasn't expecting this, but of course I was pleased. If he had waited one more day, I would have been gone."

"How did my father lose the varta?"

"It was because of something." He frowned. "He heard a sound."

"A sound?"

"A voice."

"A voice? Whose?"

"It was a *vila.*"

I'd never heard that strange word before.

"I'm sorry, Ivan. I don't understand."

"Forgive me, Mikhaylo. Of course you don't. Let me explain."

15

◇◇◇◇◇◇◇

The accident

"I HAVE BEEN TO A PLACE in Drury Lane called the Promenade of Wonders, have you been there, Mikhaylo? No? It is an interesting place. You should go," Ivan said. He opened a drawer in a tall desk and produced two glasses and a bottle of Ruthenian horilka. The name comes from *hority*—to burn. The Russians call it vodka, from the word for water, *voda*, but if you think you're tasting ordinary water, you're in for an unpleasant surprise. Ivan said he wouldn't explain what happened to my father until we toasted his memory first. He filled my glass, and even though I knew what it would do to me, I gulped it down, hoping for the best. My throat burst into flames.

"Ivan, please," I said, gasping. I started coughing. He poured me a glass of water. Real water this time. I drank some. "Please tell me. What happened to him? What was it?"

Ivan laughed.

"Too strong? Don't worry. By your third glass you won't feel your throat anymore." He gulped down his, stomped the floor, and croaked like a frog. He didn't follow it with water.

"I went there, to the Promenade, because someone in our shop said there was an exhibit of strange and fantastic specimens from Eastern Europe. I think I was feeling homesick for our village, and that is why one of the tailors told me about it. I asked your father, but he couldn't go. So I went alone. I purchased my ticket and went inside. Right there, in the main corridor leading to different halls of attractions, there stood an enormous wood tank. It was filled to the top with water, and the surface was thickly covered in lily pads. You couldn't see a thing. The water started stirring, and suddenly the head of a golden-haired woman peeked up between the pads. I thought she was just a swimmer, an ordinary swimmer, until she twisted her body and kicked under the surface again and disappeared. I saw her large green fishtail flash in the air. Everyone gasped, and a barker announced she was the first mermaid ever to survive in captivity. She was enormously friendly, he said, and when her head bobbed up again in the center of the tank, she waved and slyly smiled at us. She had a big, beautiful smile. Many of us were so hypnotized by it, Mykhaylo. We started emptying our pockets and flinging coins into the water before we realized what we were doing. That's a part of their power, you know. They can make you do anything they want. When I said a *vila* caused your father to lose the varta, this is what I meant. A water sprite. They live all over Galicia, in its lakes and rivers. That's what our old stories say. They're very similar to the Russian *rusalki*. Also the ones the Greeks have.

"Of course I didn't believe the one at the Promenade was real, even if she did hypnotize us (there are more ordinary explanations for that), and I can tell you this: If a real *vila* had been in that tank, not that friendly mermaid with good English manners, she would not have smiled so innocently and waved so politely. She would have tried to grab you and pull you in.

"They are terrible creatures, Mikhaylo. Our stories say so. They are very dangerous. They dwell in the deepest pockets of the Dniester; and sometimes they slip down into the Zimn and her tributaries and stay there a while. That is when they cause us problems."

Broken fishing lines, damaged boats, missing farm animals—every kind of misfortune was blamed on them, he said, even though, as one discovers about the supernatural realm, such things are rarely seen by the human eye. Ivan said these creatures sleep in the mud of the deep river bottoms for most of the year. Around May they start to wake and rise from the mud. They're ravenous after a long hibernation and will eat just about anything that strays too close. They have the power to assume beautiful human shapes and features and disarm the unsuspecting—I can't help thinking of poor Paul Melnyk—in the same way that an orchid mantis tricks its prey into thinking that it's a flower. And they aren't completely water-bound. They don't have fishtails, only webbed feet; they can leave the water for brief periods of time and stretch their naked bodies along the riverbanks and leaning boughs. They like to hum to themselves, and the sound is as shimmery and light as the highest notes on a violin fingerboard—easy to mistake for something else, the chirping of crickets or a ringing in the ears ... and impossible to ignore.

I thought the fumes of the horilka must be getting to me. I couldn't believe Ivan was treating Ruthenian folklore like it was something real. He talked about the *vily* as he would the latest news from Parliament or a recent crime. For God's sake, I thought, watching him finish the bottle, what about the imp?

"Please, Ivan, I still don't understand. What does any of this have to do with my father? You said you would explain."

He sat back and wiped his brow. His face was flushed and clammy.

"You're right, Mikhaylo, I'm sorry. Where was I?"

"You said my father heard a voice."

On the night of his walk, my father thought someone might have gone to fetch water in the Zimn and fallen in. The banks are steep and rocky. It's easy enough to take a bad misstep in the daytime. But he didn't see anyone. He didn't have a lamp with him, but he didn't need it—by then the moon was already peeking above the trees. It was nearly full, and everything was covered in a silver glow.

Then it happened again. He heard the sound. It was coming from up near the church bridge. His heart pounded in his chest as he rushed towards it. There was something in the water, right against the bridge's piers. At first he thought it was a tree limb that had fallen in or a big clump of pussy willows that had torn loose from the banks, but as he moved closer he saw that it was a young woman. She was struggling. He heard her sobbing and wailing. It looked like the strong current had nearly swept her under the bridge.

He told Ivan that he ran to the bridge's middle, directly above her, and reached down for her hand. She grabbed his and looked up at him, and when he saw her face, he gasped and tried to pull away. He said she laughed at him then and started pulling him down, and that's when he lost the varta. It fell out of his arms and hit her before landing in the water. She cried out and let go of him.

"Why did he pull away? What did she look like?" I asked him. He shrugged.

"She wasn't human. That's all he would tell me. I tried asking him what this meant, but he was very upset. I didn't want to upset him more."

My father said the creature laughed, even after getting hit by the imp, and pushed away from the bridge. He watched her take several long, graceful strokes before disappearing in the darkness. He spent the next hours frantically searching for the varta. He followed the river all the way down through the fields. By the time he reached the mill, a sick feeling of hopelessness had spread over him. It was gone. He'd never find it. He didn't know what he was going to tell the villagers; he didn't think anyone would believe him. Then he thought about his lazy cousins. It was all their fault. They should have done the duty, not him. He walked back to the village in a rage. His anger blinded him so much that he didn't pay attention to where he was going until he stopped in front of Ivan's house. He could see a lamp burning in the barn.

A few hours later, as Ivan's buggy was turning onto the main road, my father was in the back, sleeping on the floor. His eyelids grew heavy. Ivan had given him some horilka to settle his nerves. Before he drifted off, he realized the night felt different. It was completely silent. There wasn't even the sound of a single insect. It was as if a thick blanket had dropped over everything. But then, even though Ivan didn't, my father heard it—a faint, high, shimmery sound that seemed like laughter.

LOSING THE TOTEM BROKE MY FATHER'S HEART. He was convinced he'd left the village vulnerable to supernatural attack. Ivan tried to reassure him. Natalka's mother was the village healer at the time. She was a tremendously resourceful old woman named Eudokia. Before they crossed the channel to England, Ivan received a letter from an old neighbor and learned that more wormwood and garlic had been planted all over Prehovinka on Eudokia's orders. *Vily* hate the smell, which is why I'm carrying garlic and wormwood tonight. It doesn't hurt to carry them even though we have the imp.

Tragedy still found its way into Prehovinka despite these measures— in the years after they settled in London, my father and Ivan learned that typhus spread throughout Galicia like fire through dry brush. It was unusually fierce, and when it ebbed, finally, all the Ruthenian villages were decimated. Even though it happened all over the region, Ivan knew my father would take it personally. He knew he would blame himself for what happened to Prehovinka. Thankfully, around this time, he met my mother, and she helped him through his grief.

"Thank God for her, Mikhaylo," Ivan said. "She saved your father. She made him think about good things. Happy things. Making a life together. Having a family."

After their marriage, after I was born, this special grief remained a frequent visitor in our home. My mother never complained, and I only remember them arguing once. When I was little, I recall them having a big fight about Prehovinka at dinner. It was the first time I'd ever heard the village's name. My father said he wanted to go back for a visit. I told Ivan I'd never seen my mother so angry.

He nodded.

"Yes, I remember. She made your father sleep at my house that night. The next morning, he apologized to her and said he was a fool. She was right; there was no reason to go back. Nothing would change what happened." He pointed at the imp. "Not even him."

But one thing did change. My father's name. Soon after their arrival in England he'd translated Moroz into Frost, which suggested our family hailed from Suffolk, not a village halfway around the world. Other immigrants didn't do that. Ivan stayed Ivan; so did Giuseppe Montini. But Volodomyr Moroz decided to become Walter Frost. Ivan's story helped me understand why. He wanted a fresh start. He wanted to separate himself from his past. He wanted to put up a wall between his new and old lives even though he wasn't successful. Guilt still found its way around that wall. A new name wasn't enough.

When I left Ivan that night, I promised to come and see him again. I was grateful for his story. I didn't know what to make of his incident with the vila, but I felt closer to him after hearing it. Death may have separated us, but it didn't matter. I felt closer to my father after that. I finally understood the cause of his sadness, and it comforted me in a way that's hard to explain. It made sense why he changed his name. In fact, his reasons were similar to mine when I arrived in Prehovinka. I needed to become someone else, too. I needed to build a wall for my peace of mind and safety, and all these years it's kept away something even more terrible than guilt.

16

◇◇◇◇◇◇◇◇

Evenings with the Ashburnhams

IVAN'S STORY HELPED ME. I didn't feel complete relief, but at least I understood why my father had made the imp. What also really helped me in these difficult times were the friends I made while I was at Saint Martha's. The most important were the Ashburnhams. Their regular invitations to supper were the highpoint of every week.

Lionel and Kitty lived in a beautiful three-decker in Mayfair. The door opened on a wide, charmingly tiled entrance hall with high-paneled wainscoting in warm, golden oak, a feature that prevailed in all the rooms of the house. I would arrive, shaking the snow from my boots, and feel instantly at home. I first joined my new friend and his lovely wife as the Christmas holiday approached. Over the ensuing weeks, I lost track of the venison-stuffed game pies (and fish on Fridays), charlotte russes, and Savoy cakes that I ate at their table. It was also there that I first experienced a very fine cigar and a glass of Tokay in Lionel's exquisite study. He charmed me easily, and I shrugged off the irritation I'd felt when he deserted me after Rossetti's party. I decided it was just one of those missteps inevitable in any new friendship. I'd invested it with more irritation than it deserved—like the sighting of him and Antonia Cox leaving the party. I decided that was a mistake, too. I'd just misunderstood what I saw that night. Lionel never mentioned any of it, and I never did. It was all in the past—better to leave it there.

The best part of my visits with the Ashburnhams usually took place after dinner. We'd go up to Lionel's study and sit in big comfortable chairs, reading and swapping the latest papers. We'd smoke cigars and read out loud the amusing passages from the theater reviews. Sometimes I'd hear a door locking somewhere—the servants retiring—and soon the study door would open and Kitty would glide in, with hardly a sound from her satin shoes. She always made a deliberate effort never to disturb us, to slip into the room so quietly that we wouldn't be distracted from our reading. It never worked; I was always aware of her entrances—I looked forward to them. Passing behind us, she'd drag a finger lightly along Lionel's shoulders as she went to her chair by his desk to work on her knitting. No words were exchanged—only her touch and the slight nod of his head. I was included in this affectionate communication once: when I felt her caress on my shoulders, it startled me, and I swallowed suddenly, nearly choking on my spit.

My yearning for Kitty began as soon as I met the Ashburnhams. We'd been told in seminary—*warned* is probably a better word—that one of the greatest difficulties of any new priest's life is witnessing the small intimacies of a married couple, of a happy family, because he will never have that for himself. We'd heard that warning many times, but words are never enough, even when they're repeated. It's experience that really shows you what it means, that it's going to be more painful than the chastity vow you spent so much time worrying about (even though the two are related). I knew that a young priest's prayers, which should have been focused on asking for strength to be a good example for his parishioners, were probably spent on coping with a longing for their domestic bliss . . . and resisting despair over the choice he'd made. After befriending the Ashburnhams, I found myself doing the same thing when I should have been praying for my flock.

"Yes, it's a cruel sacrifice in some ways, I will not lie to you," Father Cremins used to tell us, "but we all must accept it and trust in the Lord." Easy for him to say. I think he came from a large family. "And besides, there will be compensations. You won't have a family of your own, but you will guide many families. You will be the father to many who will need you very much. That is a blessed compensation."

Well, it wasn't a blessed compensation to me, not when I looked at Kitty. When she entered the study, I didn't care about being the father to many. When I looked at her, I became aware of my humanity to a troubling degree. I realize how this must sound now, but I didn't understand what was happening to me at the time—that I was already rejecting my vows even though my priestly life had hardly begun. It was a half-formed rejection . . . half-buried in my thoughts. I didn't treat it as something more significant than that; I just assumed my doubts were common to new priests and that if I ignored them for long enough, they'd die like a vine deprived of water. Or maybe I'm only making myself look better now—maybe I did know what was happening to me and just didn't want to admit it. Every Friday, I eagerly looked forward to Kitty joining us in the study. I'd catch myself waiting, not reading the papers too closely yet, until she'd settled in her chair . . . and then I'd discreetly glance over and admire her profile: head bowed to her work, long strands of blonde hair falling carelessly over her shoulder.

Sometimes I tried to bring her forward, out of the background, by asking her a question. If I spied a book on the table in front of her, I might say:

"What is that next to you, Kitty? *The Lancashire Witches* . . . Ainsworth? Really? I didn't know you enjoyed Ainsworth! Is he one of your favorites?"

She'd smile and put her needles down.

"Not my favorite, Michael. I like his work, but there's another writer I like more," she'd say, glancing at Lionel. "I would have to say Ainsworth is my *second* favorite." He was busy reading his paper; he seemed hardly to notice what she said. I, on the other hand, noticed everything.

When she wasn't knitting, Kitty read her Ainsworth or some other book she kept in the knitting basket at her feet. I always noticed she had a different book whenever I visited. She was a very fast reader. I also noticed her taste ran to novels with happy endings, with a few exceptions. She adored *Wuthering Heights*, and who doesn't, but when she finished *Hypatia*, whose titular heroine gets murdered by a Christian mob, I remember watching the book sail across the room one night and land in a corner. At first, I'd thought Kitty was throwing it at a spider on the wall, but there was nothing there. She threw it because she just didn't like—*really* didn't like—how the book ends. Lionel chuckled.

"My wife has very strong feelings about fiction," he said.

As her earlier remark about Ainsworth might suggest, Kitty regarded Lionel as a writer of importance. I routinely heard about a manuscript of poems he was assembling, but this elusive work never seemed ready to share. It was a situation he sometimes acknowledged, referring to the poems as "my eternal work in progress." What he didn't hide from us was the journalism often calling him away from the house. He was one of several pens hired to produce The Eye, a theatrical column in *London Illustrated* much like the Sketchist's column in the *Telegraph*. He kept up a demanding and sometimes unpredictable editorial schedule. Often I'd arrive for our weekly dinner and find Kitty alone with the children. "The newspaper, *again*," she'd say, irritated. Usually Lionel would appear before I went home; he'd burst into the room and apologize for being late. He always made a point of kissing her in front of me, and I think it was because he knew I was attracted to her. I'm sure I did a poor job of hiding it, and these displays of affection seemed intended more for me than Kitty. No matter how late he was, she always forgave him—but the sadness never quite left her eyes . . . not even later, when the room filled with our laughter and cigar smoke.

Not every family is willing to explain its circumstances, and I only learned about the Ashburnhams' situation from casual references dropped over many evenings: how their dependable income was thanks to Kitty—her family owned a large estate near York and supplied her with a lavish allowance—and the glorious Mayfair house belonged to Lionel. The house meant a lot to him; it provided a link to a family that otherwise didn't acknowledge him because he was considered an outsider. He was what the proper people call "the product of an indiscretion" committed by one of the younger daughters of George Ashburnham, the third earl of Ashburnham, a family that produced the immortal Swinburne. Some families acknowledge their bastards; others don't. The Ashburnhams belonged to the latter. Swinburne sympathized with Lionel about this—after all, he was accustomed to being treated as an outsider, though for other reasons. Thanks to the poet's solicitations, Lionel was given the house, and a warm, affectionate relationship grew between them. Lionel said Swinburne deeply adored Kitty. That didn't surprise me. Her skin was beautifully pale, translucent. Her figure reminded me of a Greek warrior-maiden. Swinburne had based several poems on her beauty, and that was no surprise, either—but when Watts-Dunton insinuated himself into Swinburne's life, their interactions with the poet dwindled.

AS I WATCHED THEM TOGETHER, I thought Kitty was far too gentle for a man like Lionel. She seemed to concede to him on any disagreement; she met every disappointment with Botticellian downcast eyes . . . at least that's what I thought. But during one of our happier suppers together, one that hadn't pulled Lionel away to some editorial business, I saw my impression of her was wrong. She wasn't meek or helpless. Far from it.

What happened was that Charles, their little boy, misbehaved at the table. He wouldn't stop pulling his sister's hair despite several warnings. It didn't bother me, but I could see his behavior in my presence was embarrassing his parents.

As a result, after the meal, Kitty called Annie, one of their maids, and told her to take away Charles's prized toy—a key-wound locomotive—and hide it from him. Charles howled in anguish as soon as Annie left the room. In the kitchen, she found a spot for the toy on top of an old white cupboard of solid oak, standing on four short, thin legs. Twin doors opened on a space containing crockery intended for daily use, and the very top of the cupboard (behind the scrolled facade) was smooth and flat—an ideal spot for the toy. So she thought.

Charles wouldn't stop crying and whining, and it was a relief to finally escape upstairs to Lionel's study. Even with the door shut, you could hear his muffled cries. It was a long time before the upset lad finally quieted down. Finally, thank God, a deep silence fell over the house as we settled into our chairs. Unfortunately, it didn't last. We were just trimming our first cigars when the stillness was rent by a woman's terrible cry. It was Kitty. Already displaying that stubborn attitude of his father's, the boy had crept into the kitchen and climbed the front of the cupboard to take back his cherished toy. As he did, his additional weight compromised the furniture's old legs, and they buckled with a loud crack. The cabinet's bulk lurched forward, throwing Charles to the floor. The cupboard wobbled, its doors opening and dishes crashing to the floor, and Kitty rushed in at the sound. She saw the entire cabinet slowly tipping forward onto him. She threw herself against it, crying out for him to crawl to safety.

"That's my lamb! That's it!" she cried as we ran into the kitchen.

We found Kitty in tears, red-faced, shivering against the large wood frame as we stepped in and took her place. When she moved out of the way, one of its legs suddenly crumbled and it toppled forward. Lionel and I braced ourselves, and I was astonished at how heavy it was, especially for two grown men. We groaned as we pushed it back until it was upright. A servant came in with bricks from the back garden. These were wedged underneath next to the broken legs. I looked over at Kitty. She was on her knees, hugging her little boy and sobbing. "Don't cry, Mama, please don't cry!" Charles kept saying, terrified. Her tears seemed to scare him more than what nearly happened to him. I was astounded by the strength she'd shown. Her protectiveness of her child made her capable of things I'd never imagined.

This isn't the end of the story.

Her strength wasn't the only thing I saw that night. Later, once the children were in bed and the broken crockery had been swept up and thrown away, Lionel and I returned to the study. Our evening went on, finally, almost as if nothing had happened. Lionel called for a decanter of brandy, and soon there was a light tapping at the door. Come in, he said, and it was Annie, carrying a tray with the decanter and two glasses. I was absorbed by something in my paper, but I looked up when she set down the tray. I noticed a large bruise on her cheek. An angry purple bloom. It hadn't been there an hour before. I was sure of it. When Kitty had given her the toy train to hide, I remember looking at Annie and appreciating the simple beauty of her face. But now her eyes were red and glistening with tears as she hastily left the room. Lionel noticed the change in her appearance as well.

"Our lioness is quite protective of her family," he said after she'd gone. "Didn't know that about her, did you?"

His flippant tone bothered me.

"Kitty did that? My God, Lionel, it's not Annie's fault what happened with the cupboard. You need to say something to her. It was an accident."

He shrugged.

"Maybe so, but I wouldn't expect you to understand," he said, turning a page. "Next time, she'll think more carefully when she's asked to do something, won't she?"

17

◇◇◇◇◇◇◇◇

Bad dreams

WITH THE EXCEPTION OF WHAT HAPPENED to Annie, the time
I spent with the Ashburnhams was usually uneventful. My presence was
so regular and frequent, I felt like an adopted member of the family. I
was the bachelor cousin. Or uncle. The servants always recognized me
at the front door; even the children fell into the habit of running up and
giving me hugs when I arrived. I always made sure, before heading off
to Mayfair, that I had an ample supply of toffee or licorice allsorts in my
pockets for them.

I loved my time with the Ashburnhams. It took away the loneliness
that no one ever really warns you about in seminary. I felt like I belonged
somewhere. But even then, Lionel's behavior could be odd sometimes. I
might be reading some sobering account of how many had been killed in
the Boer conflicts or chuckling over a theater critic's exasperated remark
about some actor, and that's when I'd feel it: the pressure of his gaze. He
never asked what I was reading or what I found interesting; if I happened
to look up and catch him, he'd quickly avert his eyes. It turned into a little
game that probably would have lasted God knows how long if I didn't
force the issue one evening. It was getting late, and Kitty had retired and

gone to bed. I was thinking of doing the same. I put down my paper and yawned, and that's when I felt his eyes again.

"Well?" I said, staring back at him.

"Well what?"

"I can't read your mind, Lionel. For God's sake. What's the matter? What's wrong?"

"Nothing is wrong. Why do you ask?"

"Why do I——?" His evasiveness annoyed me. "Something's wrong. I can tell. There's something on your mind. This isn't the first time I've noticed. You've been doing it for weeks. You keep looking at me. You're not very subtle about it, either. Look, there's something you want from me, so tell me what's on your mind. Go on. Get it over with."

He put down his paper and stared at the fire. He still didn't say anything.

"What is it?" I said. "Is it Kitty? The children? Is something wrong with them?"

He shook his head.

"Is it your work? Are you having trouble with that *Telegraph* editor again?"

He gave the back of his head a vigorous scratch—a nervous habit.

"No, there's no trouble with him. Or the others."

"Then what is it?"

"It's Gabriel. He's not well."

"Gabriel?" I said. It took a moment to remember who he was talking about. "The artist? Well, yes, he's certainly not well. I could see that. I think all the guests could."

He shook his head again.

His physical condition is fragile, but that's not what I mean. Gabriel suffers from something else. It's difficult for me to explain." He looked up as if there were words on the ceiling. "It's a kind of . . . *bewitchment*, you might say."

I considered the word. "Are you referring to a woman? Is he having troubles with someone?"

He frowned.

"A few years ago I might have said so, but no. The only women involved in his life now are his sister and mother . . . and the nurse. It's not that. What I mean is"—he scratched his head again—"you said yourself they're all around us. I heard you. The whole church did."

"What did I say?" I couldn't hide my impatience. "Lionel, I'm tired and it's late. If you can't be direct, let's leave this for another time. I want to go home and go to bed." I started to get up.

"Now wait, for God's sake, just wait," he said, irritated. "Very well. What I'm talking about is . . . a spirit. His wife's spirit."

I studied his face. There was no sign of humor or irony there. Nothing. This wasn't a joke. He was completely serious. I didn't expect this sort of talk from him. I sat back down.

"He's never stopped grieving for her," he said. "But it's changed into something else. You saw. He's obsessed. It's madness now."

He relit his cigar and took several long tucks. We talked about what happened at the party, how Gabriel interpreted the fallen painting as a sign that Elizabeth, who had died more than ten years ago, had come back to him. Anyone else would've interpreted it only as a sign that someone did a very bad job of hanging the painting. Not Rossetti—not an artist who spent his life delving into the hidden meanings of things. He took it as more than that, and it wasn't the only sign. Lionel said there had been other incidents in his house, but everyone who knew Rossetti just dismissed it all as the product of grief. No one challenged him—no one wanted to risk upsetting him.

"There are some who really do believe it's her," Lionel said.

"You said there have been other signs. What kinds?"

"Just knocks and raps. The sounds any old house makes. I don't know what to think, but Gabriel is convinced. So are his brother and some other associates. They think it's her, and I can't understand why. If there really is a spirit in that house, why would anyone assume it's Lizzie? She was a very gentle person, and the stories I've heard about this presence don't sound like her. Something's playing a cruel trick on him. I'm sure of it. There are so many spirits out there, aren't there? You've said so yourself. Why would it have to be her? Why couldn't it be something else?"

To hear such talk coming from him was incredible. Lionel Ashburnham, mighty critic and relation of the great Algernon Charles Swinburne, was telling me a ghost story. It didn't fit the man I knew. He seemed too much of a materialist, sensualist, pragmatist, and all the other -ists—what interested him were the pleasures and possibilities of the physical world.

And yet, on that night, we sat in his comfortable study, high above the deserted streets of Mayfair, discussing something far beyond the taste of a Turkish cigar or English politics or a beautiful actress or even a grieving husband's strained mind.

"I can see this amuses you, Michael. Stop it. Stop smiling like that. I'm being serious. Do you really think it's easy for me to talk this way? I don't like abstractions. I don't like thinking about things I can't touch with my hands. But that's what we're dealing with here, and I'm worried. Cold as Lizzie was to him sometimes, she'd never make him suffer the way he's suffering now."

"What do you mean?"

"You saw. His nerves. They're badly frayed. He can't sleep, and when he tries, he has bad dreams. He confessed to me once that when he sleeps, when he manages to, he has one recurring dream. He sees his wife, dressed as a sorceress, perched in a tree above a field of dead men. All the corpses have the same face. His. To me, it all sounds like a trick. I couldn't make sense of it until I went to Saint Martha's and heard you. You opened my eyes, Michael. You helped me understand what is going on. You said Ezekiel describes the mental tricks that evil spirits use to tempt and hurt us. That's what it is."

I was shocked he'd paid such close attention.

"Not Ezekiel, Lionel. It was a desert monk named Evagrios. But couldn't this just be stemming from what you said before, his grief?" I thought of my father. "Grief is powerful. It can make us see and believe in incredible things. Shouldn't we start with that?"

He shrugged.

"I suppose so. But Antonia detected something. That's why I wanted you both at the party."

He sat forward and flicked his cigar into the fire even though he hadn't finished it. Absentmindedly, he reached for another. The mention of Antonia Cox irritated me.

"Ah, the illustrious Madame Cox," I said. "I never expected to hear her name again. What great discovery did she make?"

He ignored my sarcasm. He said she was a great practitioner of the tarot and that her cards suggested Rossetti had been singled out by what she called a "supramundane intelligence." She'd hoped to get a clearer understanding of it with a reading during the party.

"She did her best, but there wasn't enough time." He gave me an embarrassed look. I knew why.

"There wasn't enough time because of me, right? I interrupted her when I fell. If she's as good as you say she is, it's too bad she didn't read my fall in her cards. She might've warned me."

Lionel looked at me.

"Maybe she did see it and just doesn't like you."

"It sounds like Gabriel isn't the only one who's bewitched."

"Oh, shut up."

When he talked about Antonia, Lionel's eyes had a look in them. It reminded me of the look my mother sometimes gave my father. I felt sorry for Kitty. Lionel said Cox's abilities were extraordinary, but I didn't think so. If she was everything Lionel said she was, why did she need my help? Or anyone else's help? He said Cox was arranging for someone else to assist her in identifying Rossetti's spectral guest, a powerful practitioner of the dark arts named Khristiana Lumens. Lionel and Cox had met with her, and this solemn high priestess was already preparing a powerful ritual. Lionel said he hoped I would join them for it. He pressed a card with Cox's address into my hand.

"We're meeting with Antonia to discuss the ritual. Can you join us?"

I slipped the card into my coat pocket.

"Me? What would you expect me to do, Lionel? I'm a priest, not a magician!"

"Yes, but you understand things the way a magician does. You possess a real knowledge of the occult that's valuable, Michael. We need you. You might notice something that we won't."

"I don't possess anything special, Lionel, I really don't. I just tell stories on Sundays. That's all."

"You talk as if stories don't matter. But they do."

I knew he was right. Stories are important. We tell them constantly to ourselves. We tell ourselves what will happen to us, what to do, what to expect, who we think we are, and what we're meant to be. Our lives are nothing without stories. Our lives are nothing but a long stream of them, good and bad. I couldn't help remembering—as Lionel kept talking—one that my mother liked to tell me before bed. There was a little boy stuck in an unhappy orphanage who saved every penny he found in the streets to buy balloons at the county fair. The orphan keeper and the other orphans all laughed at him. They thought he was wasting his money. One day, when the little boy finally had enough pennies, he bought a big spray of balloons, tied them to his bed frame, and floated away—off to a faraway land where his parents were waiting for him.

Lionel kept asking if I would join them. At that moment, I wished I could do the same thing.

18

◇◇◇◇◇◇◇

The chapel library

I LEFT MAYFAIR THAT NIGHT without agreeing to anything. I don't know how I managed to escape without giving Lionel an answer. He kept pressing me, and I just kept telling him my head ached and that I needed to go home. The whole next week we didn't speak, and I knew he was angry. How did I know? It was simple: my regular dinner invitation never arrived. By the next Friday morning, I was still waiting for it, and I knew he was punishing me. He was withholding the one thing he knew I cherished.

On that invitation-less Friday afternoon, I found Father Bramble down in the common room, thumbing through the latest number of the *Catholic Herald*. I heard him cough—he had a disgusting habit of hacking up mouthfuls and choking them back down as he skimmed the issue— and I couldn't bear the thought of eating dinner with him. Father Veach would be taking care of the benediction that evening, so I went to the kitchen and told Nessie not to include me in her meal preparations. I grabbed my coat and ducked out the kitchen door. A few streets away, I found my supper in a penny pie shop before heading off to the library of Father Gerard Balfe. Gerard was another friend who meant so much to me when I was in London. He never required a note, never sent an invitation. His door was always open.

I discovered Gerard quite by accident because of my regular rambles in a place I've mentioned several times already, the book stalls of Paternoster Row. The Row is a narrow street just north of Saint Paul's Cathedral that monks and priests once strolled as they prayed their Our Fathers (hence the name). That little stretch of road—just about two hundred yards' worth—had been the heart and soul of the British book trade for more than a century. It was during one of my visits that a bookseller told me about an interesting collection of arcana.

"What? Here on the Row?"

"No, not here. It's a dumpy place in Brompton near an old hospital storage building," the man said. "There's a square there. And an old bronze statue of Wellington covered in bird droppings. It's not open to the public, though. And the fellow's more of a book *keeper* than a seller. Not very pleasant, either. Mind yourself if you ever go there. I wouldn't."

Despite the warning, I went to look for it. I was intrigued. I found the spattered statue and the square without any trouble, but I spent a frustrating hour searching for the shop. I was about to give up when I spotted a plain little house, flat, single story, tucked back in a courtyard hemmed in on all sides by tall buildings. The courtyard was lost in shadows, and the house looked deserted. Some curious designs in the loose plaster around the front doors caught my attention. I squinted in the gloom and could just make out a bull's head, an eagle, and part of a wing that belonged either to a bird or an angel.

It was odd; here were two (quite possibly three) symbols of the four evangelists—not something you'd expect to find on a house. I went up to the front doors and knocked. No one answered. When I pounded harder, the doors cracked open. They were unlocked. I decided to look inside.

I had no idea I was stepping inside a relic of the Roman Church's history in England. That small building, like others in the country, had been a covert place of worship until the 1850s and the new freedoms given to the Catholic faithful. For centuries, such churches had kept as low of a profile as our priests had. No ornaments on the exterior were allowed, nothing to call attention to, especially no crucifixes, statues, or stained glass (which makes you wonder about those images in the stucco, why the people using this house took a risk)—it was almost as if, thanks to Henry VIII, English Catholicism had traveled back to its first-century roots when Christian houses of worship were just that: houses. After the emancipation, most of these recusant churches were abandoned . . . most, but apparently not this one. Inside, I found myself staring at an incredible sight in the church's nave.

An ocean of books.

They weren't scattered around in rubbish piles; they'd been organized. The old wood pews once forming two sections of seating had been unbolted and moved into new positions. Some pews were set against the walls and stacked high with books. An obvious effort had been made to segregate and group everything, even if it wasn't immediately clear what the organizing principle was. The front of the church was used the same way; books had been stacked on the altar table and on each of the steps leading up to the altar. There was no gilded tabernacle there anymore, no home for the Most Blessed Body and Blood . . . just books, books, and more books.

And no human beings.

The place seemed empty, but if it was, who had lighted the lamps? Or forgotten to lock the doors?

I heard a noise coming from behind the altar—it sounded like papers being shuffled—and then I heard a cough. I found Gerard sitting in the sacristy, which had been turned into a study. The old priest looked up and growled at me until I identified myself as another priest. And when he heard my name, his expression brightened.

"Oh, Frost—wait now—*Michael Frost?* The new priest at Saint Martha's? I've heard about you!" Evidently, Gerard was a reader of the Sketchist.

Though he called the place a library, it wasn't one. There were no regular visitors (only accidental ones like me), no lending cards. He explained that the place served as a storehouse of sorts for a variety of Catholic (and non-Catholic) literature that had been circulating all over England.

"I had a parish once. You could say these are my parishioners now," he said, pointing at the books. "And the mice, too."

I smiled at him. His shaggy beard and clenched jaw reminded me of a very friendly mastiff. There was still something boyish and good-looking about his face, even though he had a bug-eyed expression that was slightly unnerving—caused by an apoplectic fit years ago that never went away.

"There's nothing quite like this in the country," he said proudly. "We have things here even the Bod doesn't."

Now, *that* was a ridiculous claim, but as I became more acquainted with Gerard and the library, I realized he might be right. Many of the books were refugees from the Gordon Riots against the Catholics a century before. In the late 1770s, Parliament wanted to make the situation better for us—and gain more bodies for its thinned-out army ranks—but the antipapists wouldn't have it. They staged protests that ended, as almost everything eventually does, in violence, fires, and looting. The protesters attacked government buildings and any houses suspected of being secret churches or of supporting us in any way. Many books were rescued from destruction and found a home in the chapel library; others were acquired later by various unnamed hands, avid collectors, all of them contributing to what became a vast, disordered, moldering pile of knowledge until Gerard came along.

Because his legs were weak, Gerard used an old hospital chair on wheels to move among the pews. He rolled down one of the rows and stopped with a loud squeak.

"Here," he said, reaching for a book on one of the stacks. "You mentioned your father was a child of the Rus. This may interest you."

He handed it to me. I read the title. *Le catholicisme Romain en Russie* by Dmitry Tolstoy, published in 1866. I smiled at him.

"What an extraordinary variety of books you have," I said.

"We should probably thank the Prohibitorum for that, Father." He gave me a sly wink with his good eye.

The library's contents, he said, included many on the Holy Father's index of forbidden titles. I followed him around the room as he explained the library's organization. He pointed to stacks of books written by adherents of the Arian heresy, of gnosticism; others on divination; texts by Copernicus, Kepler, and Brahe. There were books of prayers and practices used in the Orient. Interspersed among them were loose pages of translations of old Greek poems—Gerard had produced these himself, he said proudly. Along the room's eastern wall were books devoted specifically to poetry and literature. He patted one volume atop a stack and smiled. "Browne," he sighed. "*Urn Burial*. Sublime." From another stack, he picked up a book with German script stamped on the cover. He showed it to me.

"A German edition of Marlowe's *Faustus*, a 1685 edition," he explained with a shiver of pleasure, "with annotations by a devoted follower of Agrippa."

I couldn't understand why Westminster would ever allow something like this, allow the storage of forbidden books. In the seminary, we'd been taught to treat such titles like poison, as if they'd been written by Satan himself.

"If these are all prohibited," I asked, "why would the diocese want to keep them? It doesn't make any sense."

He grinned.

"Oh, I thought like you once, but if the Church has learned anything over nearly two millennia, it's this: Knowing what your enemies are thinking can be very valuable. It increases your chances of survival."

GERARD WASN'T THE SORT OF PRIEST any bishop wanted in the pulpit. Early in his career, as assistant pastor of Saint Aethelryd's in the Fenlands, he'd worried his superiors each time he delivered a homily. Usually, he just confused people with esoteric ideas, but sometimes, he cut uncomfortably close to heresy in ways that were all too clear to everyone, even the ignorant farmers and canal workers who formed most of his congregation. Gerard didn't do this because he disputed Catholic doctrine: his fault was his curiosity. He just couldn't help himself. He never turned his back on anything interesting, even when he was expected to deliver a simple sermon about forgiveness or the graces found in small acts of mercy. His circumstances had been so different from mine; I realized how lucky I was to have Cardinal Manning's blessing before venturing into the sorts of dark subjects and provocations that had gotten him in trouble.

At first, the people of Saint Aethelryd's gave him a chance because he was young. But not for long—they were a crusty bunch of old Fenland families with practical outlooks and a similar expectation of their clergy. They wanted good edifying pearls of knowledge to help them through the rural hardships of the week, not Gerard's musings over whether Virgil truly echoed Isaiah in his fourth eclogue. His assignment there was soon over, and the same thing happened in his subsequent assignments until, thankfully, he was moved here.

GERARD'S LIBRARY FED MY WORK, and it sheltered me when I needed it most. He was the person who gave me a place to stay after my argument with Bramble and Veach. The early assumption I'd made about him based on the Row bookseller's warning—that he was a cold fish who hated human interaction—was completely wrong. Gerard was generous and social; he threw open the doors of the library to me and didn't mind an unannounced visit. I enjoyed his company, and I know he felt the same way. Occasionally, another clergyman or some collector from the Row might stumble into the place, and he was always cheerful and receptive, but his interactions with people were few and far between.

I decided to leave the imp with him because of his familiarity with the occult. I told him about its discovery among my father's things and what I'd learned from Ivan. He asked my permission to show the totem to an old friend who was knowledgeable about the occult.

"He's been something of a business partner to me. A real expert on arcane things. If you think I know a great deal, wait until you meet him," he said. "Don't worry, Michael. I know how special this little fellow is to you. I promise to be discreet. I'll keep him safe."

I knew he would.

AFTER BEING SNUBBED by Lionel for Friday supper, I went to the chapel library and found Gerard in his chair in the study, with the imp at his side. Gerard was eating a bowl of stew. I sat down in a chair across from him, and he offered me a bowl. He said his legs were cold, and he'd built a roaring fire; it was so hot I had to move my chair back several feet from the grate.

Firelight danced on the imp's face and Gerard's cheeks. When he picked it up, Gerard handled the imp like it was a holy relic.

"So," I asked him, "what do you think it really is? Any ideas yet?"

He rubbed his jaw.

"It's a tutelary deity. I just don't know which one."

"That makes sense," I said. "I've looked at all kinds of ritual night walks. I've found plenty of descriptions of village sentries. No mention of a totem with horns, though."

"Well, night watches have always been common across Europe," he said. "Don't worry. We'll get to the bottom of it. Let's eat first. And have a little drink."

He poured us each some whiskey, and we toasted the imp. He was wearing the horns Ivan had asked about—I'd found them at the bottom of one of the crates in the cellar. Thank goodness I hadn't mistaken them for trash.

In the firelight, I inserted the ends into the discreet holes on the imp's head, just as Ivan had shown me, and the result was amazing. A change came over the imp. With the curled horns in place, it seemed less ghoulish than before. Almost regal.

19

◇◇◇◇◇◇◇

Afternoon tea

I RETURNED HOME THAT NIGHT and found fried mutton waiting for me in the rectory kitchen. Nessie was always so thoughtful; I told her I wouldn't be eating with my associates, and she'd left me a plate anyway. She was always doing nice things for me. I think she felt sorry because I didn't have my parents, especially my mother. Fathers are important, of course, but a mother brings you into the world. She's the doorway into life. There's a saying among Ruthenians that if you lose your father, you're considered a half orphan, but if you lose your mother, you're a whole one.

I shouldn't have been hungry, not after the penny pies and Gerard's stew, but Nessie was a good cook and knew how I liked my mutton—heavily salted and peppered and fried until the skin was crispy and black. I ate like I hadn't eaten in weeks. The thought of it makes my mouth water even now. She also left a letter by my plate. I ate the mutton and opened it. I thought it might be an apology from Lionel. Maybe he regretted snubbing me, or maybe Kitty had forced him to write it.

I was wrong. It was from Dante Rossetti. He wanted to see me. I couldn't believe it. I had to read the letter several times before the words finally sunk through my thick skull. He asked if I would come the next afternoon to 16 Cheyne Walk. The shock of his invitation was matched only by the shock that he'd known where to find me, but I knew Lionel must have told him. Rossetti wrote that there was an urgent matter he needed to discuss but didn't say more. I don't know if it was my excitement or eating too much, or a combination of both, but my stomach hurt that night, and it was hard to sleep. I rubbed rosemary oil on it, but it didn't help.

The next day, I left early and took a carriage down to the embankment to make sure I wasn't late. It was a beautiful sunny afternoon. The wind was blowing the stink of shit from the Thames in the other direction. Rossetti answered when I knocked. I was surprised; I had expected one of the servants to answer, but he told me they'd been dismissed for the afternoon.

"I'm so glad to see you, *Father*," he said, smiling. I wore my black cassock, the little cape like a soldier's, and my biretta. Oh yes, and my rosary beads, which hung from my waist and clicked at the slightest movement. There wasn't a reason to hide my identity anymore. I thought my clerical dress would please him.

I followed his little figure into the entrance hall, past the beautiful women with forlorn expressions and seductive open mouths. The word *extraordinary* risks becoming meaningless in my story, but that's the best way to describe our meeting. By that time in his life, the gates around the artist were being strictly managed by his brother and Caine—and by Swinburne's man, Watts-Dunton. Few people slipped through, and few things from Gabriel (gifts, notes, invitations) ever slipped out. The party had been the exception, an exception I'm sure William Rossetti regretted. He had established a highly controlled environment in his brother's best interests, even though it seemed more like a prison sentence. I understood why he did it, to protect his brother's health, but it was clear to me that Rossetti craved company even if his guardian was against it.

The house was quiet. Caine, who had moved in with Rossetti that fall, was away on business. We had the entire place to ourselves. As I looked around, it was hard to believe this was the same house where the party had been held. The rooms seemed so lonely without guests filling them. Rossetti led me to a small sitting room that had been used for our coats. The room was almost as simply furnished as my own, except for two chairs in front of a roaring fire. There was a small table with a plate of biscuits, two teacups, and everything one needed for a nice cup of tea.

Rossetti took the kettle from the fire and poured us some hot water. He looked the way he did the night of the party—same poor color, same clamminess—but he also seemed somehow different. His eyes were more alert, more animated. He chuckled to himself about something as he filled my cup.

"Father, Lionel says you are a solid individual, a person to be trusted. I'm very good at sensing things about people, and I believe him. I'm certain I could trust you even if it weren't for your chosen vocation in life." He indicated my dress. "I don't know what you know about me or what Lionel may have told you, but I've had many trials in life, and I've been helped by many people. Their love and concern are very humbling to me, even now. In all honesty, I don't think I deserve it."

"You're very fortunate to have so many concerned about you, Mr. Rossetti. I understand what you mean, but I don't think you should feel guilty about that. It's a blessing from God. It's something to be grateful for."

"Please. Call me Gabriel."

Our conversation started out well enough. Rossetti talked about his family—his doting brother, his overly concerned mother and sister, the famed poet Christina—and then asked about mine, about my education and experiences in the seminary.

"I'd hoped I might enjoy your excellent counsel, Father. When Lionel first asked if he could invite you to my party, I recognized your name immediately. Does that surprise you? It shouldn't. I'm a great admirer of the Sketchist's articles. Like many, I read about the successes of the new young cleric at Saint Martha's! I'm not nearly as isolated or immersed in my work as some think. I know what is taking place in the world. And I'm aware of your sermons, though I haven't had the chance to come and hear one for myself. How I desperately wish I could. Nothing would make me happier. My own knowledge of the occult surely pales next to yours. That is why I asked you here today. I was hoping you would help me understand something. I was hoping you might help me make better sense of my wife's new presence in my life."

I felt a sinking feeling in my stomach as he described my accident with the painting and how the fact that it involved *that* painting—which meant so much to him and his wife—was undeniable proof of her return. In the days after that incident, he said the sweet spirit of his beloved wife was making herself known to him in many comforting little ways—with raps and knocks on the walls and tables that followed him wherever he went. Or if it wasn't a knock, it might be the movement of an object—a paintbrush might suddenly slide across a perfectly level table while he was working. Or a book might fall open to a page she obviously wanted him to read. He had enjoyed such experiences of her after her death, but her spectral presence later vanished from his side for many years. He said this happened after he exhumed his celebrated volume of poems. He knew why she left him—even though the book made him successful and restored his confidence in his poetic powers, desecrating her grave had angered her. But he'd suffered long enough, and now she'd clearly forgiven him, and he asked me if I'd ever heard of anything like this before.

I didn't know what to say. I had no experience with ghosts. I hesitated. I worried that if I didn't say something right away, the silence would become awkward. But Rossetti didn't wait for my answer. He started talking again. He eagerly explained how he'd read that the dearly departed sometimes appear as glowing balls of light or leave behind sticky strings of ectoplasm. Nothing like that had happened at 16 Cheyne Walk; he said those manifestations sounded more like the entertainments found on Drury Lane, mere parlor tricks. He said he didn't want to turn his queries about the supernatural world over to one of the many spiritualists flooding London in those days. There were too many hucksters and confidence men among them; it was too risky, too easy to be taken advantage of.

"Which is why I needed you here, Father. I am so grateful that you came to see me. I am so grateful to Lionel for bringing us together."

"I'm honored to have your trust, *Gabriel*, but I must be honest with you. I am no expert. I know my sermons may make me sound like one, but that's not the case. I'm a neophyte. A beginner. There was another guest of Lionel's at the party, wasn't there?" I tried not to sound irritated. "A Miss Cox. What of her? From what I understand, she is a true expert. From what Lionel has told me, she's able to help you."

His expression darkened.

"She hasn't been as helpful as Lionel made me think. He said more needs to be done before she can, although I don't know what 'more' means. I'd hoped the card reading at the party would be enough. She and Lionel are apparently very concerned."

I knew this "more" involved Khristiana Lumens, and I waited for him to mention her. But as he continued, it was clear that Lionel hadn't told him anything about her or the special ritual.

"Concerned? What are they concerned about?"

"That what I've described to you isn't my wife."

"Why not?"

"They say this presence is harming me."

"Harming you? How?"

"They say she's making me ill. But they're wrong." He frowned. "I know they're not the only ones. I've confided in some friends who share their opinion. They can all think what they want. I don't care. They can just leave me alone. Leave *us* alone. I don't need to explain or justify myself. To anyone."

I took that last part as a warning to me.

"And besides, if this spirit wasn't her, if this was something else, something as dark and terrible as Lionel and Miss Cox think it is, it wouldn't like my having a priest around, would it? Yet here we've spent the better part of an hour enjoying a pleasant chat, and nothing's happened to you. Nothing has flown off a table or wall at you." He smiled. "And you're even wearing your Roman dress and those beautiful rosary beads! Lizzie loved such clerical raiment even more than I do! If it wasn't her, if it was something malevolent, this visit wouldn't have been possible. That is convincing proof all on its own."

He smiled and looked off to the side of the room.

"Don't you agree, my dear?"

I turned my head, half expecting to see someone there.

"Please, show Father Frost it's really you. You know I don't need proof, but please show our guest, my dear. If you are happy about his visit, give us a little sign. Something small. No flying objects, please. Nothing to frighten him." He lifted a finger. "And if you *aren't* happy that he's here, well then, don't do anything at all. Don't give us any signs."

It was at that moment, so long ago, when I truly became a believer in the spiritual world. I know how this must sound, especially coming from a priest, from someone who stood in the pulpit on Sundays and spoke forcefully of things seen and unseen, but there's a difference between the beliefs we learn and the ones we experience. I think we're all mildly skeptical by nature—we're all rooted in the material world—until something comes along that points us toward hidden realities. How does skepticism finally turn into belief? What causes the change? How long does it take? For some, I think it's a gradual slide over many years; for others, if the experience is powerful enough, it doesn't take years. It was like that for me. A plunge down Alice's rabbit hole. I entered Gabriel's house of one mind and left it in another.

Nothing happened at first. It seemed that his invisible spouse—if it really was her—had chosen the second option. She wasn't happy I was there. Several minutes passed in silence. The only sounds in the room came from the fireplace. Gabriel grew anxious. At first he fidgeted with his hands and tried to fix another cup of tea. The kettle shook in his hand. At that point I decided to stand up. He was getting agitated, and I didn't like that there was no one else in the house. What would I do if he was overcome with an attack of hysterics? How would I explain it to his brother?

"I should probably go, Gabriel. Your hospitality has been so generous. Thank you."

"No, no. Wait. Please, Father," he said. He looked around us again. "My dear? We're waiting. Please, won't you show us a sign? The more we wait, the more I worry you're angry with me! I couldn't bear it if you were! Oh, please, show me you aren't! *Please.*"

The way he begged the empty air was unnerving. It was madness, just as Lionel said, and I suddenly saw the wisdom in William Rossetti keeping his brother away from the world. But then it happened. I was about to turn and go when I heard a soft knocking sound on the table between us—not too hard, just enough not to be mistaken for something else. It happened several times, and Rossetti sighed and sat back. I peeked under the table, looking for something, a mouse perhaps, but I didn't see anything. I sat back down again and looked at Rossetti. He smiled at me. The knocking sound continued. It moved to other parts of the room. We heard it on the fireplace mantel and the walls, and then there was a sudden sharp tap on the top rail of my chair, directly behind my head. This one was harder than the others. It sounded like a nail being driven into the wood. The sound was so sharp and loud, I involuntarily pitched forward and stood up again. My biretta fell on the floor.

"Oh, she can be *so* mischievous sometimes!" He laughed. "She's always been that way! My sweet Lizzie. And a little stubborn, too. It took time to coax her, but you see now, don't you? She's just as pleased to have you here as I am! Is everything all right, Father? I understand how you must feel; it takes time to accept these new manifestations of her. It did for me. Would some fresh air help? Would you care to continue our talk in the garden?"

20

◇◇◇◇◇◇◇◇

Hiss of steam

I REMEMBER A GOOD DESCRIPTION of the spirit world in one of Gerard's books that says it's like the ocean. "In the cold black currents which come up from the deeps," the book said, "there are strange and sinister creatures lurking—evil intelligences which tempt and corrupt and destroy, malignant elementals, astral corpses, zombies, nightmare things. . ." The writer uses a good metaphor. I've never found a better one. What you soon realize when you study the occult is that it isn't a single unified thing; it doesn't have canon law or a legislative charter listing all its bylaws and rules. There are plenty of systems that may try to explain everything, but none neatly mesh and dovetail with the rest. Instead, it's all chaotic and contradictory, which is why I'd say—to continue with the ocean metaphor for a moment—the faith I was born into is like one of those solemn, magnificent, very orderly-looking suspension bridges one sees in Europe and America, and the occult is the inky black sea underneath. When anyone casts a line into it—with a séance or tarot cards or some other practice—there is no guarantee they'll catch exactly what they want. If you've ever been on a ship before, when you look at the water, how do you know what's swimming down there? You don't. You make assumptions. They're not always the right ones.

Out in the garden, Rossetti happily chattered on about what had just happened inside. I didn't share his excitement; I was thinking about my school days. I was thinking of the times I showed off in class and felt the hateful glares of my Mortimer classmates on the back of my neck. I could truly feel it. You can feel hate like that; it can travel through space and be felt like sunlight or a loving glance or a breeze or a thrown rock. That's what I felt when Gabriel's companion announced itself. Hate. I was sure of it. That presence wasn't some loving spouse, no matter what he believed, and it wasn't happy I was there. That tapping on the back of my chair had been hard, not playful. Insistent. Irritated. Like an insult. Or a slap in the face.

Though the afternoon was cold, I was glad to be outside. I felt safer there, even though I'd never read anything that said supernatural entities had an aversion to lower temperatures. As we walked, I could see the effect of the opiates Gabriel was using to break his insomnia. He walked with a slow, halting gait, and I had to assist him down the steps into the garden. His footing was unsteady, and I worried he'd stumble on anything, even the slightest stone.

"I enjoyed your recitation of Propertius. It was masterful, even if it came at poor Lawrence Klein's expense. Many of my friends are very unfavorable toward him even though I've told them to be patient. He is a bit of a fop, I know, and his poetry is very derivative, but one day, I'm sure he'll discover his voice. We all must struggle to know ourselves. Gifts aren't so easily given. We wage a war to uncover them. But maybe I'm too presumptuous in speaking for us both, Father. It was effortless the way you displayed your knowledge of the Roman poets at my party. Effortless and commanding. How lucky your congregation is."

"Thank you. I wouldn't have my abilities with the Latin poets or anything else if it weren't for my mother. She deserves the credit. She adored them. Her affection for them was something she gave me before she died."

Rossetti smiled.

"Our loved ones certainly do affect our lives' quality." He gave me a queer look.

We walked on in silence under lime and mulberry trees, passing statuary that seemed too large, too unnatural for a private garden—looming classical figures with fierce faces that I wouldn't have wanted to spy from a window after dark. Aside from these imposing forms, the garden was empty, even though Lionel told me Gabriel had a reputation as a great keeper of animals—apparently, he was the gentlest of benefactors since Francis of Assisi. And yet, I didn't see any—no peacocks, deer . . . not even the wombat about which he'd famously written. Perhaps the animals fled because they had sensed something wrong at 16 Cheyne Walk, too.

We reached a small marble bench, set in a half arbor, and the poet wearily sat down even though we'd walked hardly fifteen or twenty feet. From here, the house had a chilly aspect in the late-afternoon light, and more than once, I felt as if we were being watched from its windows. To be alone here at night, I thought with a shudder, to be unable to find the peace a common laborer knows after a hard day's work—I felt dread and pity for Rossetti. He seemed to read my thoughts.

"It is a very big house," he said, "ideal for my many collections, less so for its occupant. That is why I enjoy parties so much. I wish there were more, but my family won't allow it."

He said he was contemplating a trip. A friend's kind offer of a seaside bungalow in Kent seemed an appealing retreat, not the least because he had no doubt his wife would be with him. "She's always adored the sea," he said. He hoped I would come and see him again before they—it unnerved me the way he used the plural—departed for the coast. He wanted me to recite more of my translations from Propertius. He said he felt a sharp attraction to the Roman poets.

"I think I understand how much their love poetry really isn't an expression of romance at all," he said. "It's clear to me they wrote out of grief. I didn't see it in my youth, but an old man who has suffered his losses does. Grief is just as powerful as any love . . . and more lasting."

The artist shivered and rubbed his hands together and said his neck was cold. He asked me to go back inside for his scarf. He said it was on a chair by the garden doors. I didn't want to; I felt a very strong "No!" congealing in the pit of my stomach, but when I saw the pleading look on his face, I couldn't refuse.

The scarf wasn't where he said it would be. The chair by the door was bare. By the time I found the scarf, hanging on a hall tree next to the sitting room, our conversation about grief had worked a change in me. I found myself thinking of my father again. Yes, Gabriel was right. Grief does last. I missed him, but I'd been so preoccupied that I hadn't given myself a chance to grieve. I don't think I wanted to. I don't think I was ready. As I walked back to the garden door, I found myself thinking about his death, about the moment when the undertaker came. I saw my father's closed eyes and fallen jaw. The purpling of his forehead—how quickly it darkened the moment he was gone. The coldness of his cheeks. When I'd touched them, when I'd kissed him one last time, they'd felt hard like wood or stone, like anything but flesh. In that moment I'd become more aware of the bones in his face than I'd ever been before. With that sensation came the realization I wasn't touching *him* anymore; those weren't the cheeks that had tickled me with their roughness when I was a child. Death had changed him with its withering touch. Even the fairness of his skin, which had always had a soft, rosy glow, was gone. It was difficult to stay there, by the bed, watching the undertaker measure something I didn't recognize anymore.

I reached the garden door and could see Gabriel outside. He was rubbing his arms and hugging himself. I took a step closer to the door and stopped. I felt a wave of dizziness and couldn't understand why. I tried to think of the last time I'd eaten anything that day. I closed my eyes and inhaled deeply, but it didn't help. I felt the room start to spin. I stumbled forward and grabbed the back of the chair by the door to steady myself. There was a warm, coppery taste in my mouth.

I didn't want Gabriel to see me this way, but I needed to go back to him. He was waiting. I knew going outside would help me. The cold air would help me. I reached for the doorhandle and was surprised to hear a voice softly calling my name from somewhere behind me in the house. It wasn't one of the servants; they were still away, and besides, even if they had returned, none of them would have known to use the Ruthenian form of my name.

My memory of what happened next is still unclear. I remember feeling terrified and stumbling outside. By the door was a trellis covered in a thick brown mass of grapevines. I hid there a moment and waited. My teeth were chattering. My breathing was wildly uneven. I felt tears in my eyes. I didn't want to alarm Rossetti; I didn't want him to see that anything was wrong. I just wanted to give him his scarf and get out of there as quickly as I could.

I waited several minutes. When my breathing slowed, I wiped my eyes, stepped out from the grapevines, and closed the garden door with a loud bang. I made quite a show of rushing down the steps to him. He looked up as I handed him the scarf, and I apologized for taking so long. I said the scarf hadn't been where he said. He studied my face, but I avoided his eyes. He had to have known there was something wrong, but he didn't say anything. He only asked to be helped back to the house. He said it was too cold now, and he wanted another cup of tea.

I walked him to the door and told him I couldn't stay. I hadn't realized the time, I said. I had forgotten another appointment.

"If I don't leave now, I'll miss it."

"Yes, of course, one mustn't do that."

I could tell he was disappointed, but he was gracious. And generous. He offered to pay for my cab—it was probably his way of apologizing for the fright I'd experienced earlier. I declined, thanking him and telling him our afternoon together had been payment enough.

When I left Gabriel, he watched me walk out through a side gate to the street. A carriage was parked across the way, and I waved to him as I climbed in. I'll never forget how he looked then—his little figure leaning against the railing, waving back. Behind him, the house looked like a face: two windows above him were unblinking eyes; the open garden door was like a mouth ready to gobble him up. The carriage started pulling away. I imagined him wandering the halls that night, happy and content as long as he heard that dreadful knocking whenever he called his dead wife's name.

It was on the ride home that I changed my mind. I decided to help Lionel and Antonia Cox. I'd join them for the Lumens ritual. I didn't know what would be expected of me, but my experience that day convinced me that Gabriel needed help. I couldn't let him down. Experience had given me what Lionel's words couldn't. I didn't know what Lionel truly hoped I could do—I was still a mere researcher on these matters, not a practitioner. He was investing me with far more credibility and expertise than I deserved. Still, after tea with that poor man, I knew it didn't take a practitioner's experience to know he was in danger. What was the word Cox used? *Supramundane.* She'd said there was a supramundane presence in the house. I thought about the night of the party again and the accident with the painting. My throbbing fingers. I realized what happened to me then had been a warning not to get involved. And then, on this visit, I'd felt that malignant quality again, vibrating in the air, knocking on my chair, and creating the voice I heard behind me that nearly broke my heart.

Mikhaylo.

It was like a hiss of steam.

My father's voice before he died.

21

◇◇◇◇◇◇◇

The bridge

2:00 a.m.

THE NIGHT WALK ISN'T AS BAD AS IT SEEMS if you're able to spend some of it next to a warm stove.

Some villagers don't take the duty seriously enough. They wander around for a few hours and go home. Or they come out right before dawn, pretending they've been walking all night. No one ever bothers to check, and someone should; it would be tragic if something happened because someone wasn't where they should have been. I'm not like that. It's only one night. I can sleep tomorrow.

I can't help feeling guilty for what I'm doing now, but there's nothing I can do about that. It's still raining. I can't go outside until it ends. If it ends.

I said before, in one of my sermons, that supernatural beings hide from us, and I'm sure that description would offend them. Most consider themselves superior to us. The thing that was haunting Rossetti certainly did. Our faith teaches us that we are the greatest of God's creations, but all my research in Gerard's library taught me the opposite. When it comes to the angels, even the fallen ones, one memorable phrase stands out: we are to them what ants and fleas are to us—something to be ignored, unless we prove to be a nuisance. Saying that they hide from humans is insulting to their pride because it suggests they're afraid, and they're not. The reason we don't notice them isn't because of their concealment; our eyes are just defective, our minds are too small, and they don't care to involve themselves with us . . . most of the time.

Until the recent disappearance of Paul Melnyk, there hadn't been any supernatural incidents in Prehovinka since I arrived years ago. A few of us, Natalka included, believe that something supernatural is involved with Paul's disappearance. But no one here really wants to talk about it. Villagers get upset if you bring it up; they want to pretend that something else happened to him. For them, it's simple: If you stop thinking about it, you'll stop worrying about it, and it won't exist anymore. That's what they want. And that's why I think there's been a falling off in the night-walk duty, too. It's been a long time since anything frightening has happened here that's hard to explain. Most people feel less urgency about the duty even though there are still practical reasons for doing it.

There was that same ignorance, or indifference, whatever you want to call it, before my father lost the varta and left with Ivan. After that happened, and typhus swept through, Natalka says people became afraid again, and there was a big renewal effort to keep the village safe. But in the years since my arrival, that apathy has returned, and that's a bad thing. I don't want to criticize or disparage my fellow villagers. I wouldn't call them lazy—that would be unfair. And inaccurate. They're not. They're some of the hardest-working people I've ever known. It's just that we've been distracted by too many other things, human matters, to worry about anything else: new demands from Gradwolski, new costs imposed by the Minkins, poor weather, worries about the harvest. There have been other tensions and disputes, too. Ruthenians have experienced a great deal of hatred in recent years for insisting on our own identity as a people and calling for formal political recognition. Not long ago, a large group of Hungarians held a protest in Stanislau against us, claiming this whole region of the empire is an ancient Hungarian land and should be given back to them. They might be right. It's hard to argue with history. Like many, the Hungarians look to the past for their sense of identity. Ruthenians can't do that. If we did, we'd only find despair. We have to look to the future. That's where we find ours.

As I'm refolding my coat under me and settling back again, there's a flash of lightning in the dome, followed by a loud crash outside. But it doesn't sound like thunder; it's more of a terrible groaning—the kind timber makes when it's being ripped apart.

I grab my lamp and go outside. The rain's subsided to a drizzle now. At first, I only hear the roar of the river, but as my eyes grow accustomed to the dark, I can see the frothing surface. It's very high. Tree branches and clots of river grass and old logs sail by, touched by my lamp's light.

Some of the debris isn't branches and logs; it's carpentered wood—sawn beams and planks—and I realize with a sick feeling why. I know where it's coming from. I move up the embankment, and it's just as I suspected.

The current has torn away the piers from underneath the bridge, and it's sagging at the middle and sinking. I look over at the other side. It seems so far away now. I can't get back that way.

I don't have many options. I could wait inside the church until morning or take the only path on this side of the river. It winds along the back of the fields at the forest's edge. We take our carts and wagons on it when we're gathering wood. It's a long trek down through the fields, but it leads to the mill, where there's another bridge that I might be able to use—if it hasn't been damaged, too.

Staying inside the church would probably be wiser—and more defensible, especially on a night like this—but I don't want to. I don't want to give up on my duty. And I want to get home by first light. I'm not thrilled at the prospect of taking that lonely path, especially since it's so far from the village. But I have the imp with me, and I know I'll be fine. And besides, Rudy lives out there. He manages our harvest sheds. And eventually the path will take me to Natalka's cottage. I'd like to see her before the night is over.

Thinking of her and Rudy makes me feel better about my choice. Knowing that their homes are out there reminds me of the comfort mariners feel when the torch at the top of a lighthouse appears in the fog.

WHEN I FIRST MET GERARD, I felt sorry for him. He seemed lonely to me—like he didn't have any company in the world except for his books. He never mentioned any relations except for an ancient aunt living somewhere west of Dublin. He seemed completely alone. Not long after my unsettling visit with Gabriel, though, I went to see him and discovered I was wrong. Gerard did have friends. Well, he had one. I arrived at the library and heard laughter coming from the study. I walked in and found him talking to a man dressed in a plain dark suit. At first, I mistook him for another member of the clergy.

"Michael, at last!" Gerard said. He gestured at an empty chair and handed me a glass. "I'd like to introduce you to someone!"

There was an odor of strong spirits in the air, and I saw an uncorked decanter of brandy on his desk. The imp was there. He was couched on a cushion and looked like he was enjoying their conversation.

The other man jumped up from his chair as I approached.

"William Ige!" he announced, stepping forward and extending his hand. "It is a supreme pleasure to finally meet you, Father! I've been waiting to meet the famous subject of the Sketchist's column . . . and the owner of this *exquisite* specimen," he said, pointing at the imp. "What a remarkable little fellow!"

His enthusiasm took me by surprise. Gerard introduced him—"that's *Ige* as in *league*," he said—as an old friend who earned his living as a collecting agent for several private clients and museums. He acquired rare items for them from auctions and private collections all over the country and across the channel, especially in France. It was a good living, judging by the fine cut of his otherwise wrinkled suit.

"William and I have had many adventures together," Gerard said. "We wouldn't have solved several interesting matters if it hadn't been for his brilliance. In fact, William has some intriguing ideas about your varta." Ige cleared his throat and stood.

I sat back in my chair and listened to what this odd-looking man had to say. Ige was a short, frumpy figure in a shirt with billowy sleeves and a silk waistcoat all covered in tobacco stains. His nostrils flared like trumpets, and the gray pallor of his cheeks and forehead made his face seem as if it were entirely made of wax. His hair was gray and curled, growing in frizzy patches on his head like a neglected garden. He had a look more serious than a Calvinist's, but as his eyes darted between Gerard's and mine, he gave us both a delighted smile that reminded me of a church mouse.

He embarked on a lengthy description of horned deities and their primacy in some of the world's oldest faith traditions. As he talked, the sweat glistened on his forehead. He became so heated from his exertions that he finally removed his waistcoat and tossed it on a chair. He spoke quickly but with a gentle air, and he displayed a supple knowledge and ease in discussing the occult. Something about him made me like him instantly. He wasn't showy with what he knew—not like Lionel or Lawrence Klein—and he seemed unaware of his own innate brilliance (as most genuine disciples in any discipline usually are). He gestured at the door, which led to the library's main room, and said the answer to my father's imp had been out there all along.

"But I looked," I said, "and I didn't find anything. What did I miss?"

He held up a volume from the stack where Gerard kept the library's holdings of books on religious anthropology. *Barbarian Deities: Their Cults and Practices*, by the great scientist and adventurer Sir Herbert Harken, published in 1873. Green calfskin with red lettering. I confessed I hadn't noticed it before.

"What you've asked about the varta, about its identity, is all in here," he said, "but I wouldn't have known to look if it hadn't been for one crucial bit of information. Gerard mentioned that you'd almost thrown away his horns. Thank heavens you didn't!"

He poured a sloshing measure of brandy into my glass. Then he reached for the two horns and inserted them into the sides of the imp's head.

"These are the key to this marvel's identity."

Ige said the curled branches were "like the ones worn by a very powerful ancient god of the Slavs. Veles." I looked at him blankly. "He's a figure similar to the Celtic Cernunnos." I gave him another blank look. "See here."

He opened the book to an illustration of a man with a long black beard standing in a forest clearing. He was dressed in a white robe and wore curled horns on his head. This was Veles.

"Isn't it lovely?" Ige said. "Some images show the moon rising behind him so that it encircles his head. Almost like a halo. Or an aura of protection."

Another illustration depicted Veles in half-human, half-serpent form, locked in battle with Perun, the Slavic god of thunder.

"The serpentine element helps us understand these," he said, stroking the patterns of intricate lines on the imp's body. "Don't these resemble a snake's underbelly to you? I think they're supposed to."

Along with the Celts, he went on, one finds a similar kind of deity—
always with the horns—among primitive cults around the world. He said
all the gods of these religions are just fallen angels in disguise. When they
rebelled and lost, they fell to earth and found consolation as objects of
worship. They became the central deities of many different creeds.

Gerard interrupted, quoting some lines from Milton:

Then were they known to men by various names,
And various idols through the heathen world.

"That's exactly right," Ige said, smiling. "And the fallen one who became Veles is quite high in the diabolic hierarchy." He gave the imp an
affectionate pat on the head. "Veles is decorated with more honors than
an old general covered in medals."

That night, I learned so much from William, and I couldn't believe
my luck; what he shared in an hour would've taken months for me to
discover on my own. He explained how Veles holds special authority over
many things—death, the underworld, magic, trickery, wealth, music, cat-
tle, even poetry. He ran his fingertips over the curling lines carved on
the imp's chin. He said they reminded him of Veles's flowing beard. I'd
thought they were only decorative.

"Gerard told me the stories about your father and your father's friend.
I hope I'll have a chance to meet Ivan one day. I have so many questions
for him," he said. "If we think of this totem as a representation of Veles,
it helps explain why it had such an important role in your father's village.
And why your father was so worried after it was lost."

My initial excitement soon gave way to another thought. If Ige was
right, if the object my father created represented this demon, then he
had committed idolatry. And that meant Prehovinka's villagers had, too.
I took a big gulp of whiskey and closed my eyes. Was his soul in hell after
all? Gerard could see something was wrong. When I explained that I was
worried for my father again, he tried to comfort me. Bad things, he said,
get put to good uses all the time.

"Like building churches over old altars. Or taking Christmas away
from the pagans. It's the same with your father's totem. He was just trying
to right a wrong, Michael. You shouldn't be so concerned. God knows.
God understands. Think about the guilt your father must have carried

his entire life. He was punished enough already. I think Our Lord understands that you must fight fire with fire sometimes. You can't just love everybody and toe the line *all the time*, for God's sake."

I was glad to hear this very unorthodox view of orthodoxy. It's what I needed. His words helped me. So did what William said next.

"Father, if you would be willing to consider it, I would very much like to purchase this totem."

"What? You want to buy this? What for? For you?"

"No, not for me, Father. For a client. He's a collector of curiosities," he said. "An American businessman. He adores exotic things. What I'd like to do is approach my client on your behalf—I would ask only for the normal mediation fee, of course. I'm certain he would pay handsomely."

At any other time, I would have welcomed a chance to be free of the imp. As much as this new information unnerved me, the imp had given me a special connection to my father. Maybe he'd wanted me to find it after his death, even though I didn't know what I was supposed to do with it. Maybe it was his final gift to me. Is it strange to call it that? A gift? I wasn't sure what to think, but I knew I couldn't part with it. Not yet. I could see that William was disappointed when I declined the offer, but he was very gracious anyways. I liked that about him. I was grateful Gerard introduced us.

That night, I told them about everything else that was troubling me. I described my involvement with Gabriel Rossetti, Lionel, and Antonia Cox. I know now that I should have been more careful, more circumspect, but I had no reason not to trust them. They had given me helpful information about the imp that was brilliant and sensible . . . and they were both good, honest people. But the one problem that Gerard and William had was that their enthusiasm for esoteric things, for arcana, was so blinding, so complete, that it ignored simpler, more ordinary explanations for things. I didn't realize this weakness in my friends until later, when too many things had already been set in motion.

As William refilled our glasses, I described Gabriel's party and the accident with the painting, his strange outburst about his wife, my afternoon visit, and the chilling manifestations of something in the house—the rapping sounds that couldn't be explained, the ghostly voice of my father in another room. Describing what happened was upsetting—it felt like I was reliving it again—but neither man seemed shocked or troubled by anything I said.

When I explained that Antonia had been upset because my accident interrupted her card reading, William chuckled. I took his reaction to mean something significant.

"I knew it," I said. "She's a fraud, isn't she?"

He cleared his throat.

"Well, no, Father. She could be, but I'm not sure she is."

"But you know her. When I said her name, it was clear that you knew her."

"No, I've never heard of this woman. But I know her kind. There are many such spiritualists in London. That's all."

When I mentioned Khristiana Lumens, though, his reaction was completely different. Far more dramatic. I said Lumens was planning a special ritual to help the artist. The mention of her name caused Gerard to nearly drop his glass. William whistled.

"Lumens? Here in London?" he said. "You didn't—well, this changes everything. I have heard of her! This is extraordinary! How fortunate for you! For us! Have you had a chance to meet with her yet?"

"No, I haven't. In fact, I wasn't going to participate at first. But after what happened with Rossetti, I changed my mind."

"Good, that's good. Khristiana Lumens is a very important practitioner, Father. Very important," Ige said. The composure he'd exhibited all evening was suddenly gone. His reaction seemed a little like mine when he'd offered to buy the imp. "If Antonia Cox is seeking out Lumens for help, well . . . she is a *legitimate* authority. She is *known*, Father. The fact that she's here in London and willing to help is an incredible opportunity. I may not know Cox, but if she's associated with Lumens, I'd be more inclined to trust her."

Ige asked if he could also attend the ritual with me. Gerard agreed. He said he didn't want me to go alone. Lionel and Antonia would be there, I said, but this didn't seem to satisfy either of them. Gerard said I shouldn't participate unless William attended. I didn't imagine any problems in arranging that—I rather liked the idea of having him there. As the evening wore on, I realized I'd made another friend. I agreed, promising to let William know as soon as I received information about the ritual's time and place.

I expected that my agreement with Gerard's request would make him feel better, but it didn't. I caught an exchange of worried glances between them when they thought I wasn't looking. Then Gerard added more wood to the fire and settled back in his chair. He was quiet for the rest of the evening.

22

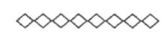

Ariel

THE OCCULT PRIESTESS KHRISTIANA LUMENS was staying in Lambeth, just on the other side of the Thames. I was excited to meet her, and during the ride over, William gave me a brief history of her life. He told me she'd studied the black arts in Prague using rules set down by the Holy Roman Emperor Rudolf II and his circle of magi. Her pedigree was impeccable, Ige said. She was especially renowned for helping families contact the spirits of lost loved ones. She commanded sizable fees wherever she went—and never disappointed.

Lumens's lodgings were located above a chemist's shop on North Street. Little did the customers know that while they were purchasing prussic acid and valerian for their ills, upstairs, a ceremony was being prepared to call on Ariel, a very powerful spirit reputed to have the power and authority to reveal all hidden secrets.

Lionel climbed the stairs first and knocked on Lumens's door. We heard two people arguing inside. A woman's voice was chiding someone for something. He knocked again. The argument stopped, and we heard her voice on the other side of the door.

"Who is there?"

Lionel identified our group, and the door opened. Lumens stood in the doorway and looked at us. After what William said about her, I had expected her to be dressed in a swirl of prophetic scarves because isn't that what we expect of our sorceresses? Instead, Lumens wore a man's dark coat over a long skirt and a pair of lace-up men's boots. She looked so strange, so unlike the wanton, sensual images of witches I'd come to expect from Rossetti and his Pre-Raphaelite brethren. There was a military plainness about her. Her hair was pulled back into a small, severe bun, and her old face was very pale, plain, and wrinkled. But her skin's pallor was leavened by the brilliant smile she flashed at our group—which included only Lionel, Antonia, William, and me. Lionel started to thank her for this meeting, but Lumens, still smiling, shushed him and led us down the hall to a sitting room.

THE SUN WAS NEARLY DOWN, and the only light came from a single candle. It sat on a small writing table at the room's center. There were four wooden chairs for our group, a fourth having been added for William at the last minute. We didn't sit together; each chair sat in a corner of the room. That was it. No big caldrons bubbling with eye of newt and wing of bat. No weird altars, swords made of virginal steel, or upside-down crosses.

The only thing that seemed unusual was the child. At the table sat a well-dressed little boy. Lumens had obviously been arguing with him when Lionel knocked—probably telling him to sit still and behave. Was that her son? Lumens ignored him and asked everyone to take a seat.

As my eyes adjusted to the dark, I watched the child and had a sudden fright. When the child looked up from the table, which had a big stack of blank sheets of paper and several pencils on it, I realized it wasn't a child's face at all. The child was a little old gnome staring back at me.

"Evenin' sir," the man said. He had a raspy voice like a hot coal makes when water's poured on it. Shocked, I looked over at William, who seemed just as surprised.

The sitting room had large windows on three sides, and all of them were wide open. The shutters were thrown open, too. The sounds of the street floated up to us, as did a chill, and the room grew colder as the sun went down. I shivered and watched Antonia wrap her coat more tightly around her. If she'd been sitting next to Lionel, I'm sure she'd have nuzzled against him. It was obvious, even to me, that they were on intimate terms. Earlier, when William and I arrived at the chemist's shop, they were already there, waiting outside. I saw her lean into him for a quick kiss as our carriage pulled up.

Lumens apologized for the delay in answering the door, explaining that Wallace, which was the name of her little associate at the table, had been rather reckless in placing the four chairs and had nearly forgotten to open the windows.

"Do we really need them open?" Lionel asked, rubbing his hands. "It's cold, and I'm sure I'm not the only one who'd be thankful if we closed them." He looked at Antonia.

Lumens sniffed.

"I am afraid your comfort must be sacrificed, Mr. Ashburnham. Yours and everyone's. Comfort is not important here. It is not the point of this evening." Lumens had a very precise, very mechanical way of pronouncing English. "The spirit Ariel commands the winds of the world's four corners. When it comes, it comes in a great burst of air. With thunder. And sometimes lightning." She eyed Antonia. "I have heard stories, very sad ones, about people calling Ariel who didn't know this. They performed the ritual in an enclosed room, and it was very unfortunate. The calling was a great success, for Ariel is always faithful, but there was a—how do you say?—a great concussion, like a bomb. Some lost their hearing as a result. We don't want to make that mistake, do we?" Lionel shook his head. "Very good. That is why I have left the windows open. You should have worn a heavier coat if you were worried about the night air."

Her description of the spirit's power made me uneasy. William looked over at me and made a little gesture with his hands as if to say, "Relax, don't worry." I tried, but it was impossible.

Despite the poor lighting, I had a good view of Antonia, who was sitting just across the room from me. She was certainly very attractive, even though I didn't want to admit it—this was the first time I'd seen her since the party, and I'd been too drunk then to fully appreciate her looks. Now, as we waited for the ceremony to begin, I noticed her pouty, kissable lips and an angular chin and cheekbones that projected delicacy and strength at the same time. She wore her hair in loose ringlets the color of dirty gold coins; it fell loose on her shoulders. Her dress was simple—made of serge, very plain and untrimmed, which was the style of the times, and it would've looked too mannish and severe if it weren't for the way it hugged her hips and waist. Over this, she wore a dark cape, almost like the one I always wore with my cassock, and her sleeves were long and billowy, adding drama to every movement of her hands. I had never seen fingernails so long or so many rings and bracelets (not even on the wealthy wives of Saint Martha's) that glimmered as they picked up the candle's light.

"Tonight," Lumens said solemnly, "I believe there will be many great revelations for you. That is my hope. I will do my best to make it so."

I've had one already, I thought as I watched Lionel and Antonia. The glances they exchanged reminded me of my parents. Yes, she was attractive, but I still couldn't understand why Lionel would ever choose someone besides Kitty. To me, she was an angel, even despite her shocking treatment of Annie. I found myself suddenly thinking that there must be advantages to having a wife with weaknesses like hers. And surely these extended to the bedroom—wouldn't she be willing to do anything, even learn a little perversity, if that's what the man she loved wanted? I couldn't understand why Lionel would waste his time with Antonia. If things were dull in his marriage, couldn't he change them? That's what you're supposed to do, isn't it? Yes, in normal situations. Yes, with normal, reasonable people. But Lionel was anything but that. During the months of our friendship, I realized he lacked the patience for almost anything requiring a concentrated effort. He was forever looking past whoever was engaged in conversation with him to notice the new person entering the room. He was forever seeking new distractions, new sensations. That's probably why I didn't see him very much anymore. And that's probably why he preferred flitting from theater to theater, dashing off his column, rather than taking the time to settle down and finish his book of poems or write a book-length piece of criticism like Klein. That required too much discipline. He couldn't even muster the patience to sit still as the high priestess of magic was quietly conferring with the little man at the table about something. Lionel loudly cleared his throat.

"Excuse me, but how long must we wait? When will this ceremony begin?" he demanded.

Lumens glared at him. She started to say something, but I gasped loudly, and everyone—even little Wallace—looked at me.

"Lionel, I think it already has," I said, pointing at the floor.

WHEN OUR GROUP entered the room, we'd assumed we were walking on an old, delicately varnished wood floor. We'd walked as lightly as we could, but the floor still crackled under our feet. By the time I called attention to it, everyone's eyes had adjusted enough to see that this floor, *the entire floor*, was covered in paper. Blank sheets overlapping each other to create a single large surface. And upon this, an enormous sigil—with complicated squiggles and patterns just like I'd seen in one of Gerard's grimoires—had been painted (with lamb's blood, Lumens said).

"You are quite right, sir," she said to me. "Ariel is being called right now. At this exact moment. With this sigil, we are opening up a pathway *between worlds*."

William, who hadn't muttered a word until this point, couldn't help himself, either.

"My God. I have never seen a signature of this size before." He looked at her. "In the spiritual realm, this must be deafening."

Unlike what happened to Lionel, this seemed to please Lumens.

"You are correct, sir. Exactly so. We must transcend the babble. We must be the loudest. This is also why we must tread *delicately* in this room and not ruin what has been so carefully prepared." She shot a glance at her partner.

Then Lumens took a small pouch from one of the pockets in her bulky coat and sprinkled some powder on the candle. It was just enough to make the flame spit and turn blue. It was a purifying mixture, she explained, that slowly filled the room with a mild scent . . . far from the cloying incense that sometimes turned my stomach during the benediction. The odor was pleasant, and I soon forgot about it.

Lumens explained that Ariel's signature had been written the night before and that she'd spent the entire day sitting on the floor in the room's center, reciting the prayers that would set everything in motion. Somewhere in the lines and squiggles, she said, she had written Gabriel Rossetti's name. Lionel started to interrupt her again, but Lumens hissed like a cat.

"Not now, *please*. No more questions. I have called upon Mercurio, and I must be ready for him. Mercurio is my spirit guide. In life, he had been a French envoy sent to arrange loans from Cosimo de' Medici. Just as we have mediums in this world, we must have them on the other side, too. We have known ours a long time, haven't we, Wallace?" she said, but Wallace didn't answer. His chin had tilted down as if he were asleep. When she noticed, Lumens chuckled.

"Mercurio," she said in a cunning tone, "are you here with us now?" With his position unchanged, the slumbering Wallace spoke.

"Yeeeeeeeessssssssss."

At the sound of his voice, my neck felt brushed by pine needles. Wallace's voice was completely different; where it had been gruff and thick before, it was thin and reedy.

"Excellent, my dear," she said. "Now, can you say whether Ariel will heed our call?"

Wallace sighed heavily. He sat up in his chair and lifted his head. His eyes were still closed.

"Ariel is not far off."

"Soon, then?"

"Perhaps."

Unlike other spiritualists, Lumens wasn't the medium; she didn't channel the spirits. That's what Wallace was for. I had never heard of anything like this before. Even William seemed a little uneasy as we listened to Wallace's strange voice coming in spurts. Lumens could see the shock and fear on our faces, and several times, she reassured us that Mercurio was an ally and that this had happened many times before. As we watched, I looked past her pale face at the open windows, and one of the shutters quivered even though there wasn't the slightest breeze. Was this a sign? Was Ariel here? I looked back at Lumens, and she was intently focused on Wallace, who was now writing on one of the sheets at his table.

"What are you writing, Mercurio? I see all manner of scripts, but none that I can comprehend."

For the first time, Lumens seemed a little uneasy herself, and William made her agitation worse by standing up.

"May I?" he said, stepping forward. He was eager to see what Wallace was writing.

"Sit down, *now*," she said, irritated. "No one must interfere with Mercurio."

"But it's not Mercurio anymore," William said. "I believe it's our long-awaited guest."

As Lumens stood at Wallace's side, the little old man scribbled furiously. Lumens's eyes wandered around the room, as if she were expecting someone or something to appear at any moment above our heads. Every so often, her eyes stopped on Wallace, and when she looked to see what he was writing, in a steadily growing pile of papers, her expression became more flustered and confused.

Finally, she raised her arms in a gesture of supplication.

"Mighty Ariel, we have called you for your generous aid. The cause has been written," she said, indicating the sigil on the floor. "Your vast knowledge spreads to the far corners of all creation. We implore you to help us in revealing the agency behind the torments of the artist known to the world as Dante Gabriel Rossetti. Will you reveal this now? Do you agree to help us, O wondrous and mighty spirit?"

Wallace emitted a loud guttural sound as he continued scribbling—the poor man's hand was going to be sore when this was over. His growl was incoherent, but the tone seemed impatient, as if Ariel were thinking, "Well, of course I'm going to help you! I'm here, aren't I?"

Lumens looked above Wallace's head, and everyone's eyes followed hers. There seemed to be a pooling of the room's darkness above him, but it was hard to see for sure.

"Ariel, I don't understand," Lumens said. "You must be clear."

Her tone was firm.

"Will you help us? I cannot tell from what is being written. Do you agree to help us?"

Wallace let out another sound, this time a roar. Lumens was unmoved; her bearing grew more authoritative as she glanced at the paper under Wallace's moving pen. She sighed impatiently.

"O, you will not? You dare to defy us then? After all that we have done to honor you?"

From a pocket of her coat, she took out another small pouch and flung something in the air, another powder, directly into the blackness above Wallace's head. The poor little man's movements didn't stop; in fact, the speed of his hand increased, moving even more quickly down the page. Mechanically, his left hand snatched away the sheet, and he started writing on the next one.

"You are being very obstinate," Lumens hissed. "You will do as we wish!"

Wallace's writing hand was a blur like a hummingbird's wings. His hand moved steadily down each page, and later—when the pages were reviewed—everyone could see it wasn't random scribbling; the writing was incredibly accurate, clean, and clear as if it had been printed by a press. He produced incredibly precise characters, evenly spaced, which seemed impossible—for any normal human. William gasped in astonishment and kept muttering "extraordinary" under his breath. Antonia's eyes moved between Lionel, me, and William, but she didn't say anything.

The toll of the writing was beginning to show on the poor little man. Sweat was streaming down his face, and his breath came in short, sharp gasps. He began whimpering. His hand and wrist must have been hurting; his eyes were still closed, his hand still frantically traveling down the pages, repeating a phrase that was making Khristiana Lumens angry.

Suddenly, he wailed and fell from his stool to the floor. He lay there, motionless, and that extra quality of blackness and quiet in the room was suddenly gone. The ceremony was over.

The bell on the chemist's door rang downstairs.

Lumens ignored her prone companion and turned to the group.

"I'm sorry. I don't understand why this happened. I will need more time to make another preparation," she said, "one that no amount of stubbornness will resist. I cannot tell you the cause of Mr. Rossetti's troubles yet. I'm very sorry."

Wallace sat up and started rubbing his right wrist. He had a blank expression on his face. Poor man. The sigil had torn underneath him when he fell. Was that what disrupted the ceremony? Would Ariel have stayed if Wallace hadn't fallen? I wanted to ask Lumens, but she seemed irritated and distracted. She had taken Lionel aside; she was ready to speak to him—about her fee.

William walked over to the little table and glanced at the sheets of Wallace's writing. He looked at Lumens, who was preoccupied with Lionel, and then at Wallace, who was slumped over like a marionette with cut strings. He took a few of the sheets, the top ones, and slipped them into his satchel. Then he walked over to the door and waved for me to follow him.

23

◇◇◇◇◇◇◇

Dante's secret

WHENEVER I WAS INVITED to dine with the Ashburnhams, I didn't wear my cassock. I didn't like doing that. I wasn't going there on official business; I was going as their friend. But on the night that everything changed, I wish I had. Maybe it would have made a difference. Maybe it would have reminded me of my responsibilities. I don't know.

I grabbed my coat, tucked a book under my arm, and slipped out the rectory kitchen door. As I walked up Cadogan Street to the corner, where I usually found a carriage, I remember thinking the timing of the invitation was odd. It wasn't a Friday; it wasn't our usual night together. And even though it was written in Kitty's hand, not Lionel's, I knew he must be behind it. Somehow, he found out that I'd visited Lawrence Klein that week and wanted to know why. He didn't want to wait until Friday. That's why the invitation arrived on the wrong day.

I'd gone to see Klein because I wanted information. I visited him a few days after the Ariel ceremony because of something Gerard said.

What we'd witnessed in Lumens's lodgings had been an incredible display of that special angelic writing that occurs when a spirit guides the hand of the medium. Each page that William hid in his satchel was crowded with words and phrases, written in Wallace's incredibly precise hand, from all the world's oldest languages. Some were readily identifi-able—Hebrew, Arabic, Latin—but others weren't. William wanted Ge-rard to see.

It was late when we left Lambeth, but we still found him in the chapel library study. The old priest studied the stolen pages and emitted sever-al meaningful *hmphs!* before telling us that some phrases and fragments appeared to belong to languages that had died out in humanity's earliest days. When Lumens kept asking if the spirit agreed to help us, this stream of ancient tongues ceased, and a single string of letters in English repeat-ed itself across the rest of the pages:

idonotidonotidonotidonotidonotidonotidonotidonotidonoti-
donotidonotidonotidonotidonotidonot

Seeing this made me understand why Lumens had gotten so angry. In response to asking the spirit if it agreed to help us, Ariel kept telling her "i do not" until poor Wallace fell to the floor. Though the spirit's refusal seemed clear, Gerard studied the letters closely anyways. He wondered if they were actually saying something in Italian, not English. One of the repeating *O*s, he said, looked suspiciously like an *A*, and he suggested Ariel might have said "donati," not "i do not." That startled me. I'd heard that word before. It took a moment to remember that Lawrence Klein had mentioned the Donati family when he described his new book at Gabriel's party. His theory, he said that night, was that Gemma Donati, the wife of Dante Alighieri, had sabotaged her husband's masterpiece. I told Gerard and William about this, and Gerard suggested that I go and talk to him. Maybe, he thought, it might shed some unexpected light on Ariel's mes-sage even though it was obvious the words were a refusal, not an Italian name. I thought it was a fool's errand, but I agreed to go anyways. I had an entirely different reason for going: It would give me a chance to make up for my poor treatment of Klein at Gabriel's party.

When I arrived at his beautiful Holland Park home, Klein's reaction surprised me. He showed no animosity, no suspicion—in fact, he seemed delighted to see me. Though our conversation didn't yield any insights where Ariel was concerned, I was grateful for Gerard's suggestion. We spent the afternoon discussing Klein's fascinating book, and he responded to my sincere questions with a warmth and generosity far from his behavior the night of the party. In return for my interest, he rewarded me with a copy of his new book. That was the book that I took along to Mayfair.

On the ride over, I imagined what Lionel would say about Klein. He'd tell me I was wasting time with him, and I rehearsed my response. I wanted to be ready, just in case. That's why I had the book. As I've mentioned, Lionel hadn't written anything more than pieces of journalism while his enemy had published a book—two, if you counted another book of poems Klein published years ago. I hoped showing him this study of Dante would derail any interrogation he had planned for me.

When I arrived at the Ashburnham home, I was met with a surprise. In the entrance hall, Annie informed me that Lionel was out. It took a moment to register the news as I stared at her plain face. (The bruise on her cheek, finally, mercifully, was gone.) I looked in the dining room and saw settings for four. I heard a voice behind me.

"We will be dining without him."

I turned. Kitty was watching me from the stairs in the entrance hall. At a height of a few steps, she towered over me, and the sight of her overwhelmed my senses . . . how lovely she looked, how perfect, like a work of art come to life. I felt an ache in my chest. Her dress was dreamlike and lovely as ever—soft pink with frills at the neckline—and the light from the lamps along the stairs made her face and hair glow. I smelled honeysuckle in the air. I heard a chorus of angels in my head. The only detail out of place was her eyes. They looked tired and red.

"Why? Where is he?"

"He's been called away. By his work. Again."

"Now? At this hour? Another deadline?"

"That's the excuse he gave me this time," she said. "I didn't believe him, and when I said so, he became angry. We argued."

I thought she was going to cry, but she didn't. Instead, she asked me a question I wasn't prepared for.

"Michael, what has she done to him? Why does he abandon everything, and everyone, at a word from her?"

I looked in those sad, pretty eyes and didn't know what to say. I couldn't deny Lionel's involvement with Antonia Cox. If I'd tried, if I'd offered equivocations instead of taking her side, I knew I'd lose her trust. I didn't want that. She meant too much to me. What Kitty needed was consolation. As she descended the stairs, I tried to say something encouraging, but I faltered as she came closer. I'd never seen her look so unhappy and confused. I stammered out the only thing I could think of, a very general apology for her unhappiness, for this sorry state of things, but the sound of her children loudly coming down the stairs drowned out the rest of what I said. Her expression altered as they rushed by us. She loved them so much; she thrilled at everything they did, even the small gestures. I knew it must be a mother's love that was keeping her from surrendering to the sorrow and darkness I saw in those eyes. Her smile flashed suddenly in the old familiar way, and she chuckled as they dashed ahead of us into the dining room.

"They were waiting for you, Fr. Michael! Weren't you, little ones?"

Charles nodded. "Oh yes, Mama. Let's eat!"

The sudden change in her mood surprised me.

"But Kitty, is there anything——"

She gave me a withering look. She gestured at the children, who were settling in their places at the table.

"There is a time for this, Michael, but *not now*. Let's enjoy our dinner. Can we do that? Please?"

The kitchen servants had been given the night off. Kitty prepared and served everything herself. I felt uncomfortable watching and waiting, and I offered to help, but she wouldn't hear of it. A clear, savory beef soup, followed by lamb cutlets with asparagus and salad, beetroot, celery, anchovies—cherry water for the children, wine for the adults. All of this done with her own hands. I marveled at it; I've never forgotten how delicious it was or what she served. Over the years, I know I've forgotten many things, things about my life and the world in general—even its grander historical movements—but my stomach hasn't. It has an impeccable memory. I can still recall the taste of the pasta my mother made every Sunday, the roasted pecans Giuseppe gave me whenever I visited his shop, and all those dishes Kitty made for us on that long-ago night. I remember the special atmosphere of our dinner, too. The absence of servants and the silence of the house increased the intimacy around the table. The rest of the world seemed to have vanished. Even the street was quiet outside. There was us, only us. The children were friendly and talkative, even though the girl regarded me a little strangely—at least I thought she did—when her mother tended to my plate the way she usually did for Lionel. I tasted the soup.

"Kitty, this is superb! Did you really have no help with this?"

She shook her head proudly. There was an embarrassed smile on her lips. Then, her daughter addressed me.

"Shouldn't we have said grace, Father?"

Of course.

"Goodness, little one, yes, you are right! What was I thinking?" I said. I set my spoon down and held up my hands.

They bowed their heads, and I prayed a blessing over them. As I did, I studied each of their faces: the little boy looked so much like Lionel, and the girl had her mother's pretty eyes and smile, the same long blonde hair . . . I wondered if she had her temper, too. I used a longer form of the prayer before meals. I wanted the moment to last. I invoked many saints, many angels, more than I needed to, and I asked God to grant them happy days ahead. When I was done, Kitty looked up.

"Thank you," she said. Her eyes were shining.

Usually, whenever I ate my meals in the rectory, I was silent—I had no interest in sharing anything with my associates. I'm sure they weren't interested in what I had to say, either. But on that long-ago night, I found myself eagerly telling the children funny stories about the leashed monkey and dog I saw that day near Piccadilly as I walked past several street performers. Charles and Flora laughed despite their yawns, and I could tell from their eyes they wanted more stories. But I looked up at the small porcelain clock on the mantelpiece and saw it was late. Kitty shook her head. "So soon? But why? Why don't you take your usual place in the study? I will join you once the children are in bed. Stay for a little while. Please?"

Can anyone imagine how I felt at that moment? When that beautiful woman suggested, no, insisted, that I stay, a window opened . . . and I heard Father Cremins's warning again. For the first time, I think I truly understood what I'd given up becoming a priest. I looked at Kitty and her two children—who could have been mine if life had been different—as they waited for my answer. At first, I hesitated. Without Lionel? I thought. Could I really do that? Would it be right? And then I imagined my empty rooms in the rectory, the plain walls, and the draft blowing down the hall and under my door. Kitty repeated her request, and I agreed to stay.

I'd been in Lionel's study a thousand times, but I felt like a trespasser that night. I sat down very carefully, very stiffly, as if I were being watched. But why? There was nothing wrong with this, was there? It wasn't dishonest to want the company of a friend. I'd helped ease their loneliness over

Lionel's absence . . . and they were helping mine. I was grateful for the time I spent with Kitty, for she was just as much my friend as Lionel was.

And yet.

I looked out the window. The street was dark; the streetlamp by the front door was out. Their marriage was in trouble, and Kitty knew it. I could feel her suffering in her every look, every movement she made, even when she smiled. What causes a man to turn his back on someone who loves him so much? I know it's a naïve question, but I didn't understand back then. To be honest, it's hard for me even now. I took some matchsticks from my coat pocket to light a cigar, and several papers and other bits of trash spilled out on the desk. I left them where they were, lighted my cigar, and blew a plume of smoke into the air. I sank into one of the low-backed chairs, kicked the pillow off the other one, and put my feet up though my boots needed a shine.

I could hear Kitty sending the children up to their rooms and bedtime rituals. She would be a while. I sat back and opened Klein's book to the title page. *Dante's Secret: An Examination of the Unrecorded History of* The Divine Comedy. Well, I thought, there's one bright side to Lionel's not being here. No scolding, no interrogating—nothing but time for reading.

After several tucks on the cigar, I plunged into the book with no idea that this night would determine my future.

24

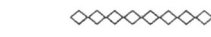

The far fields

2:30 a.m.

AT OTHER TIMES OF YEAR, this path along the outer edge of the fields would be overgrown and too difficult to follow. But now, even after a storm, I'm able to find it. The back-and-forth of the wagons has cut an obvious path in the grass here.

The path takes me east to the farthest northeastern corner of our village's fields. Then it curves down and weaves along the tree line. Following it will eventually lead me to the mill. It will take a good hour to get there. I could save considerable time, at least in theory, if I didn't bother with the path and just cut across the unplanted fields and followed the river to the mill. I'd save myself at least fifteen minutes that way. Maybe more.

But the fields are too muddy, and some farmers don't like it when you walk in theirs. The path's in good shape anyway; the dirt's packed down hard from the weight of all the wagons and horses. It's better for walking, especially for me. If I tried crossing the fields, I'd probably twist an ankle or aggravate my gout. I'd end up like one of Bram Minkin's poor horses. And I'm sure he'd welcome the chance to put me out of my misery.

Ahead, the forest rises like an ocean swell. The moon's illumined the clouds. It seems as if this path is going to take me straight into the trees, straight into its blackness, but then it veers off. To my right, in one of the fields, there's a large white stone the size of a pumpkin. I can't read it from here, but I know it marks a corner of Abel Lawryk's fields. It's painted with the letter *L*. There will be another about fifty paces away, marking the other edge. Next to the Lawryk land is the Melnyks'. The parcels don't butt right up against each other. Running in between each farmer's farmland is a long strip of soil that's about two feet wide. No one is supposed to plant in it. Most are good about respecting that even though it's tempting to gnaw away half a foot and hope your neighbor won't notice. I pass the stone painted with an *M*.

The next field over is smaller than the rest; it's a long rectangular piece of land that's short and narrow. It's also marked with stones that have an *M* on them—for Moroz. It belongs to my family. It's not our only field; it's just a small bit of land that one of my ancestors must have taken because no one wanted it. It's hard to reach this spot with wagons, and the ground is rocky and difficult to plow. It's not good for growing anything. We've never farmed it, but I found a use for it, and it's been very successful. About thirty or so feet from where I'm standing now, there are three short wood posts sticking up in the dirt. They're one of the two wickets in the cricket pitch I created years ago. I'm old now, but I was still in good shape when I arrived, and I wanted to introduce the villagers to something from my English life. I had been a good player in seminary—I was a very effective batsman—and I thought this might be a fun way to get to know my neighbors. It was. On Saturdays, even after a half day in the fields, everyone would play. Today, we still do; sometimes we play against another team from Kalush, and even though I can't move around like I used to, I still get out there sometimes.

As I pass the pitch, I know I'm nearing the place where the left fork of the Zimn runs into the woods. I can hear running water off to my left somewhere. The breeze picks up, and a cloud of mist suddenly rolls across my path like steam from a locomotive pulling into a station. It feels good on my face. It curls and dances, hanging in the air like a ghostly tapestry.

On the forest side of the path, there are several big elderberry bushes. I notice one of them swaying back and forth. It could be the wind, but I don't think so. Something's making the bushes move. I can hear snapping branches. And a grunting sound. I'd like nothing more than to move on and leave it alone, but I can't. This is part of the duty, too. I hold out the imp in front of me and take a clove of garlic from my pocket. I step off the path and slowly approach the bush. I can feel my heart in my chest, in my ears.

"Away, in God's name," I yell. More branches crack and snap. "Away, away, in God's name!" I shout louder, flinging it into the bush. Then I take another clove from my pocket and throw it even harder.

"Away from here . . . in the name of Our Lord!"

"Ow!" cries the bush.

Ow? Thank God, I think, thank God it's not an animal. Or something else.

"Who is there? Come out at once! If you don't, you'll be sorry!"

The branches part, and the big moony face of Justina Lemko peeks out.

"Easy now, Deacon, easy! I'm no demon!"

She climbs out of the bushes. She's covered in twigs and leaves. A hunter's pouch is slung over one shoulder. She tells me Natalka is paying her to look for a very elusive object, a fern flower. Something about the time of the year and the phase of the moon has made Natalka think Justina will find one. She says she's been roaming the forest and river ever since the storm passed.

"But, Justina, you know it's dangerous this time of night. You shouldn't be out here. Especially after what happened to poor Paul. Remember?"

She grins and nods, and I can see the gap in her bottom row of teeth. When I first arrived in Prehovinka, her family wanted me to marry her. If I had, that gap would be the first thing I'd see every morning of my life.

"Ah, Deacon, I know, but I'm armed just like you," she says, holding out a handful of garlic and wormwood bundles. "I just never expected to be on the receiving end of one." She rubs the top of her head. I apologize. She looks at me. "So you have the varta duty tonight, huh? What are you doing way out here? Shouldn't you be in the village?"

I tell her I was sheltering from the storm in the church when the bridge washed out, and I'm on my way to Natalka's. I ask if she wants to join me. She shakes her head. She says she can't; she's found a fern flower and is hoping to find more. She'll get paid extra for each one she finds.

"Really?" I say, surprised. "You found a fern flower? May I see it?"

She laughs and takes a thick blossom from her pouch, then holds it up to my lamp.

"Isn't it a beauty? It's only one, but it's big."

It is a beauty. The petals are red and yellow, wispy, like long filaments—they dance back and forth like a flame in Justina's big, shaky hand. I've never seen one before, but I've heard plenty of legends about them. Their elusiveness has given them a mythical status. Some believe the flower will reveal the location of a buried treasure if you boil it like tea and study the patterns the petals make in the bottom of your cup. Others say the blossom is a powerful charm against demons—more powerful than even the imp. Natalka wants it, Justina explains, for other medicinal properties.

"Like what?"

She shrugs.

"She didn't say. I don't care what she wants it for—just as long as she pays me."

I tell her to be careful. She promises she will. She smiles and goes back into the bushes. The squishing of her boots soon fades, and everything gets quiet again.

FOR THE PAST QUARTER OF AN HOUR, someone has been following me. At first I thought it was only the wind blowing in the trees or raindrops from branches landing in the mud puddles. But it's not that. It sounds like footsteps. Like someone is on the path behind me.

It's easy to let your imagination run away with you out here. I've been trying to tell myself it's nothing. I've been trying to convince myself it's just the sounds one hears after a big storm. But then I reached Elias Pauluk's strip of land, and my fears were confirmed.

The cheating with land that I mentioned before, with that margin of soil running between each family's parcel, is something Elias won't tolerate. It's understandable. One year the Semeluks, whose strip is right next to his, plowed into the margin and used up most of it. They pretended they didn't know what happened; they said they were plowing late, it was getting dark, and they didn't see what they'd done. It was a reasonable explanation. I've been in the fields when it's getting dark, and it's easy to make a mistake like that. So, I believed Vasyl Semeluk, but when Elias told him that, mistake or no mistake, he couldn't use the margin for his crops, Vasyl refused to remedy it. He said to let it go for the season. He'd fix it after that. They had a big fight. Elias was so angry he stomped into the tavern and walked right up to Vasyl and hit him so hard he fell off his stool. Several of us stopped the fight, but not before Vasyl hit him back and bloodied his nose.

It was Father Roman who finally settled the fight. He knew what was behind Vasyl's refusal. Not long before this happened, Vasyl had gone to him for confession and asked forgiveness for being short-tempered with his family. When Roman asked what the cause of it was, Vasyl told him he was falling behind on his mortgage because his crops hadn't been good the previous year. He was trying to grow as much as possible that season to make up for it. Roman told him he should have explained that to Elias, but neither man likes each other very much. He was too proud to say anything. But Roman secretly told Elias why Vasyl did that, and Elias let Vasyl's family grow in the margin. But the next year, Elias erected a fence down the middle of the margin and sealed off his swath of land. He's the only one to do that. Fencing is very expensive, and everyone noticed that Elias used up most of the fencing from his yard.

The path I'm on cuts through Elias's land. Anyone using it will encounter a wide gate that has to be opened to continue on. Then there's another gate on the other side of his fields. I reached the first gate a little while ago. It has a very simple wire latch. I let myself through and put the latch back in place. I hadn't gone very far when I heard the latch lift again. I didn't imagine it. It was very quiet. I heard it very clearly. I hurried through the second gate, and then, a little after that, I heard that one open and shut, too.

If this person doesn't want me to know that they're following me, they should have done a better job with the gates.

I walk another five or ten minutes, listening behind me for anything, for kicked stones or the squish of a foot in the mud, and then I stop suddenly and turn. I squint into the dark. I can't see anything. The moon's passed behind a thick bank of clouds. My lamp doesn't cast its light very far.

"Hey, I know you're back there. Justina? Is that you? Did you forget something?"

No answer. I know it's not her, but it's the first thing I think of. It's probably a poacher who doesn't want to get caught. We get them all the time. I should walk back up the path and tell them to leave; that's part of the duty, too. But it doesn't feel right. My insides are telling me not to do that.

Instead, I start trotting down the path.

It's terribly awkward with everything I'm carrying. And my foot's started throbbing again. But I don't care. Something's wrong. The hair's up on the back of my neck and it won't go down. I don't know what is going on, but I don't stop. In another half mile I should reach the harvesting sheds and Rudy's house. I mentioned him earlier. He's our shed manager. He's lived out here with his family for years. It's a little lonely and spooky, but he doesn't seem to mind. He's paid extra for maintaining the sheds and guarding the equipment that everyone uses. Thieves have tried to break in and steal our equipment before, and Rudy's had to deal with them all on his own. He's a big Russian fellow with a deep, gravelly voice that's so loud even big dogs will stop barking and listen to him. He always smells like bacon; he keeps his hair slicked back with hog fat. He always knows what to do in an emergency.

I'll feel better when I get to his house.

25

◇◇◇◇◇◇◇

The old maid's gambit

I WONDER WHAT WOULD'VE HAPPENED if I hadn't taken Law-rence Klein's book with me to Mayfair. Maybe I would have stayed in London. Maybe I would have stayed a priest.

Klein had a good, writerly voice. Not showy or excessive, which was a surprise considering his behavior and dreadful poetry at Gabriel's party. I spent an hour oblivious to the world around me. That was a sign of the book's quality. Klein made me forget everything—even the beautiful woman sitting across from me. The more I read, the more I understood why he had been disappointed at the silence of London's critics.

Klein's book did something wonderful with Dante: It treated him as a struggling artist facing the demands of a reading public as daunting as our own. That he even managed to finish his epic while in exile, always relying on others' generosity, hopeful that he and the members of his ex-pelled political faction might someday return to Florence, was something that impressed Klein deeply. It impressed me, too. Klein found the small places in the poem where the poet's unhappiness with exile peeks out at the reader. There's his distant ancestor, Cacciaguida, who warns Dante that everything about exile is bitter:

You shall find out how salt
Is the taste of another man's bread,
And how hard is the way
Up and down another man's stairs.

Klein argued that Dante, like any author, was under pressure because of the success of his first book, the *Vita Nuova.* That work describes the poet's adoration for a young Florentine named Beatrice Portinari and was so successful that it compelled him—*forced* is probably a better word—to do something unexpected when he wrote the *Comedy.*

Beatrice died young, and Dante's readers expected him to include her in his epic. Their expectations were satisfied. He did include her in his great poem, but their imagined meeting (which some call a reunion even though they never really met) takes place in purgatory. That didn't make sense to Klein. Why did he do that? Shouldn't heaven be the obvious place where he encounters his heavenly lady? Klein blamed the public for this. And the popularity of the *Vita.* The focus of the *Comedy* is supposed to be about Dante's journey to God, but the public was more interested in his journey to Beatrice. To deflate those expectations, Dante set their meeting in purgatory. He wanted to get it over with. And then, to discourage anyone's romantic expectations, the woman Dante encounters isn't the gentle maiden we see in the *Vita.* She's a scolding, angry figure who makes him feel so bad he cries and faints.

I liked Klein's insight into Dante's treatment of Beatrice. It made perfect sense. It made him seem wonderfully contemporary. But Gemma wouldn't have cared about any aesthetic considerations or strategies. While other members of the Donati clan—Corso, Forese, Piccarda—appear in various cantos, Gemma is nowhere to be seen. She's never mentioned in any of the poem's 14,233 lines. It didn't matter to her whether Beatrice was a shrew or a lover in the poem—the only thing that mattered to her, Klein insisted, was that she had been left out.

As he finished writing out sections of the poem, Dante would send them to his sons, Jacopo and Pietro, to copy and circulate among his friends and patrons. At the time Dante was finishing the poem, his sons were living with their mother and supporting her in their father's absence. This situation gave Gemma plenty of chances to see what her husband was writing—and plenty of chances to be disappointed. The arrival of each new section provided her with another reminder that he didn't care about her. By the time the final thirteen cantos of the "Paradiso" arrived, Gemma had had enough.

That's when she struck.

An important antagonist in Klein's theory was Smerelda, an old maid who'd raised Gemma from a little girl. Dante and Gemma's daughter wrote in her diary that Smerelda, who didn't think Dante was good enough for Gemma, was a virtuoso with Gemma's feelings. She easily stirred her mistress's jealousy against him. She was very cunning. Klein wrote that the old maid insisted on a major housecleaning in response to an early flaring of the black plague in Ravenna. That is where the Alighieris were living while Dante was on a diplomatic mission (his last) in Venice. The home was turned upside down by the cleaning. Everything was in chaos. Furniture was moved from the rooms; old linens were burned; the kitchen was cleared; and a stringent mixture of vinegar, lemon, and water was scrubbed into every inch of brick and flagstone in the house. Klein wrote that the housecleaning lasted for nearly a week, and it was during this time that the final cantos of Dante's poem arrived by messenger and vanished.

I marveled at the details Klein marshaled to create his portrait of a fourteenth-century household in disarray. I admired his care and attention to (and affection for) his subject. In a footnote, he said that he spared no expense to visit Italy's Valpolicella region and read old family letters and the diary of Dante and Gemma's daughter, which were in the possession of their descendants. Reading these was critical to his brilliant theory. They also provided him with many ordinary household details that brought his narrative to life. Reading it invigorated me. As I finished one chapter, I was eager to start another.

I should've gone home instead.

I heard doors opening and closing downstairs. The servants were cleaning up for the night. I looked up from the book. In the lamplight, the soft down on Kitty's neck glowed. We'd hardly said anything since she joined me. Only a few words and a glance when she brought us each a glass of port. That was all. This must be how old married couples are, I thought. Words aren't necessary. I listened to the clicking of her needles before turning to the next chapter. I ruffled the page and cleared my throat, hoping she'd ask me about the book, but she didn't.

Click, click, click.

Soft white hands.

KLEIN'S NEXT CHAPTER, "The Old Maid's Gambit," contained the most provocative parts of his theory. He describes a letter Gemma sent to her husband in Venice in 1325. The poet never read it—he died before he could—and it was soon lost. But Gemma's daughter helped her to send it, and sensing its importance, she copied out several passages in her diary. Klein focused on a single sentence that he felt was interesting. It was more than that. The simplicity of it all, I thought, the brilliance! *My God, this is wonderful!* I looked forward to seeing Klein again and telling him so.

"What's wonderful, Michael?" Kitty said. I looked up. She was watching me. I didn't realize I'd said what I was thinking out loud.

"Oh, it's something in this book. It was written by Lawrence Klein, one of Lionel's associates. Do you know him?"

"Yes. I've heard his name before. What impressed you?" Her eyes sparkled. "I'd like to know what intrigues you."

It didn't take long to explain Klein's theory to her. The best ideas are often the easiest to summarize, even the elaborate ones. Klein had done an excellent job of laying out his argument in clear terms. When I described Gemma's pain and anger at being ignored by Dante in his epic poem, Kitty nodded.

"It isn't fair to be forgotten. She deserved better. She did so much for him."

Gemma's letter to Dante, the one he never read, was sent to him soon after the final thirteen cantos had arrived in Ravenna. Klein believed she read them, saw that she was overlooked again, and that prompted her letter.

"What did the daughter say about her mother's letter? You said she copied the letter in her diary. Did Klein say what she wrote?" Kitty asked.

"We don't know everything. But Klein says that a single line makes Gemma's feelings evident: *'Husband, you think nothing of me—I would have it that the world thought nothing of you.'*"

She didn't explicitly say she wanted to destroy the poem, but for Klein, these words were damning enough.

"Klein believes Smerelda had something to do with that destruction. She's the true villain of his book. She wanted Dante to suffer for neglecting her mistress."

What had always astonished scholars about Pietro and Jacopo's loss of the last thirteen cantos of their father's work for nine months—that's the amount of time given in the official story from Boccaccio—was how they could have lost sight of the most important document in their family's life. Your father sends you the precious final cantos of his masterpiece, one of the three (or four) pillars of Western literature, and you don't know where they are? Klein had a simple solution for that.

His book includes a diagram of the Alighieri home. It had a large interior courtyard surrounded by an arcade. When the house was being cleaned, Smerelda had the furnishings of the rooms moved into this courtyard. Furniture, clothing, kitchen utensils, pots, books, and papers—everything was moved there. If the final thirteen cantos were among them, Klein argued, Gemma would have seen them anytime she went to get something. Of course, Smerelda could have destroyed the cantos herself, but she swore to God in front of the sons that she didn't, and such vows weren't made lightly. So Klein believed the old maid used the housecleaning to ensure the cantos were left in plain sight, and then her mistress's emotions did the rest.

Kitty chuckled. It felt good to see her smile.

"I can understand why you're intrigued, Michael. I really like his theory. It makes sense to me. Smerelda sounds like a very clever person."

Her teeth were white and perfect. I stretched my arms and looked up at the clock. It was well past eleven. I told her Klein's theory exhilarated me and also left me feeling depressed.

"If Kleins' theory is true," I told her, "I don't think any scholar will be able to feel the same awe for the 'Paradiso' again."

"Why would that matter so much?"

"It just wouldn't be the same. I know I must sound foolish." I watched her sip her glass of port. "Klein's theory is provocative. I'll grant him that. It's marvelous to read. I haven't enjoyed a book so much in a long time. But I have trouble accepting that Gemma, no matter how she felt, could have done such a terrible thing. To ruin a masterpiece like that—"

I never finished my thought. Her sad smile made me stop.

"What the world thinks doesn't matter if someone is in pain, Michael. Throwing papers in a fire is a small thing. I think unhappy people are capable of much worse."

DOWNSTAIRS, KITTY WATCHED me put on my coat.

"Don't forget your book," she said, handing it to me. Her fingertips brushed my wrist. I looked in her eyes. She still seemed unhappy, even after our time together. I let myself think it was because I was leaving.

"Kitty, before I go, let me say what's on my mind. I want you to know how much it hurts me to see you this way."

She looked at me but didn't say anything. She didn't have to. She understood. She gave my hand a gentle squeeze and looked down at her feet.

I should have turned to go. But her touch was so unexpected. It excited and confused me—and loosened my tongue. I found myself confessing to that beautiful woman how much I worried about her, thought about her, and wanted to take her unhappiness away. I wasn't drunk, but I sounded like I was. If the ways of speaking to an attractive woman could be likened to the stages of a child's growth, I was a complete toddler. Wobbling on my legs and crashing into the furniture. I didn't know where I was going or what to do.

She looked at me.

"Michael. Thank you. You may think I'm a fool, but I'm not. Not like some. Lionel's always been a good father, even a good husband. In his way. He's just a child sometimes. He picks up an interest in certain people, an affection, but it's never long before it wanes. I've learned to accept that, but this time . . . it's different this time. I can sense it. He's different with me, and I don't understand why. I don't understand what she's done to him."

She seemed about to cry as she opened the front door and stepped onto the porch. I don't think she wanted the servants to hear us even though they should have been in their quarters by then. I followed her outside. Lionel had been acting differently with me, too. I told her that. I hardly saw him anymore.

Together, we looked into the blackness of the empty street. The streetlamp near their house was still out.

"Playing with our family," I heard her mutter, "no one gets away with such a thing. Not with impunity."

"He's a fool," I whispered hoarsely. "Any man would thank God for you. Every day of his life. I would. *Kitty*."

The way I spoke to her, the way I laid my poor, vulnerable heart in her hand—it was terrifying and thrilling at the same time. I'd never done anything like it before. I'd never allowed myself this kind of vulnerability. For the first time in my life, I felt the exhilaration of truly risking complete honesty with someone. I didn't know what the result would be. I didn't know what to expect, and I didn't know what to do after that. I was a romantic toddler, remember? To be honest, I don't think she knew, either.

Kitty didn't say anything right away. She turned and opened her arms to hug me, and as I stepped forward, our heads moved awkwardly, our cheeks brushed, and before I knew it, we were kissing . . . and neither of us wanted to stop.

Think of all the romantic first kisses you've ever had. Think of the surprise you felt when you tasted someone's lips the first time. Think of the surprise, and then, how that kiss changed from something tentative and gentle into something far more exploratory, passionate . . . and the excitement of knowing you both felt the same way. Think of this, and then multiply it by a hundred. By a thousand. Then you might understand how I felt. My woolen pants suddenly became uncomfortably tight, and though the heavens didn't open up, I heard a chorus of angels singing hosannas in my ears. I sucked greedily at her lips, faintly tasting the port we drank upstairs. She relaxed into my arms; her mouth opened, and our tongues touched. I pressed against her, half expecting her to push me back, but to my surprise, she didn't. *God in heaven*, I kept thinking. Up in the study, I'd never imagined the night could get better, and it did.

And then everything changed.

I looked in her eyes.

"Come away with me."

"What?"

"Come away with me. Let's leave London. Tonight." I had no idea what I was saying. The words just spilled from my mouth.

"*Michael*. Are you mad?"

"Yes. I'm mad," I said. "I'm mad about you. You must know that. I don't care where we go. Just as long as we're together. I want—I want to give you the life you deserve."

"*Michael*—"

I tried kissing her again, but my words had broken the spell. She'd come back to herself, to her senses, to the moment. When I reached for her again, she pushed me back this time, hard, and something about the force of it made me think of Annie. Her bruised cheek. The ancient cupboard. Kitty told me that what I wanted from her was impossible, despite her own attraction to me, despite her heartbreak over Lionel's involvement with Antonia Cox. None of it mattered to her. She had a duty to keep, she said, and the whole time she spoke, I couldn't take my eyes from her lips.

I wanted to give her the world; I realized I wanted to spend my life serving her—that I would be more adoring and reverent with her than I'd been as a priest. I would be ... I know this must sound blasphemous ... *her* priest. This is it, I thought—this is what God wanted for me. In an instant, I saw all the causal links in my recent life . . . my father's death, the discovery of the imp, my assignment to Saint Martha's, the popularity of the sermons that led me to Lionel and her . . . and it was never clearer than at that moment. My life. My destiny. I was meant to be with her. The certainty I felt was incredible; it flooded through me like a river . . . and there she was in front of me, a goddess, talking about her children and obligation and loyalty to a man who didn't deserve her.

For a moment, Kitty had belonged to me, truly belonged, but now I looked at her and saw someone else—the goddess had de-metamorphosed back into Mrs. Lionel Ashburnham.

Of course she was right. I know she was right; it was impossible. But I didn't see it at the time. Like any inexperienced young man, any spurned young lover, I took the rejection personally. My body was overwhelmed from kissing her, wanting her. And I was angry that the kissing stopped.

In that moment, my reading up in the study came back to me. I thought about Gemma Donati. I felt sorry for her. I understood what she must have felt—the cruelty of loving someone who doesn't want you. I thought about Dante and Beatrice and the unhappy tensions of the romantic triad Klein described in his book. I thought about Smerelda, too, and I decided to do something that would have grave consequences beyond anything I could imagine. I turned to Kitty and told her I was going to leave, but I'd forgotten my rectory key up in the study (even though it was in my pocket).

"I'm sorry," I said. "I don't know what came over me. It won't happen again. I promise. Please forgive me. You're right about Lionel. And about your duty. I should be ashamed of myself. After I get my key, I'll go home. I do hope you will be able to forgive me."

I didn't mean a single word of it.

WHEN I ENTERED THE STUDY, I didn't linger. I didn't have to. My idea was simple. Obvious. And completely unoriginal. I hurried back down the stairs to Kitty.

"Found your key, did you?"

I thrust a hand into my pocket and held it up. I avoided her eyes.

"Well, that's good," she said. Going up to the study had given her time to compose herself. She seemed calmer now. "I'm glad you found it. And I want you to know I'm glad you came here tonight. Michael"—she looked down—"your care for me means so much. It really does. You are a good friend to me. And to Lionel. I want you to know that." They were words I didn't want to hear. "I hope you understand. I hope you understand one day."

I looked away. I was still angry. I walked past her and muttered a quick goodbye.

In the vest pocket of my coat, I kept various address cards from my home visits with the sick. Among them was the address card Lionel gave me for Antonia Cox. When I was in the study, I went to Lionel's desk and left it on the little pile of trash I'd made earlier. Kitty might see the card if she went upstairs to wait for him to come home.

Why did I do that? To help Kitty. That's what I told myself. She deserved a chance to defend the honor of her family and marriage, didn't she? Lionel was messy and disorganized about many parts of his life, but he was orderly and discreet when it came to Antonia Cox. I wanted to change that; I wanted Kitty to have a chance to go and confront her—if one of the maids didn't clean up my trash first.

I put everything in God's hands. I'm sure Smerelda would have approved.

On my way home, as I watched the houses slip past my carriage window, I thought about how beautiful Kitty looked when I said goodbye and she closed the door. I caught one last glimpse of her face in a sliver of golden light, her full lips and troubled eyes, and didn't realize—I couldn't have realized then—that I would never see her again.

26

◇◇◇◇◇◇◇

Walking

THE DAYS AFTER MY DINNER WITH KITTY were difficult. It was Lent, and my life was busy—so many soup kitchens and charitable activities to organize, so many confessions, novenas, and Stations of the Cross—but I wasn't busy enough to stop worrying about her. I waited and waited for news from Mayfair. I waited for news that something had happened to the Ashburnhams. But nothing came. No urgent messages, no signs of Cox's sudden departure from the city (which is what I wanted most)—no invitations to dine with them, either. All activity at the Ashburnham home seemed to stop.

I found myself walking more in those days ... more than was usual even for me. I was restless, and long walks in the city helped settle my nerves . . . aside from a glass of whiskey now and then. I couldn't go to the chapel library and share my anxiety with William and Gerard. William was away on collecting business, and the library was locked up tight—Gerard wasn't feeling well. I couldn't go to the Ashburnhams—not until I was summoned. I fought the temptation to go to Mayfair many times.

So I waited. And while I waited, I did what any lonely person does: I took advantage of the many distractions found in a city of three million. Despite any complaints about London's filth and crowding, I do miss

some things about it, even now . . . now that I live in a place that sometimes feels as if it hasn't been touched since the creation of the world.

Nothing ever stopped in London. Its character changed constantly—
by the hour, by the neighborhood—and I'd walk far and wide and lose
myself in its many distractions. That may be another reason why I enjoy
our monthly trips to the Stanislau market so much. I think they remind
me a little of this part of my former life. There were so many interesting
faces to study in the streets, so many interesting little shops filling the first
and second floors of high and narrow buildings . . . displays of dingy
dresses and coarse eatables, awful-smelling cigars . . . and gin shops at
nearly every corner. The doors of these seemed like the gates of Dis; each
time they swung open, a cloud of pestilential fumes poured forth, and the
vapors filled my nostrils and burned my eyes, and I wanted to get away.
Other passersby didn't—the smells seemed to attract them, and they'd
plunge through the murky doorways and disappear.

Whenever I felt any pangs over what I'd done or imagined Kitty's
troubled face or the touch of her lips, I'd walk faster. Farther. And soon it
left me alone. Sometimes I attended free public lectures, even making my
way all the way up to Great Ormond Street and the Working Men's Col-
lege, where Gabriel himself had once lectured. If I didn't have the time
or enthusiasm to sit and listen to the droning of some expert, I'd spend it
peering into shop displays or counting the top hats on the heads in front
of me as the crowds marched in slow procession like a regiment of soldiers. On one of these occasions, when I wasn't far from the amusements
of Drury Lane, I even remember—to my great distress and disappointment—seeing Antonia Cox.

She was far ahead of me, and I didn't notice her at first. I saw a
gaudy pink parasol floating above a sea of heads, and then, at a break in
the crowds, I recognized her profile—snub nose and smirking lips, dirty-
blonde curls. She looked well, too well, I thought; from what I could tell
from her body language, she didn't seem troubled or in any hurry. She
was walking with a very light step, and she seemed to be smiling about
something. The sight of her discouraged me, and I forgot to tell myself
that this, even this, was God's will, even if it wasn't what I'd wanted.

But what was she doing in this part of the city, so far from her lodgings in Marylebone? I tried following her, but the traffic was too heavy,
and her parasol drifted farther and farther away from me. The crowds

were especially thick at the intersection ahead, where there was a popular coffee stall. By the time I reached the same spot where she had been, she was gone. The parasol was nowhere to be seen. I couldn't understand it. She wasn't walking fast enough to outpace me—not by an entire block. The foot traffic wouldn't have allowed it. One of two things must have happened: She either took down her parasol and was somewhere up ahead, or she'd entered one of the shops. I looked around. The colossus of Drury Lane loomed to my right—it was the immense facade of a menacing giant, club in hand, plastered to the front of the Promenade of Wonders entertainment hall. This was the place where Ivan had seen the mermaid. Whoever painted that monstrosity hadn't given him black pupils of equal size. As the colossus glared down on the crowds, he looked a little cross-eyed, and it reminded me of Gerard.

For a moment, we exchanged glances. Then I gave up my search and walked on.

EASTER WAS COMING, and I'd done little to prepare for it. I'd been too preoccupied by all that I've described so far. In the weeks leading up to the holiday, I was gripped with panic. The prospect of what was needed—so many details and arrangements for the liturgy and the baptism ceremony—was overwhelming.

I frantically assembled a small committee of devoted volunteers. They were a wonderful group of men and women: enthusiastic, willing, steady—all the qualities my associates lacked. We accomplished so much in a short time. Thanks to their discretion, no one knew about these rushed circumstances. Everything we assembled suggested long premeditation and care, not the handful of days we'd had.

As the great triduum wheeled closer—Holy Thursday, Good Friday, Holy Saturday—my loyal little committee and I were ready. We had a small army of servers, deacons, singers, and musicians assembled … and plenty of fresh lilies and bolts of scarlet and purple cloth for the church. Everything looked so beautiful by the morning of Holy Thursday, and the evening's service—which centered on washing the grubby feet of some selected parishioners—was a great success. That night I was exhausted but in high spirits.

When the service was over, Nessie left a loaf of rye bread and a pot of stew simmering for us in the kitchen; it was a delicious, greasy mess of chopped carrots, celery, and potatoes—no meat, not until Sunday—and I ate to my heart's content. My associates didn't join me; they were tired and went up to their rooms. I didn't mind; I didn't have to worry about my table etiquette. I filled a second bowl of stew and tore off several pieces of bread, soaked them in the bowl, and stuffed them in my mouth. I ate like a savage, like a Viking—the juice spilled down my chin as I chewed and dripped on the tablecloth. It made a brown puddle next to my bowl. I tore off another piece of rye and sopped it up.

I hadn't noticed before, but there was a small envelope propped against the bowl of salt that stayed on the table for all meals. My name was on it. Nessie had left it there for me. The note inside said:

Rev. Frost,

It is with immense reluctance that I write you. My brother has asked for you several times. At first, I didn't respond for I believed his words were only the fevered products of his delirium. Of late he has been so insistent that I cannot ignore them any longer. It seems he has a craving for an absolution that no one else can provide except you. I know this must be a very busy time for you, but I would be grateful if you would come. Please do not delay—his periods of clarity are exceedingly short.

The address is enclosed.

William Rossetti
Birchington-on-Sea

I dropped everything and rushed to the Pancras station to catch the last evening train for the coast. I didn't even finish my second bowl of stew.

27

◇◇◇◇◇◇◇

Birchington

BAEDEKERS CALL BIRCHINGTON the "site of a great and natural mixing" on England's eastern coast, a place where the currents of the Thames and North Sea meet. There are salt marshes and mudflats, chalk cliffs, and a monotonous flatness that abruptly drops off as you approach the water. The sea there is full of roach and dace, pike and carp. Seabirds are everywhere, dropping from the sky like little feathery imitations of Icarus. It's a very elemental place, elemental and plain. My experience there was brief, but it was enough time to observe how the temperaments of its denizens are very much like their environment. Curt replies from the stationmaster and the ticketing agent, a grunt for "yes" or "no" from the dogcart driver. I doubt the place has ever given birth to a poet—though I know one who stayed there and never left.

Only a few small cottages slipped past my window as the night train slowed and pulled into the station. Though Birchington sits on the coast, the weather was very warm. I can still remember it. I was wearing my heaviest coat, in expectation of the cold, and soon took it off. My cheeks and forehead were perspiring. The air was still and heavy. The clouds were swollen with a rain that wouldn't fall.

I waited for nearly an hour inside the little train station house before walking down to the Rossetti bungalow. I decided to wait until the sky lightened. It didn't seem right, even if I was expected, to intrude on the house before the dawn.

During the train ride I'd reread William Rossetti's note several times, parsing the words, wondering if I had overlooked something. *It seems he has a craving for an absolution that no one else can provide.* What did that mean? I couldn't be the only priest his family knew. What did he expect me to absolve?

I SET OUT on foot for the Rossetti bungalow rather than hiring the dog-cart in front of the station. It wasn't far, and I thought the walk would be good for me—clarify my mind and help me prepare for what was ahead. The bungalow sat at the end of a long road leading out to the cliffs and shore. Beyond it, the ocean was a flat expanse of gray. There were hardly any waves; the surf murmured groggily as if it were waking up. Angry seagulls fought over mussels in the shallows.

The morning was windless and uncharacteristically still. I say "un-characteristically" because a big sign at the railway station had greeted me with a boast about Birchington's bracing atmosphere. It promised excursionists that they'd find "twice as much air as you get in London!" I was glad I didn't have to contend with a stinging wind in my face as I walked toward the bungalow.

I followed a narrow-rutted lane down to the shore. It curled around several sandy, grassy knolls; the bends in the lane and the height of the knolls made it impossible to see very far ahead. For a quarter of an hour, I wondered if I'd taken the wrong one by mistake. But then the angle of the land suddenly grew steeper, the lane gradually rose higher than the knolls, and I saw my destination. There were several houses up ahead.

I crossed a wide, flat lawn used for croquet; another, behind the house, reached down to the sea and bathing sands. Unlike the others, the Rossetti bungalow was a simple affair, long and single-storied, with a few small trees and a garden and little else to screen it from the winds usually blowing in from the sea. The Rossetti family was afforded good privacy in this time of crisis by a wide stretch of mud on either side of the house that separated it from its neighbors.

As I neared the front steps, the door opened. William Rossetti stepped onto the porch.

"Hello, Reverend Frost. I cannot thank you enough." His voice was strained. It sounded like he hadn't slept in days. "My brother is not well this morning. He's declined very quickly. More than I expected when I wrote to you. I'm sorry you made this trip. I'm not sure it even matters now."

A train whistle screamed behind us. The tracks were just up the road. I had crossed them on the way down.

"I understand. I'm very sorry for you, Mr. Rossetti, and for the rest of your family. Please accept my condolences. May I see him anyway? I would like to give him a blessing, if you would permit me. It would be good to still honor his wishes in some way."

Rossetti sighed and stepped back from the doorway.

"Yes, of course, I understand. Why should I deny him that? I'm expecting the rest of our family this morning. Fifteen minutes with him should be enough, shouldn't it? His room is at the end of the hall." As I passed him, the brother added, behind me, "Brace yourself, Reverend. This illness has changed him. He's not as you may remember him. As any of us do. I will be in the sitting room with some of my brother's associates. Call us at the first sign of trouble."

28

◇◇◇◇◇◇◇

Viaticum

GABRIEL WAS IN A GLOOMY LITTLE BEDROOM at the end of a dark hallway. The nurse was standing by the bed, arms folded, watching him. Her name was Mrs. Abrey. I never learned her first name. She was a big, buxom old lady with meaty hands and a tired look on her face. She'd probably done this kind of sad work all her life. The bedsheets were pulled up to Gabriel's chin, and his body was hidden so completely by the thick blankets and a large quilt that I didn't see him at first. I remembered his brother's warning to be prepared. The pillow cradling his head was stained yellow; sweat, or water from the wet cloth on his forehead, had nearly completed a halo on it. The sour smell of his breath reached my nostrils the moment I entered the room.

I asked the nurse how long he'd been asleep. She wiped her hands with a rag and tucked it into one of her apron pockets.

"Hard to tell now if he is or isn't, *Father*," she said, spying my collar. "Can't really call it sleep. It's more an in-between. Sometimes he lets me feed him some soup or eggs. Or else opens his mouth and starts cursing at me. But it's awright. I don't take it to heart."

There were muffled voices out in the hall. William Rossetti and another man. I opened my viaticum bag and retrieved the oils. The little jars bumped together and made a clinking sound. The nurse moved to the door. I told her she didn't have to leave.

"I understand if you aren't inclined to my papist ways, but it's unnecessary for you to go. I won't be long."

"I'm not disinclined to anything, Father. I just need to go and check on his breakfast is all, even if he won't be eating it." She opened the door. "Call me if you have any problems with him." She closed the door behind her.

That was the second time I was warned. Problems? What problems? I couldn't imagine this poor man giving me trouble of any kind. I hurried through the rite anyway. I wasn't given much time. I put oil on three fingertips and left glistening marks like a snail's trail on Gabriel's lips, forehead, and breast and said the old prayers—and nothing happened. He didn't move. Didn't wake up. It was like any other time I'd administered the rite to someone near their end.

His bedroom window, which looked out on the beach, was wide open. The sash was partly up, but the air in the room seemed stale anyway. There was no breeze. No relief. Even the candles by the bed burned low and blue, as if they were at the bottom of a mine. I wasn't expecting anything but a sick man in Birchington, but I'd brought the imp with me anyway. Something told me to bring him, and I'm glad I did. He was there next to my viaticum bag, wrapped up in a thick sheet so that no one would know what he was. If William Rossetti had asked—he didn't—I would have said the bundle was my bedding from the train.

I went over to the window and raised the sash higher. It didn't do any good. The air still felt stale. On the table next to his bed were several small medicine bottles of colored glass. A few of these were on their sides, like fallen chess pieces. I straightened them and adjusted the pillows behind his head. I took the cloth from his forehead and fanned him with it, and he groaned. He didn't wake, but he started moving—shifting and twisting, seeming to try to find a more comfortable position.

I pulled back the quilt, thinking it was too heavy on him, and he thrust one of his arms in the air. His hand fluttered about in a strange kind of waving, and I softly called his name, worried that I had disturbed him too much. I hadn't; he was still asleep. His eyes didn't open at the sound of my voice. Then he whispered, *"Where is it?,"* and the sound of his hoarse voice made the hairs on the back of my neck turn as stiff as the teeth on a comb.

I tried putting his arm down, back under the covers, but it wouldn't move. It was as solid as a post. I pulled on it, and nothing happened. No matter what I did, it wouldn't move. It was incredible. I couldn't believe his strength. I took his wrist in both of my hands, as if I were gripping an axe handle, but before I could do anything, he suddenly flung me back with so much force my feet lifted off the floor. I fell backward and banged my head against the wall.

Gabriel started to make sounds. He was muttering something. It was incomprehensible. Gibberish. An infant's babble. Rolled *R*s and gargled words. I heard a carriage pull up outside, and then William Rossetti's voice out in the hall. I turned back to the bed.

"There now, there now!" Gabriel rasped. "Easy, easy! God forgive me!" His jaw worked as if he were chewing on something. He wrung the bedsheets in his hands. "Careful! Careful! Did you not hear me? Is one of them broken? Careful!"

I could feel a bump growing on the back of my head. I stood and went over to him. I shook his shoulders the way my mother used to do when I was having a bad dream, but it had no effect. It didn't matter how hard I shook. His eyes stayed closed. I took a step back when I heard the bedroom door creak open. Mrs. Abrey peeked in.

"Is everything awright? Do you need me?"

I thanked her and said he seemed the same as before, except that something was bothering him in his sleep. She nodded.

"Yes, right, that's how he's been," she said. "Just so you know, his mother and sister are here now. Everyone wants to know if you're done."

"Not yet. Tell them five minutes more. Please." She shut the door.

Gabriel raised his fist and shook it in the air. "All's not perfect! What do you mean?" he hissed.

The mind's ability to make sense of fragments is extraordinary. Despite such an upsetting and disorienting situation, I knew what he must be dreaming about. His death was so close, so close I could see the skull rising behind his cheeks and eyes, but even then, Gabriel was using the little flame of life left to him—hardly more than what those bedside candles were burning—to return to the night of his wife's exhumation to retrieve the book of poems.

His ravings were indiscreet, gruesome, and I heard things I wished I hadn't—the kinds of ugly details only someone who had been there would know. Did he act this way with Mrs. Abrey? Had she heard anything about this? Or his brother? What sputtered from those dry, cracked lips contradicted the official story—that Gabriel had been far from Highgate, waiting at home in a torment of impatience and guilt.

The exhumation of Elizabeth Siddal was a fixture of London gossip. Its long life reminds me of a warm coal—hidden, cooling under a layer of white ash until someone new comes along and blows on it. There was the exhumation's gory aspect to attract the public's gutter sensibility, of course, but that couldn't be all of it—the story's longevity had to be on account of more than that. I could think of other disturbing stories floating about London society, murders and acts of vengeance gorier than digging up someone's coffin, and these all faded eventually. But this story about Gabriel never did, and I think it had to do with it being such a nakedly selfish act committed by someone with such a pure, refined sensibility. In those days, it wasn't unusual to hear, either in the papers or among my congregation after Mass, some story about a precious ancestral ring or bracelet recovered from a grave. The logic of such an act was understandable enough, but what had been Gabriel's reasons? All he wanted was to get his book back—and chase after fame with it. His story remained an abiding cautionary tale of the desperate depths to which even a celebrated artist could plunge.

The few newspaper and memoir accounts that emerged in the months and years after tried to counter this, and they all had an unmistakable air of conspiracy about them—of course, they must've been engineered by someone, William Rossetti, probably. They were all in remarkable agreement that the deed had been handled by friends and strangers, with the blessings of the home secretary, while Gabriel sat alone at home, wringing his hands, surrounded by the same kind of aura one finds in his paintings of the saints. It was said he'd agonized over the entire morbid enterprise, but his friends insisted on it because they said he owed those buried poems to the world. How convenient—placing the blame on some unnamed, anonymous friends. That allowed him to stay pure and innocent in the public's memory . . . the ever-faithful, ever-grieving husband.

But what came out of his mouth that morning in Birchington challenged everything I knew about the official story.

The last time I saw Gabriel, he'd seemed as fragile as a sparrow's egg-shell; his hands shook and his teeth chattered as we'd discussed Propertius and walked in the garden. But the person on this deathbed was different. He was angry and fiercely impatient.

"Christ, what ninnies you are. It's there, don't you see?" he roared. "What are you waiting for?"

I saw something flit across his face. A shadow. He gnashed his teeth, and his cheeks stiffened. His face looked somehow different. It's difficult to explain. I was still looking at Gabriel, but he looked like he was wearing a mask of himself. Then he raised his arm again and thrust it at the ceil-ing, and I realized, horror-stricken, that he must be reaching for the book again, searching for it next to his wife's corpse.

Gabriel rolled up on one elbow and reached high above his head. His face flushed as the sweat dripped from his forehead, his tongue hanging from his mouth . . . and then, suddenly, he fell back on the damp pillow with a loud gasp. "There, there!" he murmured elatedly. The phantom book must've been in his hands.

It was terrifying. I tried shaking him awake again. There were loud footsteps out in the hall. I recalled what Mrs. Abrey had said about his mother and sister being there. Gabriel started coughing again, an attack so violent I thought he was choking—a deep, phlegmy rattle that coated his lips. But the coughing stopped suddenly, and he struggled to say some-thing.

"Meh," he gasped. "Meh. *Meh.*"

"What is it, Gabriel? What do you need?"

He didn't open his eyes. Whatever he was dreaming about now, it wasn't coming as easily as before. I heard more voices out in the hall. I was nearly out of time. I knew they'd come in soon and ask me to leave. I looked at Gabriel again. I wished he'd wake up. He coughed, and it took a great effort to bring out what he was trying to say. When he finally said the word, I thought I'd misheard him. It didn't make any sense.

"Meh . . . Kai . . . Low."

He coughed and said it again. This time, the sounds ran together, and I understood.

Mikhaylo.

29

◇◇◇◇◇◇◇

By the sheds

3:00 a.m.

THE HARVEST SHEDS ARE LONG and stand in a neat row on the eastern side of the far fields. Some of them abut the forest. We use them for threshing or for storing crops before they go to market or when the weather suddenly changes. A bale of hay is heavy enough when it's dry; when it's soaked with rain, it becomes heavier than a block of granite. We put as much as we can inside the sheds, especially when there's little time between harvesting and distributing.

There's also a locked barn that contains a variety of implements and tools we use in the fields. It would be too expensive for any villager to buy his own, so this equipment—plows, chains, harnesses, scythes, sickles, wagons—belongs to everyone. It's also very tempting to thieves; so are the sheds when they're full. Rudy keeps a watchful eye on all of it. His cottage is right next to them.

It's a thankless job, but he's willing to do it. He's an outsider here like me. He came here from a village near Moscow around the same time I did. I think he arrived a little before me. He spent three years in the Russian army and left before his conscription was over. Six years was too much. He hated army life, but he didn't go back to the village when he left. He couldn't—he would have been arrested for desertion. He was able to escape because he was assigned to help the regiment cook with the gathering of vegetables in a nearby village—"gather" meant steal—and he went out one night and never came back. He kept heading west until he reached Galicia. He told me he spent three of his six enlisted years sleeping in a leaky shack in some outpost, assigned to keep order in a place that didn't need it. Every night he said he dreamed of a village like ours. Having a cottage of his own. And a wife and a family. When he stopped in Prehovinka, he heard the shed manager had recently died and asked to take his place. Ruthenians don't normally like Russians. They treat our brothers in the east like animals. Like slaves. Natalka once told me they call us *malorusse* there. She said it's a stupid word. There's nothing little about us. I agreed.

"Try telling a Scotsman he's 'Little English' sometime, and you know what you'll get? A black eye," I told her.

The Russians have the colonizers' arrogance. Not all of them, of course. Not Rudy. Prehovinka adopted him as one of its own. He took over the sheds' management and later married Nastya, one of the Orlik daughters. They have three teenage sons now.

I said it's a thankless job. It's also lonely. I think that may be why everyone was willing to let him have it. No one else wanted it. The nearest building to his cottage is the mill on the other side of the bridge, and then, farther on, you find Natalka's cottage, which sits at a curve in the road before it bends back into the village. You are very much on your own out here if something bad happens. But Rudy doesn't seem to mind. He said he faced worse situations on his long walk from Russia. Over the years, he's thwarted several robbery attempts and seems to like the solitude. He keeps a rifle oiled and loaded by the front door.

Nastya doesn't like the solitude, which is why their cottage has been blessed and sprinkled with holy water several times by Father Roman and me. They have all kinds of religious pictures, icons, and crosses on the walls inside the house. I think they have more than the cathedral in Lemberg. The blessings are enough; they are powerful prayers. But I think having those holy relics around makes her feel safe. I can understand that.

I've been running ever since I heard Elias's second gate click shut behind me. I'm stomping and splashing on the path and making quite a commotion. I've given up trying to be stealthy about whoever's following me. It sounds like they've given up being stealthy, too. I can hear their feet splashing in the puddles. Up ahead is a light. Rudy leaves a small lantern hanging on the gatepost just inside his yard. I run toward it.

I am panting and coughing by the time I reach the gate. I think of what Jacob Minkin said again. A man my age shouldn't be out here, and I'm starting to agree with him. The copper glow of the lantern is comforting. I feel safe enough to peek back at the path, but there's no one there. It sounded like there was someone right on my heels. Maybe there never was. Maybe I've been imagining everything. I've been walking around tonight with too many ghosts in my head.

The circle of light from the gate lantern extends maybe ten feet in all directions. I look over at Rudy's house. There are candles burning in several windows, but I can tell that no one's awake. I know they like to keep several candles lit throughout the night as a normal practice. Nastya says they do it to keep evil spirits away. Rudy's more practical; the light discourages thieves. Either way, it seems to be effective.

Considering how loud I've been, I'm a little surprised Rudy hasn't come out to see what the ruckus is all about. I'm surprised his dogs haven't come out to see me, either. I think they were out pheasant-hunting all day. I was going to bang on his door and ask for help, but I don't want to disturb him. I don't think I need to. The back of my neck is still tingling, but I think I'm OK. I look back again and still don't see anyone. I'd hate to wake him for nothing.

My foot is really throbbing now, and the sweat is pouring down my face. I'm glad I ran. I needed the exercise. I'm more awake now … and … I'm closer to the mill bridge. It won't take long to get to Natalka's from here. I'll rest when I get there. She'll let me stay as long as I want, especially if I need her advice. I comfort myself with the thought of a chair in front of her fire and a hot cup of tea.

The path I'm on runs by the side of Rudy's house and leads all the way to the mill bridge. Before I continue, I stop next to the house and take off my coat. I'm burning up in it. It's too much to wear after running. I set the lamp down and lean the imp against the side of the house. I take off my coat and pat the back of my neck. It's slick with sweat. There's something in the corner of my eye. I give one last look back at the gate. That's when I see her. She steps into the light of the gate lantern and stops where I was standing only a few minutes ago.

It's a young woman.

She has long brown hair and is wearing a faded white dress. She is barefoot and tall, wearing just a shift. I squint to get a better look at her from this distance, but I don't recognize her. I'm not going to call out. I'm right under Rudy and Nastya's window. I can hear his loud snoring. At least I think it's him. This girl is tall, her dress just falling to above her calves, which look white and firm even from here. Her hair is wet, tangled, and hangs down to her waist. She was probably caught in the storm like me.

I wave to her and chuckle. I try to slow my breathing. I wipe my clammy forehead with the back of my wrist.

"Oh, was that you? Were you behind me all this time?" I say in a loud whisper. I feel relieved. She doesn't answer me. She just stands quietly by the gate with her hands at her sides. "Is everything all right, miss? Are you all right?"

From time to time, we get people in Prehovinka who are lost, who venture out into the woods from the other side and get separated from their families. After meandering for hours, they'll stumble into our fields and have no idea how they got here. We never give them any trouble. We know most of them are just poachers of some kind—for wood or animals or herbs—and the best time for that is in the middle of the night when the Minkins aren't out on patrol. I don't think she's one of these, though. She's not carrying a basket or a sack. It looks like her arms are empty.

I've never been a good judge of age, and it's only gotten worse as I've gotten older, but this maiden's long arms and sleek calves make me think she might be somewhere in her late teenage years. Not much younger than my youngest. I'll be able to tell better when I get closer, but I don't want to scare her by moving too fast.

"Can I help you? Are you lost? I'm a deacon in this village. I know I don't look like it, but I am," I say as I start to walk slowly toward her. "I don't recognize you. You aren't from our village. Did you know you're in Prehovinka?"

She smiles.

"What's the matter? Can't you hear me?" I whisper a little louder. "Is this better?"

She still doesn't say anything. I don't think she can hear me, but I'm not going to yell. I hear the droning of Rudy's snoring in the stillness. The girl is still some distance from me, about the full length of the house, and I don't want to raise my voice. Maybe she's too scared to say anything. I'm sure it was terrifying to get lost in the woods. And I'm sure I must look frightful with my messy hair and mud spattered all over my boots and pants.

I'm expecting her to run away, but she doesn't. In fact, she does the opposite. She smiles and starts walking toward me.

I wave again and start to apologize for startling her. She passes the first window on her left, and the glow of candlelight finally gives me a chance to really see her. I was right. She looks about sixteen or seventeen. No more than that. She has a very pretty face. Even with wet hair, she is one of the prettiest young maids I've ever seen. I know she's not one of ours. She has the kind of face you can't forget. If she was one of ours, I'd know.

As she gets closer, I can see there's something wrong with her gait. She's limping. It must really hurt because she's clenching her jaw. She must have injured herself. It's not a surprise, not on a night like this. If she came through our woods, in the dark, with no lantern, there are any number of breaks and drops in the ground that will catch and twist your ankle before you can do anything to stop it.

"It looks like you might have slipped. That's OK—I almost did myself," I say. I remember the other flask inside my coat, which is filled with the English traveler's whiskey. "Wait, miss, don't come to me. Please stop where you are. I think I might have something to make you feel better."

I hold up my hand and signal her to stop. I don't want her to keep walking with an injury; the path by Rudy's house is uneven and muddy, and she might slip and make it worse. She seems to have heard me. She pauses.

"Good. Let me get something for you. Wait right there. Don't walk on your bad foot. I'll bring it *to you.*" I turn and hurry to get my coat and the imp, which are still under Rudy's window.

As I'm searching in the pockets, I hear the squish of mud. When I turn to look, I see her coming down the path. Will anyone ever take my advice? I'm surprised to hear her softly humming something as she limps toward me. She's still gritting her teeth.

The candlelight from another of Rudy's windows suddenly bathes her face in a soft glow.

She looks more beautiful than before, and I'm starting to wish I was her age. I can't understand this. Of all the times. I've been surrounded by beautiful farm girls all my life here, and no one's ever struck me this way.

Her skin looks soft and white. She has clear blue eyes and freckles on her nose. I forget to breathe a moment. She smiles with full lips, and it seems obvious she knows the effect she's having on me. She's just a child, but her expression makes her seem older. She chuckles softly to herself in that way all women do when they're enjoying their power over a foolish man. I felt this way when I was falling in love with Eugenie. And with Kitty. She starts humming that unfamiliar melody again.

This stranger's features are so captivating that I forget where I am, what I'm doing. If she were to ask my name, I don't think I could tell her right now. Or I might say *Mikhaylo* instead. My mind's getting jumbled, and I haven't even had a drop of that whiskey. I hold up the flask to offer her some, but nothing comes out of my mouth. My mouth isn't the only thing that's stopped working. My legs won't move. All I can do is stand here, watching those beautiful smiling eyes get closer.

As she passes through the light of the next window, something happens. We're just a few paces apart now, and I notice that her appearance starts changing. In the glow from this window, her long, tangled brown hair seems coarser and thicker, and the candlelight brings out an unmistakable tinge of green.

Then a more horrible change takes place. Those pretty blue eyes, sparkling like gems, sink back into her skull and disappear. It's as if her sockets have swallowed them up. She looks at me with two deep holes in her face. The skin that reminds me of vanilla cream seems rough and old now, and it has a silvery tint. She returns my embarrassed smile with a big grin of her own, and when her lips part, I see brown teeth, very jagged, and the mashed-up bits of something. The tip of a purple tongue darts in and out, tasting the air.

It's the face of a monster, and I'm paralyzed with terror. I can't move. Or speak. But I can still hear. Rudy or Nastya's snoring floats down from their window. I try to call out to them, but the words stick in my throat.

"Ruu-Ruu—Ruuuudeeeeeeeee . . . Nas-Nas-styaaaaaaa . . ." It's barely a whisper. It's all I can do.

I'm able to move my head a little even though my legs feel like they're sunk in thick plaster. In the light of the window nearest us, the one she's standing in now, I see a large plankboard icon of the Holy Mother and Child on the sill. It is a beautiful imitation of something by Rublev. Like the inside of our church, it was painted by another itinerant artist. Nastya keeps it there to look out on this lonely road. She uses fat candles to illuminate it because they take many hours to burn down. Nothing evil can withstand that holy glow. When she walked by the other two windows, this creature had looked so beautiful, but now ...

She doesn't seem to realize what's happened to her. Or maybe she doesn't care. Maybe she's too hungry to care. She keeps limping toward me. She keeps smiling with that horrible mouth, and I feel as helpless as a moth in a web when it sees the spider.

As she steps out of the glow of the window, her maidenly form resumes. It drifts back across her face like smoke. She's beautiful again. Innocent. The sudden change is terrifying. How horrible! Witchcraft! Something from a nightmare! I think about Eugenie in despair. I wish I hadn't left the house with her angry at me.

The imp's not in my hands, but it's close by, and somehow—maybe because of a surge of panic at the thought of never seeing Eugenie again—I break this strange paralysis just enough to reach it. I clutch him to my chest. I can feel my heart beating hard against the wood. My jaw relaxes, and now I can speak. Finally. I beg her to go away and leave me alone. I beg her not to hurt me. I tell her I have a family to take care of. I beg for mercy, and the word seems to amuse her. She grins but doesn't say anything. She stops just a few feet in front of me. She looks from me to the imp and then holds up three fingers like the horns of a bull. Then she turns and walks away.

I watch her limp away into the field off to my left, in the direction of the Zimn. She disappears from my sight.

As soon as she's gone, I grab my things and run down the path as fast as I can. I'm able to fully move again. I don't stop to think about what just happened. I think only of Natalka's. I need to get there. I squeeze the imp in my arms and kiss its cheeks.

The bridge isn't far, but it feels like ten miles. My knees are shaking as I'm running down the path by Rudy's cottage. I turn a corner and pass a field of unharvested corn when I hear something. She's back! The ground shakes behind me. She's coming for me now that my back is turned, now that the imp's powerful gaze is turned away from her! It was a trick! I'm not going to make it. Don't look. Run. *Eugenie.*

The sound is getting louder now. It's closer. All I can do is keep running, keep to the path. If I plunge into the woods or fields to hide, I'll only get stuck. I'll be easier to catch. My foot hurts so much now, but I can't stop. I'm sputtering bits and pieces of prayers now, saying how sorry I am I won't get a chance to tell my wife how much I love her, that her fears were for nothing. She was worried I was going to leave her. I wish I could tell her it isn't true, even though, with the sound of pounding feet behind me, I can see her dream was right. It just wasn't what either of us thought.

All of this runs through my mind like the wild currents of the flooded Zimn as my pursuer gets closer. She's nearly upon me now. I can hear deep guttural sounds and feel her hot breath at my back, but I don't dare look. Not now. I just keep running. It sounds like she's transformed into a great beast, some awful creature with sharp teeth and claws. I start another prayer, which is probably my last, when I feel something grab me from behind and my feet suddenly leave the ground. I cry out as I drop the lamp. The imp is gripped tightly in my arms as we float off into the dark.

PREHOVINKA'S MILL STANDS on the opposite side of the Zimn. Its wheel is locked; someone must've come down earlier and done that when the rain started. That's good. The current is so strong, it could have easily ripped it away. When we cross the bridge, Bram Minkin lets me down off his horse.

He'd been out in the fields when I encountered the creature masquerading as a village girl. He didn't see her; she'd disappeared by the time I caught his attention. He said he saw a glow moving fast between two cornfields; it was my lamp bobbing and flickering as I ran for my life. It took him hardly any effort to reach me, grab me by the collar of my coat, and hoist me onto his horse.

On the ride to the bridge, we sat the way married couples do in the saddle. I was too scared and shaken to mind that I was in front of him. He told me he's been out all night looking for the person who broke their window. His brothers gave up and went home hours ago, but Bram is stubborn. He insisted he'd find them. When he saw my lamp, he thought I was the one responsible. But when he came closer and saw it was me, he thought I must be running from the wolf the Lemkos saw out here.

"Thank you, Bram," I say as I climb down from the horse. He hands me the imp. "Thank you so much. I don't know what else to say."

I'm surprised by his generosity. I'd never have expected him to go out of his way for me. He put himself at considerable risk to help me. If I'd been running from a wolf, I'd have expected him not to try so hard. After all, it would have meant one less villager to annoy him. I don't tell him about the girl; I'm still in disbelief about the whole thing. I don't want him to think I'm crazy. He has a low enough opinion already. I tell him that I thought I saw a wolf but wasn't sure.

"I don't expect you to say anything." He looks down at me. "You should move along, though. You don't want whatever you saw to come back. "

Natalka's cottage is not far. It's just around the next bend. I'm eager to tell her what happened.

I feel safe standing next to Bram's horse. I look up and tell him I'm sorry for the trouble someone in the village has caused his family. I know he's at the age when the young are determined to do things their own way, but to stay out all night for one broken window seems absurd. I think of Kitty. I think of my own stupid behavior with her. It was reckless. I didn't see where it might lead, and I should have. But I was impatient. I had wanted my life to be different. Bram's horse snorts. I tell him he should go home, that whoever broke the window is probably long gone by now. He doesn't answer right away. When he does, he's irritated.

"Go home? You think you can tell me what to do?"

He sounds like he regrets coming to my rescue.

I tell him the way he and his brothers are reacting to the broken window is too much. I feel an upwelling of fatherly affection for this sullen, taciturn young man. There have been broken windows before, and other things, I tell him, and his family has never gone to such lengths. I say the cost of replacing a window compared to the risks of crippling a horse is minuscule. I offer to help him find someone who will replace the window at a reasonable price. I'm nearly eye level with his hands, which are resting on his lap and gripping the reins. As I'm talking, he adjusts the reins and grips them tighter. I'm expecting him to suddenly kick the horse and ride off without a response. But he doesn't. Instead, he sighs and rolls his head from side to side.

"You wouldn't understand if I told you, Yuri. You're just a farmer."

"But I'm not. I'm not from around here."

"No, that's right, you're not. I forgot. Jacob says you're a big man of the world."

He eyes me a moment and then tells me what is bothering him, that his family is upset with Gradwolski. The count's failed to pay back another loan. I can't hide my surprise.

"Another? He has loans with you? How many?"

I know I'm being impertinent. In the daylight, he would probably tell me to shut up. But he's tired now. His defenses are down. He just sighs.

"Several. Plenty. Too many."

Ever since I arrived in Galicia, I've noticed a strange symbiotic relationship between the gentry and the Jews. The nobility makes the rules enabling the Jews to hold important positions, especially with the banks. In turn, they're supposed to help the nobles whenever they're in trouble. They need each other. But I'm still surprised the count is defaulting on debts. He comes from an old family with vast amounts of land and several castles; he shouldn't need any loans, should he? Now it makes sense why we're suddenly being charged more at the mill. The Minkins are trying to make up for it. They're putting the count's failure on our backs.

"I'm tired of this, Yuri. I'm tired of all of it. I wish we could just go away."

He says they have cousins in Istria with a successful textile mill. The cousins could use their help.

"Why don't you go, Bram? You should. You're young. You have your whole life in front of you."

I hear him laugh. It's the kind of laugh you hear after saying something the other person thinks is idiotic.

"I said you wouldn't understand. You don't."

"But I do. I was once young like you. I know it's hard to believe, but I was. You have so much more to experience than just this place. Besides, you have two brothers. They're happy here. They will stay. They don't mind dealing with us annoying peasants."

"My parents were born here. So was I. It's not just our arrangement with Gradwolski. It's our blood. It's here. It's what keeps me here. Good or bad, this is my home. I can't go somewhere else."

My blood's here, too, I think. I'm my father's son.

Occasionally, Jacob confides some small frustration to me, but I never expected to hear anything like this, especially from Bram.

"I'm sorry. You're right. I guess I don't understand. Your situation sounds difficult. I hope you and your family find a solution for it."

"We will. We must; if we don't, he's just going to keep asking. We can't keep going on like this." He clears his throat and spits on the other side of the horse. "Look, can you just do something for me? Would you tell your people to stop throwing rocks at my house? Maybe next time you're in church you can say something? This is the third time in as many months there's been mischief, and I'm sick of it, too. We have enough to worry about. This doesn't help. In the end, it's only going to make life harder for you, you know."

"I agree. The mischief has to stop. Yes, I'll tell Roman. He'll say something on Sunday. The villagers will listen to him. You'll see. They're good people, Bram. They're not all bad."

He starts to turn his horse and walk away. He looks back at me.

"Neither are we."

"Bram, wait."

I just thought of something.

"What is it?"

He sounds annoyed, but I don't care.

"Listen, you know that we play cricket, don't you? You should come and join us."

He laughs.

"Bram, I'm serious. Come and join us. Bring your brothers. We could use you. We have a big game coming against the team from Kalush."

"Why would I want to? I have enough to do."

"That's the point. Cricket isn't work. It's play. You'll enjoy it. It's a time to have fun. To meet people."

"Why are you asking me now? You've been playing that game a long time. No one's ever asked."

"I don't know. I just thought it might help you now. With everything."

He seems to be thinking about it.

"Do me one favor before you decide, would you?"

He sighs.

"What now?"

"Don't give me an answer yet. Talk to your brothers first. See what they say. Just consider it, OK? Would you do that for me?"

He sighs again.

"Fine. I will."

30

Power

I WAS GLAD I HAD the imp in Birchington—I was glad I'd listened to my inner voice, telling me I might need it.

I held it up and faced Gabriel's bed. I wasn't sure what I was supposed to do with it, but I knew something must be happening because Gabriel suddenly stopped talking. For several minutes he'd been saying my Ruthenian name over and over and other terrible things as well:

Mikhaylo, Mikhaylo! Oh, it's so dark here! I'm in so much pain! Why didn't you pray for me more? Mikhaylo! Why have you failed me?

I knew what was going on. I knew that what was using Gabriel (the way Ariel had used Wallace) was that same hateful presence I'd felt in his home. It read my thoughts and feelings; it knew my father was dead. It was playing with me. But I didn't give it any satisfaction. After the initial shock wore off, after wiping my eyes because I couldn't help sobbing at first, I grabbed the bundle off the floor, tiptoed over to the door, slipped the bolt as quietly as I could, and unwrapped it. I didn't want to take any chances of having Mrs. Abrey peek in again and see my fiendish-looking little traveling companion.

I'm glad I did. A moment later, William Rossetti was on the other side, tried the handle, and started banging on it, cursing me. I ignored him; I was more intent on Gabriel and finding a way to make him stop talking.

The viaticum prayers are powerful. The rite's a form of exorcism; it's supposed to purify the space and help the dying in their final struggles. I've often thought about the prayers in the same way that farmers set fire to a brushy area to drive out the snakes before they start clearing it up. The prayers work like that. At least they're supposed to, but they didn't when I blessed Gabriel. Was it because he wasn't a Catholic? Did they not count? I couldn't imagine God refusing to help him, even though I'd been taught from childhood that Catholics alone are God's faithful people. Even after seminary, I believed, and still do, that God is much greater than our human understanding and that he sympathizes with all people, regardless of their creeds. I think the viaticum prayers didn't work on Gabriel's demon for the same simple reason that some of my worst classmates still caused trouble despite the threats of our teachers. They'd heard the threats so often they didn't care anymore; the words lost their meaning. Everything was too familiar—and I was glad I had something with me that wasn't.

When I turned back to the bed and slipped the imp's horns in place, Gabriel jerked under the covers and sighed. That was it. Nothing else. That was the sign of the imp's power. I felt a cool breeze on my face and neck—the first since entering the room. It felt as if something had lifted all of a sudden. The lamps burned brighter, the curtains fluttered, the waves thundered outside, and the breeze carried their saltiness to me. Everything felt, for lack of a better word, normal. The presence was gone. I felt such awe (and gratitude) for my father, for the work of his hands. I looked down at Gabriel, and he seemed to be sleeping peacefully now. He wasn't twisting around or groaning in his sleep. His body was completely still.

William Rossetti had been banging on the door while this happened, but he'd given up. I hastily packed my bag. I knew I'd catch hell as soon as I unlocked the door, but regardless of what happened, I knew I'd been victorious. I'd given Gabriel some peace. After I put my oils away, I picked up the imp and was about to remove his horns when I heard Gabriel's voice behind me again. He was saying my name. My English name this time. He was awake.

"Michael? Father Frost? You're here?"

He propped himself up on his elbows and looked at me with half-opened eyes.

"I would never have expected my brother would . . . but you are here, aren't you?"

"Yes, I am. Gabriel, I am so glad to be here with you," I said. "I think I should go and tell your brother. He should know you are awake. Your family's worried about you."

"Yes, of course, but . . . tell me first . . . what is that?" he said. He was staring at the imp. I forgot it was still in my arms. "What is this marvelous relic? Is this something for me?"

"This?" I said. "Oh, it—belonged to my late father, Gabriel. He created it. He was an artist. Like you."

He smiled and was about to say something but was overcome by a fit of coughing. Regardless of what had just taken place, the poor man wasn't cured. He was still dying. The imp's power was magical enough to scare away a demon, but it wasn't miraculous.

I studied his face. I looked for a sign of anything, a flicker of coldness, malice. I just wanted to be sure it was really him.

"I want you to know I took the liberty of anointing you. I thought you wouldn't mind. I'm sorry, Gabriel. I really am."

He coughed and reached for a water glass on the bedside table. He shakily raised it to his lips and dribbled half its contents down his nightshirt before I could help him. His speech was thick and slow and a little hard to understand.

"Sorry for what, Father? If you mean my death, don't be sorry. Please. It means nothing to me. My family has denied what is happening, but my physical state makes it impossible to do that now. They can't ignore it anymore." He lay back on his pillow again, for the exertion of conversing had been too much. "I am unafraid," he said, looking up at me, "and I am prepared to step into that darkness, knowing I won't step into it alone. She'll be there. My Lizzie. My poor, faithful girl. Despite all I did, all I did to her, she's waiting for me. She tells me so."

He lifted a hand and pointed off to a corner of the room.

"There she is. Do you hear her?"

I panicked and started to hold up the imp again. But there was nothing. The room was quiet. I looked at Gabriel and shook my head.

"Don't worry, Father. It's no matter if you can't. I do. That's all that matters. She reassures me, even now. She reminds me that death cannot be avoided. It comes for everyone." He turned his head and fixed his gaze on the window. The curtains were swaying back and forth now. *"And some are only ancient bones that blaunch, and some had ships that yester year's winds did launch . . ."* he said softly. "My little verses. They won't leave me alone. I try to quiet my mind, but they gather around me. They demand my attention. Like unruly children. Strange to think of such things now."

I heard footsteps in the hall. I told him I would go and tell the others, but he ignored me and kept talking.

"How well I remember first meeting you," he said, "and how could I have known it would lead to a moment like this? You've traveled so far to be here, and you've taken on burdens to help me, I have no doubt. I hope you will permit me to give you something now in exchange. I had a good eye once. It's all in ruins now, but once, I was able to tell so much about a person just from a look, especially when they didn't know I was watching. People show their true selves in the little things they do at unguarded moments, and I so enjoyed studying you at my party." He smiled and tried to prop himself up again. "You have such talent and ability, Michael. When you purposely stole attention from poor Lawrence Klein, and you know that is what you did, I was surprised. I felt that Lionel had been lying to me. *This man's no priest,* I thought. *He savors life too much to renounce it!* I think . . . I think so even now."

I looked in his eyes.

"If I'm not a priest, Gabriel, what am I? What am I supposed to be? I'm . . . lost."

He coughed.

"I wish I could help you. But these are questions every person must answer on their own. What I can tell you is only this: It would be terrible to never find out. Don't make that mistake. You must try." He started to cough again. "Listen to a . . . a dying man. It has taken me a long time to truly understand this. I regret the time wasted, but it's helped me to see. And I'm happy now. "

He closed his eyes. At that moment, Gabriel seemed to me the wisest man in all the world.

Our conversation ended there—with a loud crash. William Rossetti and two men burst into the room carrying a long wooden bench. They had used it like a medieval battering ram.

"What is the meaning of this?" his brother shouted. "What is that frightful thing?" He pointed at the imp.

Gabriel opened his eyes and started to say something, but his brother screamed over him.

"Get out of here, you terrible man! Help! Someone help! Get him away from here!"

Hands grabbed me. Several of Gabriel's friends had arrived while I was administering the rite. They rushed into the bedroom. I recognized a few from the party. They dragged me down the gloomy hall without uttering a word. At the hall's other end, I saw Gabriel's mother and sister, their heads covered in thick lace veils. They looked at me with stony expressions. I was thrust so furiously out of the bungalow's front doors that I fell on the porch and hurt my knees.

The imp landed with a clatter a few feet away.

31

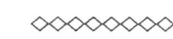

Natalka's house

3:30 a.m.

NATALKA'S DEN GLOWS WITH A SOFT, GOLDEN LIGHT. The fire crackles and pops. My coat is steaming on a peg next to it. She sits across from me. I told her that she doesn't need to stay up. I don't need company. She said she wasn't tired; it's only a little earlier than when she normally gets up. She's expecting the Melnyk boys soon to help her with her fields.

After Bram left me, I heard a branch snap in the dark and started running again. I didn't know if that creature was still out there, waiting for Bram to go. I didn't want to find out. I didn't stop running until I reached Natalka's door. I banged on it hard. She laughed when she saw me.

"Well, look who's here for a visit. Looks like you need a good warming up. Want to come inside?"

I squeezed past her without saying a word.

Her den is crowded with furniture, including the pallet that had been my bed. I put the imp down and removed my coat. There was a familiar scent of wax charms in the air. A blazing fire. I felt safe.

"I'm so glad you're awake."

"How could I not be? Damned thunder," she said. "I've been up for hours. Listen, I'll make us both a hot drink. Would you like that?"

I nodded. She told me to sit and relax, but I couldn't. After she went into the kitchen, I couldn't stop thinking about what happened. When she came back in, I was pacing in front of the fireplace.

"What is it? What's wrong?"

"It's been awful out there, Natalka. Horrible."

She looked at me.

"What happened? Tell me."

"I think I know what happened to Paul Melnyk. And the other boy in Studinka."

SHE INSISTS THAT I DRINK some tea and calm down. I tell her what just happened to me at Rudy's. I describe the girl. She says it's good I had the imp. I tell her about Bram, too; how he came out of the darkness and carried me to safety even though I probably could've outrun it. I tell her the creature was limping. She thinks it was a vila.

"It probably got hurt in the river. Banged into some rocks or the church bridge when the storm started. You know, vily are terrible swimmers," she says. "But she would've gotten you eventually, Yuri. It doesn't matter that she hurt her leg. I'm glad Bram was there to rescue you."

Natalka watches me. She seems unimpressed by this incident. I was expecting more from her than this. I was expecting gasps of surprise, but she reacts to my story like I'm telling her I just found the Kindras' lost chicken.

"Natalka, you don't understand. I could have *died* tonight."

"Yes, I understand, Yuri. You're right. You *would have* died, but you didn't. You need to tell Roman about this. He needs to say something on Sunday. Maybe it will get more people to take this duty seriously. You didn't just save yourself, you know. You and the varta probably saved anyone else who was out tonight. Like Bram Minkin. It doesn't matter if he's strong or has a horse; she would've gotten him, too."

I think of something.

"Justina! My God, Natalka, I saw her tonight! She's out there! She said she was foraging for you. We need to find her! She's in danger!" I reach for my coat.

"Sit back down and relax. She's safe. She stopped by a little ago. Right before you. She did what I needed. She's home now."

"Oh thank God. She said she was looking for fern flowers. She showed me one."

"She found several."

I hold up my teacup and ask if our tea was made with them.

"I couldn't make tea with them yet. They're not dry. Look." She points to a corner of the room. I see four flowers hanging on strings from the ceiling. "But even if they were, I wouldn't use them for you. I'm going to make a special tea for the count. He's the one who wants them."

"Gradwolski? Really? He asked you? When was he here? I've never seen him in the village."

"Of course he didn't ask. Not directly. It was Jacob Minkin who came and asked for them. It seems the count's having trouble with his new young wife." I give her a perplexed look. "Minkin said she likes taking long walks. The count has trouble keeping up. Doesn't have enough energy, understand?"

She watches my face. It takes a moment to understand.

"Oh, I see. Long walks."

She smiles.

"That's right."

WE'VE BEEN SITTING in silence for some time now, quietly drinking our tea and listening to the rain. A dog emerges from Natalka's bedroom and walks over to me. It noses me in the hand. I put my tea down and give its hindquarters a vigorous scratching.

"Peter's happy to see you," she says. The dog's named after her last husband.

Peter settles at my feet on the floor. It's hardpacked earth, but you can still see the dog's paw marks in it. That's why we keep our dogs outside most of the year. They're not as calm as Peter. They like to dig too much. Natalka asks if I've thought about what to tell Eugenie. I tell her the incident with the vila has upset me too much.

"I don't know what to say to her. I can't do it, Natalka. It's too much. I just can't understand why she'd think I miss my old life. I've never talked to her about it. If I missed it, I would have left her a long time ago. I'm older now. Smarter. Wiser. I know what matters to me. It's her. And our family."

The old woman finishes her cup.

"Well, if that were really true, a pretty young girl wouldn't have turned your old head just now. Even if she did turn out to be a monster. Look, far be it from me to provide advice on romantic relationships. But I'll tell you, a woman never wants to hear about a rival, Yuri. Ever. Don't you see? Your other life's a rival to Eugenie. It doesn't have to be another woman. It can be other things—too much hunting, too much fishing, too much gambling or drinking. Why do you think I don't have a husband anymore? He's all I need." She points at Peter. His ears perk up. "It doesn't matter how long you've been with Eugenie."

"I know. You're right. You're always right. But what am I supposed to do now?"

"Farmer's wives don't need complicated stories. You've been wasting your time tonight. All they want are things that are concrete. Practical. A firm sign of loyalty. Trust. That's the Ruthenian way. Your past . . . it's like a faraway place to Eugenie, understand? It *is* a faraway place. It didn't help that she had that dream about you, either, even though we know what she was really dreaming about now." She smiles. "What you said to her about the English traveler didn't help. All of this made a deep impression on her. Now you need to do something to make a deeper one. Something clear and obvious."

"Like what?"

She shrugs.

"How should I know? Look what you did with Bram just now. Invited him to play cricket. That's a nice, simple solution, isn't it? You didn't try debating him about religion or politics, did you? It was a very nice peace offering, even though it probably won't work. But I think you've got to do something like that for Eugenie. I'm sure you'll figure out what it is. You just said you're very wise, didn't you?"

32

◇◇◇◇◇◇◇

Exile

ON THE TRAIN HOME FROM BIRCHINGTON my throat hurt, and by the time I reached the Pancras station, I was too ill to hold the Good Friday service. My body ached and burned with fever. I was so sick I missed all the Easter services. All my marvelous plans, all my sermons, were for nothing. My associates took over, and the congregation was disappointed to find them in my place.

My parishioners weren't the only ones who were unhappy. Cardinal Manning was displeased to hear that I missed the Easter celebrations. I'd left town inexplicably to bless some dying man—who wasn't even a Catholic!—and then was too sick to fulfill my duty. What made it worse was that Rossetti's brother wrote to the diocese and complained about me. He threatened to go to the papers and reveal my "grotesque, satanic behavior" (those were his words) if the cardinal didn't do something. Rossetti's not the villain here; I don't fault him for this. When he burst into the bedroom, I was standing at the foot of his brother's bed with a crude pagan totem that didn't look like anything remotely Christian. His letter warned the cardinal that if nothing was done to punish me, he would use a legal suit to charge me with accelerating his brother's death, which happened two days later. It wasn't fair, but grief makes us do and say irrational things.

I was too sick to know this was happening. Several parishioners sent over plates of food and notes of sympathy that went unread. Bramble and Veach took care of the food, and the notes were left in a pile on my desk. Eventually, Nessie collected them all, tied them with ribbon, and left them for me to read when I felt better.

There was one note that wasn't included in that bundle. It was from Westminster and informed me that I was being reassigned to the poor-house church of Saint Vincent's in the East End. It probably wasn't what William Rossetti wanted, but it was the cardinal's only response. From His Eminence's point of view, I think it made good sense: I was being exiled to an obscure post in the city, but I was still close enough to move back to Saint Martha's if the situation improved. If Manning had really wanted to punish me, I doubt I'd have stayed in London. In the end, Rossetti must have been satisfied. Nothing about the incident appeared in the papers. No suit was ever brought against me.

My reassignment came as a shock, and I cried when I first read the note. I wasn't a bad person; I was only trying to help someone who need-ed me. But there was no point in trying to explain that; I knew there was no point in fighting it. I couldn't win. And when my tears abated, I realized my punishment could have been much worse. I was relieved no one thought to ever question me about the imp or where I'd gotten it. I decided, in the end, that all of this was meant to happen. It was my fate. One door was closing, as they say, so that another would open. Soon, the diocesan letter lost most of its sting. Most.

SAINT VINCENT'S WAS a squalid place—the church building was a far cry from the elegance and splendor of Saint Martha's. The interior resembled little more than a box, with a high ceiling and plain walls, a simple choir loft at the back, and a cheaply gilded altar. The parish had started off as nothing more than an extension of the main church of Saint Jude and Saint James in Whitechapel in the 1850s—not a church in its own right but what's called "a chapel of ease" to relieve overcrowding. So many of Stepney's and Whitechapel's poor started going there, though, that the chapel was eventually given an identity, and a font, of its own.

The church's pastor, Samuel Brink, was a fat, affable man with extraordinary eyebrows, like wings, and a gentle, cheerful disposition. He threw his hands in the air when he first met me and cried, "At last! My prayers have been answered!" Then he gave me a vigorous shake of the hand and said he was astounded that the priest celebrated by the Sketchist was coming to Saint Vincent's. He said he couldn't believe his good luck. Evidently, my circumstances hadn't been explained to him.

There were just the two of us and the housekeeper, another nice old lady named Maud Silas, to take care of the congregation. I had no time to myself anymore—no time to waste on esoteric studies or supernatural mysteries unless it was for a sermon. The people of Saint Vincent's struggled for their daily bread and liked a good story to help them forget their hardships. Sam was beside himself with joy when I offered to deliver a sermon. "How soon will you be ready?" he said. I could start that very Sunday if I wanted. I did, and I quickly discovered I didn't need to bait the congregation with the occult to get their attention. They were very generous with their curiosity, and I fashioned a series of homilies around odd questions (How many rungs did Jacob's ladder have? Who cleft the Devil's foot?) simply because I knew they would enjoy them—checking first with Sam, who chortled merrily and thought it was a capital idea.

Another difference between Saint Martha's and Saint Vincent's involved the seat rents. Saint Vincent's didn't have any. The money produced would have helped us incredibly, but when I expressed this sentiment to the pastor, he said he was not willing to take anything, not even a few pence, out of the hands of his parishioners. God's love is unconditional, he'd said. One shouldn't have to pay for it.

I don't mean to suggest that Saint Vincent's, despite its mean circumstances, was idyllic. It wasn't. The church faced plenty of conflicts and challenges. The Protestants, Sam warned me, were always dogging his efforts. He pointed to a rectory window facing the street. "See for yourself," he said.

I looked out. I didn't notice anything at first. Across from the church was an all-night shelter. It was a large, plain building remarkable only for the cracked and broken windows on every floor. Beyond it, I saw the dim outline of another church, an Anglican one, the Church of Little Saint Hugh, and that's when I finally noticed something. High up on the shelter walls, within eyeshot of the rectory, were several placards pasted there clearly for our benefit.

Dirty liars!!!
Sneaking priests!!
Rome is filthier than a German town!!!

I looked at him in shock.

"I never experienced anything like this at Saint Martha's, not once," I said to him. He shrugged.

"That's nothing, Michael," he said. He took a small slip of paper resembling a prayer card from a desk and handed it to me. Someone had been distributing them outside of the church. It read:

Saint Vincent's Catholic Church: See the Bleeding Saint!

This ticket admits the bearer to view the real
blood of Saint Vincent de Paul.

The saint bleeds daily at five. Do not be late!

The card looked authentic. "This has to be a joke!" I said, outraged. He nodded.

"We're openly mocked for our beliefs, but it's done nothing to our numbers. In fact, I'd say they've increased a little."

Here was a struggle worth fighting for, I thought. Sam wasn't the only one who reminded me of it. I was reminded constantly by the parishioners themselves—by the grateful looks they gave me, by the simple meals we shared, and even during Mass. During my first celebration of the Mass, one of the acolytes came up and held the missal open so that I could read the final benediction. My eyes went to the edges of the book where his hands were. I saw his blackened fingernails and crushed fingertips. Those are working hands, I thought. Like my father's. I blinked back sudden tears and felt a clarity about my life that I'd been missing. This is where I should have been all along.

When Mass was over, as we processed down the main aisle to the nave, I joined the manly voices of the old women in the choir loft singing the hymn "Into Thy Heavenly Home." Several of these same crones, clucking like geese, approached me outside the church after Mass. One even pinched my cheek, saying how much I reminded her of her son. She said refreshments were waiting for us in the fellowship hall behind the church. In those early weeks, the pastor spared no expense so that I could meet our congregation. Sam was immensely kind to me. As I was about to follow those sweet old ladies to the hall, a boy came up to me on the steps. I asked if he enjoyed the Mass, and he told me, very politely, that he wasn't a papist. He said he had been hired to deliver a message.

"Hired by whom?"

"A Mr. Lionel Ashburnham, sir."

I looked at his hands. They were empty.

"If you have a message for me, where is it?"

"It's here," he said, tapping his temple. "I didn't write it down. He said there wasn't time. He said just to tell you she's in a very bad way and that you must come . . . immediately."

My heart froze in my chest.

"Who is? Who is in a bad way? Did he say anything else?"

The youth shrugged.

"He didn't tell me anymore, sir. But he did say you would give me a half a crown once I found you."

.

33

◇◇◇◇◇◇◇

A terrible miscalculation

EVEN IN A CRISIS, Lionel was shrewd. He knew I wouldn't have dropped everything if the boy had said Antonia Cox was in trouble. That's why that bold little Hermes had been given the thinnest scraps of information. "She" was just enough—I rushed to Mayfair. I could barely breathe.

When I arrived at the Ashburnham home, I didn't have a chance to knock. The front door flew open before I even reached the top step. It was Lionel. He'd been waiting for me.

"Where have you been?" he said in an anguished voice. "I've been looking all over for you! All over! I had no idea you changed parishes! You should have told me!"

He grabbed my arm and pulled me inside, muttering that he had terrible news. His eyes were red, and his hair was messed—he looked as if he hadn't slept in days. He said he'd been working on an article about a Cornish theatrical troupe's traveling show when he received a message that Antonia had been attacked. He'd rushed home to be by her side. She was already in the hospital by the time he returned; one of Antonia's clients, a young woman eager to know if marriage or spinsterhood was in

her future, found her lying on the floor in the front room of her Marylebone lodgings.

He took me to see her, and it's difficult to think too much, even now,
about her injuries. I've seen my fair share of gruesome accidents over
the years—bodies broken by a fall into the mill wheel or crushed under
an animal's hooves. I've administered the last rites in many difficult circumstances, sometimes in the middle of a field under the blazing sun.
Such deaths are inevitable here. But for a London lady to sustain such
brutal injuries . . . it's too much to think about. It hadn't been an accident,
Lionel said. Antonia had been struck repeatedly by someone in a fit of
rage. Hands alone hadn't produced her injuries, either. Two of her for-
tune-telling implements—a mirror with a long oak handle and a piece of
quartz the size of a pumpkin—had been found in pieces next to her body.
Her face was covered in ghastly purple bruises. Her forearms, too—she'd
tried to shield herself from the blows. When I saw her, Antonia had re-
gained consciousness but was unable to say anything; her jaw was tightly
wrapped in bandages. Her writing hand was too swollen to use the tablet
and chalk on the table by her bed.

I brought my viaticum bag with me and gave her a blessing. I touched
her forehead with the oils just as I'd done with Gabriel and asked God
to give her strength and healing. Lionel went out in the hall to wait—he
couldn't bear to watch. The viaticum scared him; I tried to assure him it
was used in times of sickness, too. Once Antonia and I were alone, with
my hands still raised over her, I improvised another blessing. It was unnecessary, but I added it anyways—because I was worrying about something
else even though I couldn't bring myself to admit it yet. I looked up at
the cracks in the hospital ceiling and implored the Father of us all, who is
all-merciful and all-knowing, to bless her and grant her the ability to show
mercy and compassion for her attacker, "which is the greatest of God's
virtues," I said, "because what has been done cannot be undone."

I looked in her eyes—the only part of her that could show any real
expression at that point—and I saw them crinkle at the corners. They
crinkled the way they did whenever Lionel said something that amused
her. I think she knew what I was doing. She knew what I was asking her.

Lionel said the police suspected an army corporal recently returned
from India. His fiancée had been a client of Antonia's, and the young
woman broke off her engagement with him while he was away. The link

between Antonia's counsel and the young woman's decision had been compelling to them. The corporal was being held until Antonia was well enough to provide them with a full account of what happened.

When I looked at her injuries, I didn't see a soldier's work. I saw Kitty's—and mine. As soon as she was better, I knew what Antonia would tell them. She wasn't interested in forgiveness. Why should she be? I was naive to hope for it.

When we returned to Mayfair from the hospital, I asked if Kitty was home from her trip. Lionel looked at me strangely. He said she hadn't told him anything about a trip before he left; he only learned of their departure after he'd rushed back to London.

"But you knew, didn't you?" he said. "I'm surprised. I didn't realize you were in contact with her."

"I wasn't, not very much," I said, faltering. "I only learned she was gone when I tried to find out where you were. I really wasn't expecting her to be gone."

He made an exasperated gesture.

"You weren't expecting it? How do you think I feel? She decides to go off and see her family now . . . of all times! When I need her most!"

I followed him into the house. We didn't go up to the study this time; we sat in one of the drawing rooms. He asked if I wanted something to eat. I said I wasn't hungry; I felt sick and anxious. My gambit with the address card had worked. Kitty found her. I'd thought my little gesture would only lead to a confrontation—some harsh words, a warning to leave her family alone. Not this.

From where we sat, I could see the foyer and the staircase where Kitty had come down to dinner the last time I saw her. My heart ached, and I felt guilty for thinking of her rather than listening to Lionel. I kept thinking about the taste of her lips, how she'd made me feel, and how much—even then—I still wanted her … even as Lionel droned on about the investigation of Antonia's attack.

"It's only a matter of time, Frost," he said. "Even if it isn't the corporal, someone's bound to come forward. If they don't, we'll know soon enough. She's getting better. She'll tell us the full story." He raked his hair with a shaky hand.

I couldn't bear to listen anymore.

"Listen, Lionel, please," I said slowly. "This . . . all of this . . . it's my fault."

They were the most difficult words to get out, but the rest came easily. I told him what I'd done with the address card and why. I avoided putting the blame only on my shoulders. I lashed out at him for neglecting Kitty and giving his attention to Antonia. I told him I was ashamed of how he treated her and that she needed to assert herself against Antonia, against a woman who was invading her husband's life. That's why I left the card. I told him I couldn't believe someone so gifted in understanding the subtleties of characters on the stage and in books could utterly fail to notice his wife's unhappiness. As I spoke, Lionel listened to me with an abstracted look on his face like he was lost in some mathematical calculation. It wasn't what I expected. She'd been so full of despair on my last visit, I said, her pain had been obvious to me, and if it was obvious to me, I couldn't understand how he'd failed to notice.

"Your last visit?" he said suddenly. "And where was I? Oh, how convenient. I knew it. Sneaking over here. Playing tricks on her. On both of us. You're quite the resourceful one, aren't you? But not too resourceful. You couldn't even help me with Rossetti, you worthless shit."

A flood of curses rained down on me. He didn't exclude anything or anyone, not even my parents, the filthy immigrant and the woman barely rescued from spinsterhood. Those were his words. He reduced my life to a series of pathetic caricatures. I was dazed by his sudden viciousness. His abuse included every confidence I'd ever shared with him, and at some point, his words found their mark. I was so hurt I couldn't think or speak.

"Have you nothing else to say back? Nothing at all?" he demanded. His face was set hard. He called me a liar; he said he didn't believe Kitty was responsible for Antonia's injuries. I can't remember how I managed it, but somehow, I finally interrupted him again.

"Why," I said hoarsely, "why would she leave without telling you? Did you think about that?"

He looked at me as if he hadn't.

"Why," I continued, "would she go suddenly to her parents in York without a word? Don't you see what's happened? She's *fled*, Lionel. Because of what she's done."

Lionel did something then that was completely out of character. He tried to hit me. It was very awkward. He squared his legs and drew back his arm. His eyes never left my face. He threw his punch as if he were throwing a dart, as if he were following some steps he'd memorized from a book. He was too careful, too precise, and I easily stepped out of the way. This made him furious.

"Fled! Fled?" He swung at me again. "Stop talking that way about *my wife.*"

He lunged, and I caught him by the shoulders. I held him away from me, and he flailed like an angry child. He reached for my face and tried putting his thumbs in my eyes, but I gave him a hard shake.

"Listen to me! Stop it! *Stop it!* I made a terrible mistake, Lionel, don't you see? God forgive me! I had no idea this would happen! No idea! I only wanted to give her a chance to confront Antonia, to defend your marriage. I never wanted Antonia to be hurt! My God, do you honestly think I wanted that? It was a mistake, a terrible miscalculation—"

"A miscalculation? Is that what you call it? Fuck your miscalculations. And you. A nice way to describe what you've done to us!" He broke away from me and stormed into the dining room. I followed him. I begged him to listen to me.

"I won't argue with you anymore, Lionel. I swear to God I'll leave you alone. But before I do, would you just consider one thing? Please? Have you considered what will happen when Antonia recovers? Are you willing to gamble on what she's going to say? If Kitty did this to her, do you think Antonia cares enough about you to protect her? What's going to stop her from telling the police?"

My words seemed to have their intended effect. Lionel sank into a chair at the table and buried his face in his hands. He looked exhausted. I went over to him.

"You need to calm yourself so you can help her," I said, watching his shoulders rise and fall with his frantic breathing. "You must prepare yourself. You must make plans. What is going to happen when your family comes back from York? What happens if the police come for her?"

"The police," he murmured, still with his face covered.

I put my hand on his shoulder and vowed to stand by him no matter what he thought of me. I apologized again for what I'd done. Tears filled my eyes. Lionel shuddered under my touch; he seemed about to cry, too. But when he uncovered his face and looked up at me, his eyes were hard and dry.

"Get out," he said.

I RETURNED TO MAYFAIR several times after that. Lionel refused to see me each time. I was met at the front door by Annie or another servant, and they always told me he wasn't home. I could tell they were lying; they avoided my eyes and looked at the ground.

A few weeks later, I saw Lionel outside the hospital. He was leaving just as I was arriving. I wanted to see if Antonia had improved, and I wanted to talk to her about forgiveness again. I saw Lionel on the far side of a wide courtyard, and I called out his name. He stopped a moment and looked back. Then he turned and walked on.

I gave up any hope of explaining to him in person. I wrote to him, and my letters went unanswered. Desperate, I decided to go to Mayfair again. It seemed pointless, but I was out of ideas. I decided I'd stay outside the house as long as possible until he left or returned. I didn't care what Annie or anyone else said. I didn't care how long I'd have to wait. All night, if necessary. I just needed him to hear me one last time.

This trip turned out to be very different. When I knocked, a cleaning woman I didn't recognize opened the door. I identified myself as a family friend and asked who she was and where the others were. She shrugged and told me she didn't know; she was cleaning the premises for the new owners. The previous ones had left right after the sale.

"Sale? What sale?" I said, shocked. "Where are the Ashburnhams?"

It wasn't her business, she said. She didn't know.

I stepped closer to the door and tried to look inside, but she barred my way. She looked warily at me and said she had work to do before closing the door. I stood there for several long moments. I couldn't believe the Ashburnhams were gone. How was I ever going to find them? I'd have to try York first. I'd get an address for Kitty's family. Maybe one of Lionel's editors had it.

As I stepped down into the street, I turned and looked back at the house. It seemed lifeless in the late-afternoon sunlight. Empty except for that unsympathetic cleaning woman. Or so I thought. I noticed a movement in one of the second-story windows—a ruffling of the curtains in Lionel's study. Someone else was there. I thought it was another cleaning woman. Maybe there were several. The house was too much for a single person to clean. The curtains moved and a face looked out, and then another, and I knew what must have happened.

WILLIAM WAS ACQUAINTED with collectors and auctioneers keenly interested in the sales of ancestral homes, especially those belonging to old families like the Ashburnhams. I asked him to look for information about the sale of Lionel and Kitty's house, even though I didn't think he'd find any. He conducted his research on Cawdor Street, a hive of forgers and sham art collectors situated in the narrow lanes and alleys between Soho and Oxford Street. They held a special place of affection in his heart. "Forgers have the best eyes in the trade," he once told me, "and the best knowledge about who's selling what. They're more sensitive to the movement of money than the Bank of England." It was a time in the city's history when many large private homes were being sold and converted for new uses; initially, I'd thought this must be the case. The Ashburnhams' residence would probably be chopped up into several smaller residences.

But when William later returned from Cawdor Street, he had strange news for me. Strange, but unsurprising. He told me what I expected. He said there hadn't been any sale. His Cawdor associates couldn't find evidence of one. "If they can't find it," he said, "that means it probably doesn't exist."

If the house hadn't been sold, then where had the idea of a sale come from? I blamed the anonymous cleaning woman. That's what she said, and she'd been wrong. I didn't deny the fact the house had new owners; I saw them. But it hadn't required an exchange of assets. That's what happens in normal cases. The Ashburnhams' was anything but that.

WHEN THE CURTAIN MOVED in the study window, I saw Antonia Cox look out. She'd recovered enough by then to leave the hospital. Some bruising on her face was still visible from where I stood. She looked down for a fleeting moment before turning away. Then someone else came to the window.

The curtain moved again, and this time I saw the fat cheeks and severe expression of Khristiana Lumens. I know she recognized me. She tilted her head to one side, smiled, and let the curtain fall back.

34

◇◇◇◇◇◇◇◇

Objects of their choice

MORNINGS WERE COLD in Saint Vincent's rectory. I often took refuge by the stove in the kitchen. It didn't matter that I had a little fireplace in my quarters and an old, rusted brazier to warm my feet—the room felt like an icebox even when I lit both. I preferred the warmth and light of the kitchen while Mrs. Silas cooked our breakfast.

I remember sitting on a creaky little stool one morning, watching her make rashers and eggs. I was exhausted. I hadn't been sleeping well.

I've mentioned that Sam and I didn't have anyone to help us. We took care of everything ourselves. Mass was celebrated every morning; we spent our afternoons in confession, or informally listening to parishioners recite a litany of their problems, or else arranging the laundering of altar cloths and making an inventory of supplies. On Friday evenings, one of us performed the benediction service (which was just as popular there as it was at Saint Martha's). Then, when it was over, we gave out beef tea, wine, arrowroot, and whatever else we had to forty or fifty recipients of tickets distributed that day by a women's reform group in the parish. This was something deeply touching to me: my parishioners were among the lowliest of the low, and they still tried to help each other.

Our days didn't end until long after sunset; they were the kinds of days that sent us both to our beds drained and exhausted. I couldn't understand how Sam had been doing all this without anyone's help. I dragged myself up the stairs every night and dropped like a stone into oblivion the minute my head touched the pillow. But it wasn't a wholesome sleep. I never woke up feeling refreshed, no matter how tired I was.

I wobbled on the stool as I watched Mrs. Silas. I couldn't tell how much of the wobble was because of my fatigue or the stool's weak legs. The frying pork smelled good. It's funny that I can still remember a detail like that. I thought you were only supposed to remember really meaningful things when you got older—like your first kiss or the soothing sound of your mother's voice when you were sick. I remember those, and I can also remember the sounds and smells of that pork sizzling and popping in the pan. My mother used to cook our eggs and rashers in separate pans, but Mrs. Silas used the same skillet for everything before she dumped it on our plates. It was a delicious, greasy mess, and I loved it.

She was humming to herself that morning—she was in a far better mood than I was. This wasn't unusual; she was another of those perennially cheerful West Country girls always with a smile on their faces. But that morning, there was a special reason for her good mood.

A small item in that week's *London Illustrated* said a Vatican deputation was on its way to Wales. The rector of a small abbey in the Black Mountains had been visited by the Virgin Mary while he worked in a garden patch of rhubarb. He was digging at some weeds, and when he looked up, he saw her shadow outlined on one of the bushes. Then he heard her voice. She told him not to be afraid or surprised. No one, she said, not even the faithful living in a remote corner of the Welsh countryside, is ever forgotten in God's plans.

The article said the apparition was still visible on the bush and that people were flocking to the abbey to see it. Miracles were being reported already. A rainbow had appeared in the cloudless sky above the abbey. A nun touched some of the rhubarb leaves to an abscess on her leg, and it healed instantly.

Mrs. Silas's eyes were shining. She didn't say anything to me, only stirred the skillet and hummed to herself, but I knew she was thinking about the Blessed Mother's visit and her reassuring message that every life matters to God.

She seemed so distracted that when I tried to warn her the eggs were burning, she didn't hear me—her mind was off in the Black Mountains among the rhubarb bushes. I envied this simple happiness. I was still struggling with what I'd seen in Mayfair. That beautiful house was gone . . . into the hands of unworthy people. And I'd helped them. I'd never imagined Cox and Lumens were working together. I'd been too trusting, and Gerard and William's enthusiasm for Lumens had overwhelmed my wariness. Lumens certainly had been a legitimate occult practitioner at one time, but she was just another con artist now. Her great gifts must have left her. So many of the great spiritists have ended up that way. I'm sure it was just too tempting to continue on and devise ways of taking the gullible public's money. Maybe she hoped that if she continued, her powers would eventually return. When I'd looked up and saw her face and Antonia's in Lionel's study window, I wanted to charge the door and smash it down. Or go to the police.

But I didn't. I was reminded of something my father once told me.

WHEN I WAS a student at the Mortimer Academy, I was constantly teased for showing off. Usually this caused my classmates to insult me, and I was used to it. I ignored them, but there was a time when they wanted to do more.

Physically, I was bigger than the rest, stronger and thicker, and my size usually kept them away. The most they would ever do is lob a comment from a safe distance, and I took for granted that nothing worse could ever happen. But on that day, as I made some tortured point about Virgil or Ovid to impress our teacher, they'd had enough. They didn't like my show of superiority. When school was over, several of them followed me home. I didn't notice them at first; they kept to the gloomier parts of the street. They hid behind parked carriages and vendor stands. It was like a game to them. When I was almost home, they crossed over to my side and rushed at me. I was strong, but I counted six of them and knew I couldn't fight them alone. So I did the only thing I could: I ran . . . and they pursued me the rest of the way to Golden Square, throwing old cans and fruit and anything else they could find as I reached our front door and ran inside. I'd safely made it home, but it wasn't over. They stayed outside, shouting my name and calling me a coward. The fact they dared to bring their insults right to our door filled me with a boiling rage.

On a shelf in our front room was a mace my father had carved—the kind an old warrior from Kiev might have used to crush the skulls of his enemies. My father had cut a round, fat joint of oak into an octagonal shape and affixed it to the end of a long, thick shaft etched with the same kinds of spidery lines that cover the imp's body. Dowel pins, ingeniously hidden, kept the head snugly in its place. It was decorative; he never intended it for any use. It was a display piece, and my father was simply proud of it. But I was so furious and enraged that I grabbed it with one hand and flung open the front door with the other. I howled and charged down the front steps. When the Mortimer boys saw me, they froze, and I took advantage of their shock to swing at them like I was hitting a cricket ball. Two of them cried out and ran before I could reach them. Another stumbled backward and fell in a puddle of horse piss; the others I clipped in the shins with a loud *pock*! I sent them all scrambling, and then I stood there in the middle of our street, shaking the club over my head and roaring at them like a wild Slavic tribesman.

As I watched them disappear around the corner, I decided to go after them. I wanted to scare them so badly that they'd never try that again. Behind our house ran an alleyway that led up to Finch Lane, and I calculated I might intercept them there . . . but my plan was interrupted by a hand suddenly clamping down hard on my shoulder. I spun around and lifted the mace.

It was my father. I hadn't realized he was home. My mother, too. They'd both been in the kitchen when I rushed in and grabbed the mace. My mother was standing at the top of the front steps, leaning against the railing, watching us.

"Let them go, Mikhaylo," he said. "We saw what you did. You've done enough. Let them go."

Even though his tone had been gentle and his eyes full of pity, he wouldn't release his hard grip on me until I promised to stop. He held out his other hand, and I gave him the mace. He tested it, swung it back and forth, and muttered something flattering to himself as though it had been made by someone else. He smiled at me with his clear green eyes and told me supper was almost ready. He and my mother didn't bring up what happened during dinner. They didn't punish me, either.

When Lumens looked down and smiled at me from Lionel's study, I felt a boiling rage like I did on that day, and I heard my father's voice again. I recalled his face, his sympathetic eyes, long sideburns, and wispy brown hair. I missed him so much. I missed them both so much. Was that why I'd attached myself to the Ashburnhams? Had I expected them in some way to take the place of my parents? It was probably true, and that realization made me feel sad and pathetic. I couldn't blame them for leaving London. They had to, and Lionel had demonstrated something incredible. He'd performed an act more selfless and loving than I thought him capable of. The depth of that sacrifice, knowing what the house meant to him, staggered me. I left Mayfair that day thinking Kitty had gotten what she wanted: a powerful sign of his love. But to show how pathetic I was, I remember congratulating myself for this at the time—after all, he'd never have gotten the chance to show his devotion to her without me, right?

God forgive me, someone nearly died because of me.

GERARD'S DEATH WAS something else I avoided thinking about as I watched Mrs. Silas burn the eggs. Not long after I moved to Saint Vincent's, he was found in the chapel library study in his favorite chair. An old diocesan groundskeeper noticed a light in the window, and when he peeked into the room, he saw Gerard and thought he'd fallen asleep. It wasn't unusual. As I've said before, Gerard sometimes slept in the study when he was working late. But a few days later, when the keeper returned, he found Gerard in the exact same place and knew something must be wrong. His legs were stiff in front of him, as if he were sliding down the side of a hill and trying to dig in his heels to stop. And there was a smell already. The room was stuffy, and the smoldering embers in the fireplace hadn't helped. A physician was called even though it was too late.

The physician said Gerard had suffered a powerful apoplectic spasm. Through tears, William told me about Gerard's death, and he said the spasm wasn't Gerard's first; another attack years ago had robbed him of the strength in his legs. I listened in stunned silence, watching his face, watching him struggle the way I'd once watched William Rossetti struggle to tell me about his dying brother. William said the spasm had been so sudden and severe, "it was likely Gerard hadn't suffered for more than a few moments . . . that's what the physician said." I think this was supposed to be comforting.

William said Gerard's wish had been to be buried in Ireland, in his native county of Longford. There was a place for him there, right next to the beloved old aunt who'd raised him, in the Balfe family plot in the churchyard of Colmcille Parish. The yard was in plain view of a solitary dolmen, tens of thousands of years old, standing in an adjacent pasture and holding up its horizontal slab in primitive mimicry of the mathematician's *pi*. William said it was a fitting resting place for Gerard's bones— deep in hallowed ground, but with a touch of the pagan nearby. William offered to pay so that I could accompany him on Gerard's final journey home, but I couldn't. Sam Brink couldn't spare my help, and I didn't think it wise to ask for permission for a leave of absence so soon after the fiasco in Birchington.

William understood. When we parted, I asked him for the planned date of Gerard's burial. On that day, I said I'd go over to the chapel library and pray the rosary for our friend.

When the day came, Sam was very understanding and let me go after the morning Mass and confessions. I spent the entire afternoon and evening sitting in front of the fire and sipping a glass of whiskey in his honor. I had my Brigittine rosary with me, and I prayed the additional decade of beads for Gerard—it was "like extra money in the mint," he used to say about that extra set—to make his soul's journey easier. The room had been left just as it was when the groundskeeper discovered him. Papers and several books were open on his desk, and there was an empty glass and a half-eaten biscuit next to it. It felt as if I'd just missed him, that he would be returning soon. I took some comfort in that.

I thought about all the evenings I'd spent there, and I was grateful for them, for our time together as we made our misguided efforts to solve Gabriel's haunting—a haunting that never really required much of a solution in the first place. The Ariel ceremony had all been a fraud; there wasn't any spirit writing "I do not" or, as Gerard had thought, the name "Donati." But that interpretation put me on a disastrous course that nearly ruined a marriage and cost a woman her life.

I heard a creak behind me. It sounded like someone had walked into the room, but it wasn't that—I knew the old building's sounds. It was early evening, and I heard creaks all the time as it grew dark outside and the temperature fell. But I think I hoped it was something more this time. I hoped Gerard's soul really was there for a moment—taking one last look at his beloved collection of books before it left.

I cleared my throat and spoke softly.

"Is that you, dear friend? Are you here?"

If he was, he didn't answer.

The spirit world seemed so clear to me suddenly. It didn't take years of study to understand it. I thought about Gabriel Rossetti's situation again, and it seemed obvious why he'd been haunted by something demonic. Moral weakness and corruption had attracted it because that's what always attracts demons. They feast on our weaknesses, and Gabriel's had been unlike any I'd ever seen. His behavior—though I knew only rumors—with other women, other men's wives, his obsession with pagan goddesses and witches in his later paintings and poetry . . . all of these were signs of a corrupted soul. I'm sure it gave off a scent to them like blood to a hungry lion.

The last time I was in this study with my two friends was right before I left for Saint Vincent's. I had told them about what happened in Birchington and how I'd gotten in trouble. They were sorry to hear about that, but I remember them being more concerned that I'd attracted the demon's attention when I used the imp against it. These beings are full of pride, William had warned me, and they hold grudges just as humans do. I'd shooed it from Gabriel's room like some unruly child, and that worried them. But I was tired of the whole business by then. I didn't listen closely to what they said. I was getting ready for my new assignment, and I had too much on my mind. I asked them to leave this discussion for another day and secretly hoped we would forget it.

But Gerard didn't. He'd been brooding about it on the night he died. How did I know that?

Because of his books. The ones left open on his desk. The ones next to the empty glass and half-eaten biscuit. I put away my rosary and looked at them.

One of the books lay open, face downward. When I lifted it, I was careful not to lose Gerard's place. I looked at the cover. Milton. Of course. He liked to read him every day. Underneath were several newspapers; one was open to a *Punch* cartoon. Gerard must have needed a good laugh after the Milton.

I moved the newspapers and found another book. Like the Milton, I lifted it carefully so I wouldn't lose his place. The cover said *The Unseen World* by the Rev. Fr. Alexis Lépicier. I didn't recognize it. Gerard had never mentioned it to me before. Inside, he'd marked several passages in the margins with a pencil, including this one:

> The angelic intellect . . . does not, like the human intellect, proceed gradually and step by step to the knowledge of truth, nor is it subject to the hesitations which we experience. As it obtains, at a glance, a perfect intuition of things, so does it cling with immovable tenacity to the objects of its choice.

Though the bright embers in the fireplace had warmed the study considerably, I couldn't help shivering. I reread the passage and thought about William's warning again. Gerard had underlined the phrase "so does it cling with immovable tenacity to the objects of its choice" several times.

THERE WAS A KNOCK at the kitchen door.

Mrs. Silas took the skillet off the flame and went to answer it. When she came back, she said I was needed.

"Some parishioners are wondering if you can open the church early," she said. "So they can get out of the cold."

The rain from the night before had stopped, and the ground was coated in a thin sheet of ice. We weren't yet in October, but already everyone was expecting an early winter.

A crowd of people waited for me on the church steps.

"Oh, Father Mike, thank you!" said a little old woman who organized our choir. "Is it just you this morning?"

"Yes, just me."

"I thought Fr. Brink might be with you."

"No, he's inside the rectory. It's just me."

"I thought he was behind you now. I thought there was someone else," she said, squinting past me into the fog. She gave a little shrug and went inside.

At the back of the church, I asked several men to help me light two large cast-iron stoves that Father Brink had set up in the transepts. Once they were lit, the blowing sound the fires made and the bright orange light radiating through the slats of the stoves breathed life into the dark building. I smiled with satisfaction—a rare thing in those days. I went to the bank of votive candles against the building's west side. None were lit. The figure of Jesus, with his sacred heart exposed, hovered above them in the gloom. I took several notes from my pocket and stuffed them in the collection box next to the candles. Then I struck a long, thin lucifer and lit an entire row. I looked up at Jesus, who smiled appreciatively in the soft pink glow.

There were only two places where I felt truly comfortable anymore— in the circle of warmth cast by Mrs. Silas's stove and there in the church. The damp, soggy smells of the poor, the shuffling of their feet and mur- mur of their voices gave the building its purpose. Without them, the church was like any other empty building. That morning, a few said they'd heard the news about the Virgin's apparition and asked me if it was true. I told them the Holy Mother can do anything she wishes, and on the spot, I tailored a little homily for the morning Mass to fit the news. In purgatory, I said, she visits sinners every Saturday, and when she does, the purgatori- al fires die down low, and the sinners enjoy a moment's relief. This wasn't some lore I'd found in Gerard's library; it was something I remembered from Hammersmith from one of my teachers of systematic theology. He was devoted to the Holy Mother; he couldn't mention her without tears in his eyes. I thought of Our Lady quietly moving among the cells of pur- gatory, bringing a lull to the penitents' sufferings. Her visits gave them a chance to catch their breath and give thanks. Or if they wanted, to close their eyes and rest. I envied them.

35

◇◇◇◇◇◇◇

A face

I HURRIED BACK TO THE RECTORY AFTER MASS. Sam had planned a special trip for us. I ran up to my room and splashed my face with cold water from the basin on my dresser. I changed into a clean silk cassock and looked at myself in the mirror. Absolutely ghastly. Pale, red-eyed, disheveled. It was a wonder I hadn't given a fright to our parishioners. I tried fixing my damp, tangled hair, then decided to hide it under my biretta. I found the pastor down in the kitchen, eating his breakfast.

"Well, hello!" he said heartily. His smile fell at the sight of me. "Is everything all right, Michael? Are you not well?"

"Oh no, no, I'm just fine, Father," I said, doing my best to sound cheery and bright.

It didn't work. He still looked concerned. I didn't persuade Mrs. Silas, either; she was eyeing me with a mixture of doubt and pity. Sam said he'd hoped to show me the nearby market, something he'd wanted to do since my arrival. I forced myself to smile, even though the thought of going there exhausted me. But I didn't have a choice. I didn't want to disappoint him.

As we left the rectory, he looked at me and rubbed his bare head.

"I used to have one of those," he said, pointing at my biretta. "I lost it years ago. I have a cloth cap that's vandyked to look like one, but I can't seem to find it. I wonder if I might borrow yours this time?"

An odd request but delivered in such a friendly way that I couldn't refuse. I gave it to him and ran my fingers through my hair.

We walked east on Commercial Road, and Sam explained that he wanted me to know which vendors to trust, which were the most reliable, and which to avoid. Helpfulness was a fundamental quality of his nature. He said he wanted me to avoid the mistakes he made when he first arrived at Saint Vincent's, and that included being misinformed and spending far more than I needed to.

At that time of the morning, the market was crowded to nearly a standstill, the people all a shifting, stirring brown mass of bodies kicking up dust into the air. The square was nothing so formal as I had envisioned: I expected something on the scale of Billingsgate, but in fact, this wasn't a square at all. It was just a collection of street sellers who packed several small lanes off Commercial Road.

I could well understand why Sam was so eager, as he was in everything else, about introducing me to this place. Not only were there vendors of fresh mackerel and fruit, flowers and fowl, but also sellers of tobacco and lucifers, Dutch dolls and slabs of bacon, blacking, brooms and crockery, not to mention several tinkerers who offered to fix chair legs and basket bottoms right there on the spot. It was overwhelming, but he told me I'd become accustomed to it after a few visits.

Some vendors clearly didn't like members of the Roman church—they made no attempt to hide their scowls as we passed—but others were quite respectful, greeting the pastor and eyeing me in an inquisitive way that wasn't rude. Several times, the pastor took off my hat to the apple women and sellers of watercress, and I realized that this grand gesture was why he'd wanted to borrow it. We passed several stalls selling clothes.

"Don't bother with those if you're thinking of a gift for someone. Cheap quality! And right there," he said, jabbing a fat finger at several peddlers of coats, "stay clear of them, too."

He told me the coats had either been lifted off corpses—"notice the artful patches, probably hiding knife holes and bloodstains!"—or else were made of material so flimsy it dissolved in a steady rain.

"I had a most unfortunate experience," he said, "with one of those coats. It was such a nice shade of cerulean. When I wore it during a sudden downpour, I later found my white shirt underneath had turned completely blue!"

We laughed, and I watched the people swarm past us. Sam held up his hands in excitement.

"Ah, there's what we want. There," Brink said, pointing to a basket of citrus riding past on the ocean of heads. A young woman was carrying a full basket on her head. It looked incredibly heavy. All she had for a cushion was a small piece of cloth on her crown. Gavarni famously sketched market dwellers like her. I marveled at the strength of her neck and shoulders.

"Wait here," Brink said. "I won't be long."

I watched him set off after her, his own head and shoulders disappearing in the mob so that I could only follow my biretta, like a little schooner, bobbing along in feverish pursuit of the basket.

I laughed despite my fatigue. I loved Sam's kindness and simplicity, the way he'd perfected the formula for balancing innocence with the worldliness one needs in order to avoid trouble. After losing sight of him, I moved off to a side of the crowded lane and stood clear of the frantic foot traffic—as I moved, another group of basket carriers nearly knocked me over. Without Sam at my side, without his energetic talk and arm-pulling and laughing, I started feeling tired again. I felt myself slipping into a fog. Faces rippled and flashed by, and I shook my head to stay alert.

I noticed someone on the other side of the lane, watching me. It was just beyond all the jostling heads and bodies, and I felt it before I fully saw it. The skin tingled on the back of my neck and along my shoulders. I turned and looked and caught just a glimpse of someone, of stubbly cheeks and curly sideburns and thinning gray-white hair, before the crowd surged between us. I felt an electric shock go through me. It was my father.

I knew it was a mistake, that I was having one of those waking dreams the poets call daymares. It defied all earthly logic, all the rules of the natural world. But I kept looking for him anyways, for the haunting features I'd just seen—the strained, wasted look on his face and the bulge in his neck after he'd been laid to rest. There was also something else: I'd seen chains of different thicknesses and shapes and weights hanging around his neck and down his shoulders. Were these the chains of purgatory or hell?

A wagon turned down the lane and slowed as it passed, adding more congestion in the street, and I waited impatiently for it to move on. Once it did, I caught sight of him again. He was still there on the other side of the street. He smiled at me—it was a terrible smile . . . the stained grin consumptives have because of all the lung-rot on their teeth. More people passed between us, and when I looked again, he was gone. I looked and looked, but I couldn't find him.

My knees buckled, and everything started to spin. I threw back a hand and grabbed the corner of a vendor's stall just as Sam returned. He had a triumphant smile on his round, sweaty face. He had pulled up the front of his cassock and was using it to hold a large pile of fruit.

"Success!" he said, and then, for the second time that morning, his smile fell at the sight of me. "Michael, what is it? What's wrong?"

I didn't answer him right away; I felt like I was about to faint. I looked past Sam. Far back, on the other side of the lane, I saw a little old man selling dog collars. He was draped with more chains than Marley's ghost. He stood near where the apparition had been. Or had it been him? Did my mind dress him up like my father? Did my grief do that? I squinted at him, and our eyes met, and my attention on him was so intense that the little old fellow looked away. Sam stepped in front of me. He peered into my eyes and asked again what was wrong.

"Nothing, Sam, I'm just a little unwell is all. I see you were successful. That is good. Unless you have more to do, could we go home now? I'm very tired. I want to lie down."

THAT GROTESQUE FIGURE appeared to me several more times. During one of my walks, when I didn't see it right away, I dared thinking it was gone, that what had happened in the market had been some isolated bout of madness brought on by grief and a lack of sleep. But then I turned a corner and found it waiting for me, standing in a darkened stairwell as I took Eucharist to someone. On other walks it was hovering among the gloomy stalls of Paternoster Row or bobbing like a child's balloon behind the glass of a passing omnibus window—always with the same mocking smile and gore-stained teeth.

There was a chilling style—for lack of a better word—to the way the apparition pressed itself on me and robbed me of my peace of mind. It never announced its arrival in a blast of thunder or swirls of dark smoke.

I never knew when I might see it. That was the most terrifying part: half the fright came from not knowing.

There was always a distance separating us; the specter never came close enough for a confrontation, never to tell me what it was . . . *I am thy father's spirit, doom'd for a certain term, et cetera.* Nothing like that. Even when, in a spasm of sudden bravery, I tried rushing at it on a crowded street, there was always some interference, some distraction—a passing carriage, a throng of people—that facilitated its vanishing before I could reach it. To be honest, I didn't mind I couldn't reach it. I didn't really wish to get closer to something conjured to break my heart. I just wanted it to go away and leave me alone.

These visitations made me restless, and I couldn't find any peace even when I slept. That image of my father invaded my dreams. When I did manage to fall asleep, it was there, waiting for me, hovering in the void like an actor poised to deliver a monologue. It was during these delirious, sleep-deprived days that I realized I couldn't stay at Saint Vincent's anymore. Or in London. I needed to leave. I wished I could say there was a grander reason for it, but my decision grew out of those fitful, sleepless nights and my desperate cravings for rest.

Without sleep, I moved easily, too easily, into a state of mind that was disturbing. I found myself contemplating how to end my life without truly realizing this was what I was doing. Sometimes I caught myself staring up at the heights of buildings or our church's bell tower as I imagined a body falling through the air . . . or counting the yards between the Queen's Bridge and the surface of the Thames. I imagined dark things no healthy person ever would.

With each day's loss of sleep, my change became noticeable to others. One night, as I sat up in bed and watched the moon rise above the shelter across the street, I overheard Mrs. Silas and Sam down in the kitchen. She was telling him about an order of two hundred cases of votive candles that had arrived. I had placed the order, and it should have been for only twenty cases. Sam sounded worried, but Mrs. Silas said she'd managed to get the extra 180 cases sent back.

I wish that botched order had been the worst of it, but I made other mistakes; sleeplessness, like any disease, is a crippling affliction. I walked distracted and unaware into the paths of potential injury—I nearly stepped in front of a hansom cab as it raced by the church, but some kindly passerby pulled me in. On another occasion, I went down into the rectory cellar for meal tickets and struck my head so hard against the lintel I nearly fainted. When our senses are fully alive and intact, we don't realize how much they help us, how we are making continuous half-conscious adjustments to the world around us. Each day, how many hazards, big and small, do we navigate around with no awareness? Our senses are so finely attuned that they adjust for every looming obstacle—a crowded lane, a person we wish to avoid, a pang of hunger or fear—without our ever noticing. But I was losing this ability, this gift from God; I felt it slipping through my fingers no matter how much I tried to retain it.

I was losing control not only of my physical surroundings but also of the spiritual ones. It was in this world that I made my most serious mistakes—if these had been known, I would have been mercilessly crushed by the punitive measures prescribed in our canon law. Several times I forgot prayers, or used the wrong ones, in the confessional, on the altar, by the baptismal font. I'm sure on those occasions I sent parishioners home with their venial sins unexpunged . . . or with nothing more in their mouths than a wafer and some cheap wine . . . or with Limbo the only possibility for the babies I imperfectly baptized.

Still, I did sometimes manage to enjoy a few hours of decent sleep. This usually happened only after I took a brisk walk or drank a tumbler of whiskey. This sleep would last a few hours, and then the apparition would find me in my dreams. It always did. Once, though, while I slept, I attempted to do something I never was able to do when I was awake: I actually confronted the apparition. Somehow, I managed to open my mouth and demand of it, *When will this end? When, false image of my father, when will you leave me alone? When?*

I don't know how long I waited for its answer. It felt like a thousand years. The apparition glared at me—it wore an expression so ugly and alien to the loving man I'd known that I sobbed as I asked my questions. Finally, when it seemed nothing would happen and I was starting to wake, it spoke. It smiled and murmured something, and the gore burbled from the corners of its mouth. Dark red lines ran down the stubbly jaw and throat. I woke in the dark of my room, shuddering—gasping into my pillow so that Sam wouldn't hear. Long minutes passed as I was lying there, panting, thinking about what it said. Its answer had been hardly anything at all, just a single word.

Never.

36

◇◇◇◇◇◇◇

Plans

EVEN THOUGH MISTAKES LIKE THE BOTCHED CANDLE ORDER must've worried Sam, he never said anything about them. He never scolded or threatened me; he never complained. Maybe he knew there was already a black strike against me because of William Rossetti. Whatever the reason, he showed far more mercy and patience than I think I would have if our positions had been reversed.

One night he found me in the common room very late, avoiding my bed as usual. I was just sitting there; I didn't have a book or newspaper in my lap. I stared at the fire. When he asked what I was doing, I told him what was happening to me. I didn't try to hide it.

"I can't sleep, Sam. I've been seeing my father everywhere, dreaming about him," I said. "It started when we went to that market. Do you remember? How I grabbed you and wanted to leave after you found the oranges? I thought I saw him in the market, Sam. It was horrible."

There was a sad look on his face. I thought he was about to cry. He reached over and squeezed my shoulder.

"When a dear friend of mine died," he began quietly, "the shock of my loss didn't affect me for a long time, Michael. Then, some months later, I was fixing myself a little supper one evening and just started crying for no reason. I think something about the meal, about the smell and time of day, the way the sunset looked, just reminded me of him. I thought I'd forgotten by then. I thought I'd healed by then. It took a long time. Michael, I think that's happening to you. The more we love someone, the deeper the grief is. The longer it takes to come to the surface. I think yours is surfacing now. It's an unhappy visitor, I know, but you can't avoid it. It will always find you, no matter where you hide. You must bravely meet it. Welcome it. Everyone experiences sorrow in their own way. I can see you're tired, but keep praying for strength, and don't give up hope. What you're doing for the people of Saint Vincent's is important. This will help you get through. I know it will."

I spent the next hour listening to his suggestions that I set up a brisk new physical regimen to start each day and drink a tall glass of stout porter at night. He would tell Mrs. Silas to order several bottles in the morning. He rattled off other suggestions, dozens of them. He said he knew a man who could be trusted for his skills as a magnetist or that I might try pressing sliced lemons against my temples and the back of my neck before going to sleep. If the porter didn't work, he suggested milk mixed with hot castor oil before bed (no thank you) and taking a warm bath every night if it helped. He even offered—his generosity truly knew no bounds, what a good man—to exchange mattresses with me. His was a gift from his sister, who lived out in Lawton. It was a big downy slab stuffed with goose feathers, but he said it was too soft for him. It hurt his back, but he didn't have the heart to give it back and hurt her feelings. To this, and to all his offerings, I smiled and thanked him warmly but didn't agree to anything.

He finally lapsed into silence and watched me with his pale blue eyes. I think he understood he'd been talking too much. But it didn't last. He started up again, telling me more about the magnetist, assuring me of the fellow's skill—that he'd cured Brink's own sleeplessness, another priest's recurrent bouts of indigestion. . . that he'd even enabled one parish mother to deliver her baby without the slightest labor pains or discomfort.

"Not one jot!" he declared triumphantly. She even felt so sound in body, apparently, that she was up within a few hours of the delivery to cook dinner for her husband.

I told him the man's skills sounded very formidable, but it wasn't what I needed.

THE SOLUTION CAME TO ME a few nights later. I went to see Ivan Luzak again. I needed his help. Like my last visit to his shop, this one took place right at closing. Ivan wasn't alone this time, though; he was recording an order placed by a tall elderly gentleman. They were standing at the long counter near the back of the front room. Ivan's face brightened when he saw me, and he hurriedly finished up the order.

When we were alone and the shop doors were locked, he gave me a big, bearish embrace and asked if I was hungry. He wanted me to join him for supper.

"I'd be glad to dine with you," I told him, "but I also need your help, Ivan. There is something I want to do."

"Of course, Mikhaylo. Anything. You know you have it. What do you want?"

I looked into his eyes.

"I want to take the varta home."

NOT LONG BEFORE I visited Ivan, Mrs. Silas had prepared a special meal—she had no idea it was a farewell meal—in the hopes of lifting my spirits. It was truly splendid, and it did make me feel better. There was a roasted chicken on a pile of buttery green beans, boiled and rosemary-seasoned potatoes, biscuits big as top hats, and blood pudding, all washed down with the fine porter that was Sam's sole indulgence. It was far from the modest dishes we usually ate. It was more like something kept for Easter Sunday or Christmas Day.

"My goodness, Maud," Sam exclaimed, "why have you never cooked like this for me before?"

The old woman smiled.

"I would, Sam, but you've never been as nice to me as Michael," she said, smiling at me. "He's suffered through plenty of my stories in the morning, haven't you?" Then she turned to him. "When was the last time you ever sat there and listened to me, eh? "

Dinner wasn't the only high point of the evening. When I went to bed, I slept well for the first time in months. I awoke the next morning face down, and my pillow was wet with slobber. It was still very dark outside. I woke up earlier than I normally did, but I felt good. I felt rested. Clearheaded. The rectory was quiet, except for the gentle buzzing of Sam's breathing down the hall.

My window was open, and a cool breeze stirred the curtains. I heard the chirping of the little brown sparrows nesting in the eaves across the street. The chicory coffee vendor was whistling as he pulled the boards off the front of his stall at the corner. The city was waking up. It was that special time of morning when a city of millions can seem as deserted as an ancient ruin. I listened to the soft tread of someone under my window—a cleaning woman on her way home. She was humming. The bells of nearby Little Saint Hugh's started ringing. Soon ours would, too.

As I watched the sky lighten and spread its glow across my ceiling, I realized I had a plan. I knew what I needed to do. I wanted to leave and find Prehovinka. What had changed for me? A dream. I had another one that night, and it was different from all the rest.

THE DREAM HAD STARTED off in the usual way, with the darkness of a stage and the slow coalescing of the ghostly image of the ghoul upon it. But something unusual happened this time: the specter turned its head and looked off to one side as if it was listening to someone. Then its outline suddenly grew fuzzy and indistinct . . . so fuzzy and indistinct that it soon disappeared. Then I saw another shadow grow in its place. This one was different; it wasn't another human figure—it was smaller, short and thin, and I saw the outline of its rounded head and long, curling horns. It was the imp. It took the ghoul's place. I'd never dreamed of it before, not like this, and I welcomed it . . . but its appearance was short-lived. The imp suddenly vanished. I think it was there only to scare the other thing away.

Now the dream's darkness changed to the darkness of another time, another place. I saw my childhood bedroom, and it was one of those times when I'd suffered a very bad nightmare. Ugly monsters had been chasing me, their bodies shapeless, but I could see their sharp teeth and eyes flashing in the dark—and my father sat by my bed a long time to keep me company until I went back to sleep. In the gloom, I'd watched him pack a fresh pipe; in my dream, I could almost smell the pleasant odor of the tobacco again. He lit his pipe from a candle and then snuffed it out. The room plunged into darkness. Then he brought his smoky face close to mine and kissed my cheek, and I felt his hand close around mine on the coverlet. He gave it a gentle squeeze.

"Sleep, *malanky sin*," he whispered.

I touched his hard knuckles and felt the scars on his fingers and the fresh, new cuts he'd gotten the day before. They were like the routes of a private map of all the trials in his life. Beware the man whose hand feels too smooth in a handshake; his opinion of life's struggles means nothing. I don't remember when my father left me that night because he waited until I fell asleep.

When I woke in my bedroom at Saint Vincent's, one of my arms was hanging off the side of my bed. It was touching the imp. I forgot to mention that I had tried an experiment before I went to bed. Whenever I had the imp with me, the ghoulish specter stayed away. I decided to keep it by me while I slept and see what happened. I yawned and stretched, and then I brushed my fingers along its carved patterns and thought about the dream. I didn't care what it was made of; it protected me. I rubbed my eyes and listened to the birds outside.

Our church bells sounded. The imp needed to go home. I'd do this for my father. And for myself. I was sure someone there would know how to help me.

37

◇◇◇◇◇◇◇

Old letters

I TOLD WILLIAM ABOUT MY PLANS, and he didn't argue with me. He understood. In fact, he was very supportive.

He visited me at the rectory and brought some extra money for my trip. I told him it wasn't necessary, but he insisted. He said he'd gone to the chapel library and retrieved a few special books and sold them to one of his clients. Now that Gerard was gone, he wasn't sure what would happen to the chapel library. He said there was a good chance its contents, if the diocese decided to keep them, would be stored away or left for the rats and moths. He couldn't prevent that, but selling some books to help me had seemed sensible. He said it would have made sense to Gerard, too.

"Your company meant so much to him," he said. "He really appreciated you, Michael. I hope you know that."

Packing didn't take long for me; a priest doesn't carry much. I quickly filled up two canvas sacks. I planned to tell Sam and Mrs. Silas I had an ill relative who needed my help—and then write to them and apologize once I was on my way. One of the sacks contained my clothes and an extra pair of boots, the other my father's carving tools, Klein's book, and a few others.

I asked William to tell me about Gerard's funeral.

"I'm sorry you couldn't be there."

"Was it nice?"

He nodded sadly.

"It's a lovely place. There's a large statue of the Blessed Mother in the center of the churchyard. A good view of the dolmen, too. I couldn't imagine a better place for him."

"I'm glad. I wish I could have been there."

He smiled. Then he reached into his pocket for something.

"This is for you. It's something I know Gerard would have wanted you to have."

He held his fist out and let a string dangle from it. It was beaded with tiny pearls. It was Gerard's rosary. The larger Pater beads were each shaped like a skull. It was beautiful, and Gerard was rarely without it. I thought this would have gone into the coffin with him, but William said the townsfolk had put plenty of other things in there already—crucifixes, flowers, bottles of holy water, bottles of whiskey, even cigars.

"It was getting crowded," he said with a sad smile. He handed the rosary to me. "I have some other news for you, too, if you have time. Something you might find surprising. Or maybe you won't. It's about that fraud, Lumens."

It wasn't about her but about her little assistant. William said he saw Wallace inside the Promenade of Wonders. He wasn't a spectator; he was doing card tricks on a table next to several performers. William said his card pile seemed taller than a normal deck should be. No one seemed to notice; they were too enchanted by the quick movements of his hands and his deft ability to retrieve whatever card his audience requested. When he saw William, he interrupted his performance and disappeared behind the stage. William went to look for him but couldn't find him. He said the cards reminded him of the stack of blank sheets on Wallace's table during the Ariel ritual. He shook his head.

"I should have known," he said bitterly. "I was such a fool."

"We all were, William."

IT WAS RAINING and thundering the day I left London. I decided to cross the channel to Ghent. It was Ivan who suggested Ghent, not somewhere else along the coast. I spent most of the ferry ride at the rails, vomiting into the blue-green swells. When the vomiting stopped, I kept hic-

50

cupping. My bags were at my side. So was the imp—I had him wrapped up like an old baba. I felt safe with him. Thanks to him I hadn't seen the ghoul in several days. The ferry lurched suddenly, and I realized my stomach wasn't as empty as I thought.

At Ghent, after disembarking, it wasn't difficult to arrange for a train east. I had plenty of money and good advice from William—along with a passport and other travel papers that he and Ivan helped me with. There were several ordinary and express trains steaming on the platforms in the station. When I think of my departure, I remember that I wasn't scared, even though I probably should have been. I had so much to worry about—what the diocese would do when they discovered I'd run away, whether or not I'd find my father's village, and if anyone there could help me. I temporarily forgot those things as I read the signs posted in the station's main waiting area:

BERLIN/VIENNA —> WARSAW —> SAINT PETERSBURG —> MOSCOW

From Ghent I went to Berlin, which William advised, and then took a train to Warsaw before taking another one down toward the Crimea—a route similar to the one that the English traveler, Fielding, was taking when I met him. My final stop was Stanislau. The express train from Berlin to Warsaw took just two days. Two days: I marveled at the speed of it. The fare for a first-class ticket was fourteen pounds. I didn't hesitate to pay it; I had no idea if I would ever ride on another train again. The carriage was upholstered and comfortable—steam-heated, too.

The porters tried to get me to stow the bundled-up imp with my bags, but I refused. I kept him at my side. For most of the trip, I dozed against him and watched the countryside. I also wrote two letters—one to William and the other to Sam. I posted them in Warsaw and told William I'd write again as soon as I was settled in Prehovinka. I didn't give any of this information to Sam, though—the less he knew, the better.

I also read some old letters.

Nessie had bundled up all those notes the parishioners had sent me when I was sick, and I decided to read them now. I'm glad I had them. I had told Nessie that I didn't want them and that she should use them in the kitchen as kindling. But she ignored me and said I might like to read them one day.

"Even if they're about something that has nothing to do with you anymore," she'd said, "it's still nice to remember what people thought about you. I still sometimes look at old letters from my mum when I'm blue."

As the train moved farther east across the Polish plains, I realized she had been right.

Mixed in with the parishioners' thoughtful notes were other things. I found an invitation to speak to some Swedenborgians in Lambeth about the differences between heaven and hell, as well as a request from the *Telegraph* to pen an article based on a sermon of my choice. These were wonderful discoveries. I would have loved to write an article and speak to that group. But that part of my life was over.

I found an even greater surprise among the notes—a letter from Kitty. I checked the stamp and realized it had been sent right after Antonia's attack. I read it with shaking hands. I regretted never getting a chance to answer the letter, but by the end of it, I realized it didn't require one. It wasn't written in that way. When I was finished, I crumpled it up and threw it on the compartment floor—and then picked it up again when another passenger came in and sat down.

THE CLOSER I MOVED to the end of my journey, the less I worried about the apparition and the more I worried about customs. What if my papers weren't in order? What if I was forced to go back? What if I was somehow too conspicuous and someone reported me to the diocese? What if I couldn't answer all their questions when I was ready to disembark at Stanislau and leave the station? I had heard stories. The Russians sounded especially terrible; anyone coming across their frontier was subjected to heavy scrutiny, and if papers weren't in order right down to the letter, the traveler could be sent back where they came from, often in the train by which they came. What if it was the same in Galicia? What if the authorities there were just as inflexible?

Late one afternoon, my train pulled into Stanislau, and I disembarked. The setting sun filled the platform with golden light, making it hard to see. I knew my father's village couldn't be far. I stepped off the train and smelled the rich, moist smell of Ruthenian earth. It was overpowering. In some way it was familiar, too. My heart pounded, and I hugged the imp tightly. I was so nervous. My entire trip led me to this moment. I don't exactly remember what I prayed for, but I know I prayed for something good to happen. The wait in line next to the customs office was unbearable. There weren't many people on the train, and I couldn't understand why it was taking so long. When it was finally my turn, I nervously stepped forward into the office and saw why. It was an incredible relief, and an anticlimax, to all the anxiety and anticipation I felt when a lone customs official, tired-looking and bored, yawned and stamped my passport. He didn't bother to give the passport, or me, a second look. He handed it back and waved me on. Our train was the last one before his shift was over. He was eager to go home.

I followed a party of bearded and spectacled rabbis out of the station. The official never asked me where I was going; he never examined my passport long enough to register my name or destination. He didn't mark down anything in his ledger, as far as I could tell. No one knew I was here. Westminster wouldn't find me—if they *wanted* to find me. It's funny that Eugenie still worries about that. I've never worried. When I left that station, I knew I was free. My shoulders relaxed, and my back straightened; I hadn't realized I was walking like a hunchback until then. Or like a dog expecting to be kicked. I parted from the rabbis, turned a corner, and heard a loud commotion up ahead. It was coming from the square. I saw a huge crowd of farmers.

I'd arrived just in time to see them packing up their carts and wagons and preparing to go home. Some were from Kalush, others from Drohobych and Striy and smaller villages. I walked among them, and all I could think to do was say the word *Prehovinka* loudly, hoping someone would recognize it. No one did. No one seemed to notice or care. I was sure they were too tired from the long day to be curious about me. But just as I was resigning myself to finding a hotel for the night, one of the farmers came up and smiled. He nodded his head. He showed me his cart and wanted me to get into the back. "Prehovinka," he said. "Prehovinka."

A quarter of an hour later, we were on the road to the village. I was resting in the back against a large sack of potatoes he hadn't sold.

38

◇◇◇◇◇◇◇

A new life

MY EARLY DAYS IN PREHOVINKA amounted to a series of firsts. My inventory of memories about that time goes something like this:

First time I stepped in a steaming pile left by some farm animal
First stumble into the hole dug for potatoes on the side of the yard
First piece of bad sausage
First blisters
First harvest
First bewildering conversation with a farmer
First time I saw Eugenie

After I arrived, I stayed with Natalka for several months. I had to; she could tell something was wrong with me right away. She said she saw a haze around me; it reminded her of the way smoke sometimes clung to her father when he was finished smoking his pipe. She said something had followed me to the village. I didn't know the language and couldn't explain very much, but I was relieved that she seemed to understand.

When she looked at the imp, the cunning woman seemed very impressed. She patted it and smiled and said something that probably meant she thought my father had done an excellent job. And she realized it was helping me. She also surprised me with some English. Not much, but a few words that said she would find something better for me than the imp. She said I didn't want to spend my life carrying the imp around.

It took time to figure out what this something better was supposed to be, and it happened, as the best solutions often do, by accident. We were eating dinner one night in her kitchen, and she was asking me about my father and London. She said she was a child when Volodymyr Moroz lost the varta and left the village with Ivan. She vaguely remembered him.

"My mother was doing what I do now," she said. Her mother had figured out what to do after the varta disappeared. The village had been in crisis, and she ordered the planting of more wormwood and garlic everywhere.

I told Natalka the loss of the varta didn't just affect Prehovinka; it created a crisis in my father's life, too. He was haunted by melancholy and guilt the rest of his life. She said it was understandable. When you're a part of a community like Prehovinka's, she explained, every life feels connected to you. But I told her it wasn't that; it wasn't just the creation of the imp that showed me how guilty he'd felt. It may have been an obvious sign, but it wasn't the only thing he did. I told her he'd changed his name. She looked up from her soup.

"What do you mean changed his name?"

I explained the best I could how, when he met my mother, my father translated Volodymyr Moroz into "Walter Frost," even though many Slavic immigrants didn't do that. I said I thought my father did it because he was disappointed in himself and the damage he'd caused. He didn't like the person he'd been. He wanted to forget that man.

"I think he changed it to draw a line between what he was before and after. I might be wrong, but that's what I think."

I looked over at Natalka. She didn't say anything. She just stared down at her soup.

A few days later, she came into the den and announced that I was going to be baptized.

"What? But I'm baptized already."

She frowned.

"Fine. Don't listen to me, then. You can just keep living in my house with the varta. You can keep him by your bed, too. I'm sure your future wife, if you ever get one, will love that."

I told her I meant no disrespect. I was only curious how she'd determined that a baptism was the solution. It didn't make sense; it didn't seem necessary. She answered me the way many spiritual teachers do: with a riddle.

"What if Michael Frost no longer exists?"

SOON I WAS STANDING in a large steel bucket—it was used during the week for milking—and Father Roman was pouring river water over my head. I knew I didn't need this ritual to join the Uniate Church. Catholics haven't needed it since 1596. But I wasn't going to risk offending Natalka again; she insisted that it would release me from my past. Most important of all, she explained, I'd take a new name, and the old one, and my old self, would no longer exist. That person would vanish.

"Like what your father did," she said.

I think I've said before that names are meaningful here. They're powerful symbols. I thought back to what I'd learned from Gerard and William. Angels and demons are creatures of pure intellect. Symbols appeal to their essential natures. The way Natalka explained it, the baptism ceremony would take care of that. My old name and identity shone like a beacon that the demon had followed all the way to Galicia. But when Roman splashed water on my neck and shoulders, she said, that beacon went out. I became someone else. The demon lost me in the dark. Natalka didn't give me any larger metaphysical explanations the way Gerard and William might have. She kept it simple. By then, I knew not to ask for more. I didn't need a greater explanation: I could tell the baptism worked the moment it happened. I felt a change in me. It's hard to describe, but I know it wasn't just the shock of the cold water. A weight seemed to lift off my shoulders and chest. Everything felt brighter around me. Lighter. I felt happier, too. I cried with joy, and my tears mixed with the water streaming down my cheeks.

Natalka studied me carefully after I climbed out of the bucket. She told me to go outside and stand in the sunlight. She told me not to bring the imp. Then she stood back and squinted at me. She seemed satisfied.

"The haze is gone. You're good now, *Yuri.*"

She was the first person to use my new name.

When I was born, my parents chose to name me after the fiercest of the Lord's archangels. I kept a prayer card on my bedside table for many years that showed him with a spear, in his flashing golden chest armor, stuffing an ugly green reptile into a crack in the earth. My mother said the card would help me to keep away bad dreams.

But Saint Michael's not the only armored demon fighter. My first home's patron was a slayer of dragons, too. Saint George. Yuri. Natalka was the one who suggested it for me. It's a good name.

39

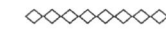

Kindling

6:00 a.m.

"YURI, YOU SHOULD GO."

I open my eyes and look up at Natalka's brown face. There's a faint light coming in through the windows behind her. I don't know when I fell asleep. The last thing I remember, I was sipping tea and asking her if she wanted my sons to come and help her with the fields next time. The Melnyk boys don't do a good job.

At the sound of her voice, I rise from my chair and get my coat. I grab the imp and pat Peter on the head one last time before going outside with her. The Melnyks are already here. They're in the barn with the wagon. When they see me and the imp, they wave. I walk up to Vasyl, the oldest.

"Morning, Deacon."

"Morning, Vasyl."

The morning's wet and cold, but the sky's clear. The storm's gone. It's probably over Krakow by now. I'm finally glad to be wearing my coat. The ground under my boots is soft and mushy, like fresh clay before it's been thrown. The rain not only softened the mud but also smoothed it out. The road before me looks as clean and blank as a painter's canvas. It's scored all over with animal tracks—the lizards and mice living in Natalka's yard, and other things. I see the tracks of a fox or maybe a stray dog. She walks me up to her gate. I think about home and feel a pang of fear.

"You should have woken me sooner, Natalka. I still don't know what to tell Eugenie. I wasted time sleeping."

"But you looked so peaceful. I figured you needed it."

"What I need is what I'm going to tell her. My whole story, my whole life in England—it's too much. She doesn't need to hear all of it."

She smirks.

"Is it even necessary? I told you she needs a gesture. Something that makes sense to her. Not an old story."

THE SKY IS IMMACULATELY CLEAR and blushes pink in the east. My heart feels light—light as it did after my baptism. I still remember leaving the church afterwards and walking around. Everything looked so new; everything fascinated me—the swirls of dust in the lanes, the thin curls of smoke from chimneys, the smells of the garlic and wormwood, the storks in their nests on the roofs . . . everything. The world seemed new to me because it was new. I was like a child. I had been given my second chance. The man guilty of so much was gone. His sins were gone. Washed away. The faces of Lionel, Kitty, Gabriel, and Antonia Cox faded as the Zimn's water dried on my face and neck. So did the grotesque apparition. I never saw it again.

On my way home, I had stopped at the tavern to toast my new life with the burning taste of horilka. After having more than a taste, I staggered down the lane to my own house, the one I live in now. I didn't need to stay with Natalka anymore. I enjoyed living with her, but I wanted to live in my father's house—and I wasn't alone. I lived with Stefan, an old bachelor cousin who'd been its sole occupant for years. We got along. He didn't mind me; I didn't mind him. He might have been the child of those greedy relatives who'd frustrated my father so much, but I didn't resent him for it. He was very kind to me.

When Eugenie and I married, Stefan welcomed her into our house, and in the years after, he welcomed the arrivals of our two sons with the joy of a grandfather. Stefan was a good man. After a hard day, all he needed was supper and a pipe to make him happy. Or his violin. I'd watch him go out in our back garden and get fresh sap from one of the pine trees for his bow. He played for us all the time; he played for us until the day before he died. I can still see him, bobbing from side to side, playing the same Viennese waltzes every Saturday night. He was gifted with his hands, too. Like my father.

AT THE CROSSING, I sign myself as I pass the crucifix in its little shelter made from the remnants of an old birdhouse. My yard's just up ahead.

I hear the distant tinkling of chains and turn to look. Wagons are already moving out into the far fields. Some of the corn will be picked today despite the rain. If it isn't, the crows will soon start helping themselves. The sight of the wagons makes my chest hurt. Old words come back to me without any prompting, any effort. *Salve fatis mihi ...* the words of Aeneas, newly arrived in Italy. *A blessing on this earth that was destined for me.* He brought Troy's household gods with him and made a new home. I did, too.

I WATCH THE WAGONS fade into the distance as the rising sun grows brighter. Its light fills my eyes. This land, this wonderful, beautiful land. It's eternal. Nothing will ever change it. It will be the same a year from now. Five years from now. Ten years. The dream we have of a country of our own, of Ruthenia, can't be far away. It's coming. I can feel it.

I have everything I want here. I have no ambitions anymore. I haven't in a long time. All I want is to work and sweat in the fields. Plant and harvest. Eat dumplings with the grandkids. Pay what the Minkins tell us to pay. Watch and wait. Harvest and plant again. Get old with my wife. If God permits it, see our great-grandchildren. It would make me happy to see three generations of Morozes in front of me. That's all. That's what I want Eugenie to understand. I see life the way she does. I'm not interested in complicated reasons anymore. I've had enough of them.

The morning breeze touches my face. I sneeze and think nothing of it. But then I sneeze again and can't stop. My throat hurts. The night's walk did this—getting soaked by the storm didn't help.

My boys will be out in the fields soon. So will the Minkins. I wonder if Bram will treat me any differently the next time he sees me. I hope he accepts my offer.

On any other morning, I'd be out there, but not today. My feet hurt, and I'm tired. I'm thinking of my bed. At the yard of our neighbors, the

Stefanchuks, I walk up to the house and put the imp by their door. I set it down gently. I don't drop it the way Sturanka did. *It's your turn tonight, Taras.* I look at the imp. *Thank you, old friend. I know we'll see each other again. Many more times, I hope.* I pat his cheek.

I turn again at the front gateposts and look back at him, grinning on the porch. Thank you—this time the words are for my father.

In our yard, I find my sons. They're preparing for another day in the fields. Walter is tightening the handle of his serp, a small scythe that can be held in one hand. Alex holds a harness for the horses. "Morning, sons," I say as we pass each other.

"Night, Father," they say.

I turn and slowly raise my hand.

"Boys, listen," I say. I can feel tears in my eyes. "I want you to know how much you mean to me."

They both look surprised. I don't try to explain. I just smile at them, and they smile back before disappearing into the barn again. I'm sure they'll talk about me later when they're in the fields.

Inside the house, I find Eugenie and my daughters-in-law in the kitchen, feeding the grandchildren. The children have finished their plates and turn to me with the glazed looks that accompany a full belly.

"Hello, my young Argonauts!" I say in English, and they grin even though they haven't the foggiest idea what the old man is saying. Helena and Irena greet me with respectful daughterly pecks on the cheek. Eugenie ladles some kasha into a bowl for me.

"How was the walk?" she says. She seems better than she was last night. "Was it good? Did you find what you needed?"

"I did," I say. I smile at her. "I did find some words. For you. The most important ones are I'm sorry . . . and I love you."

Eugenie's cheeks flush as she holds out the bowl. I take it and set it down. I'm not hungry. I take one of her hands.

"It was a good walk. I want to tell you all about it, but I need some sleep first." I'm stalling because I still don't know what to say. I pull her close and hug her before she can push me away. The grandchildren start laughing. She's annoyed, but there's a faint smile in her eyes now. Thank goodness.

"That's enough, crazy man," she says as I'm leaving the kitchen. I start to sneeze. "Look at you! Sick! I told you that you had no business out there. No more walks for you! The boys can do it! I'm going to make some tea. Helena, get me some hot water."

Helena turns to the stove. She frowns. She says the fire's gone out. Eugenie looks at me.

"Give us a moment and I'll have it ready for you. Go and undress."

I go into the den instead. I've thought of something.

From the mantel, I take down Lawrence Klein's book about Dante. There's a sheet of folded-up paper in it. I didn't take it with me last night. I didn't want to risk ruining it. I've kept it all these years like it's some kind of holy relic. It's far from that. The paper is heavily wrinkled from once being crumpled in a ball. No amount of smoothing has ever taken the wrinkles away.

Dear Michael:

I wonder what would have happened if we had met in Hammersmith when you were in the seminary. I had an aunt there I liked, and I visited her on school holidays. I remember seeing all the young seminarians on my visits. Dressed in black. So serious. Now I wonder if I ever saw you among them. I have racked my memories and tried to find you in them, but I never paid enough attention then. I had been told not to—that all the seminarians were different, not like the rest of us poor mortals. I wish I hadn't listened. I wish I could make those memories clear.

I've known other people for a long time and never felt as safe with them as I have with you. You have had a profound effect on me and my family. I'm grateful for what you did for me, what you gave me, and I suspect I should be grateful to Mr. Klein, too. I did what was necessary. I am certain Dante's wife would understand.

I didn't know what I was going to do when I went to see that woman. What had to be done, I realize now, is what God wanted me to do. I put everything in his hands. You once said in Lionel's study that we're all powerless before God. I thought I understood that lesson, but I didn't truly understand until I met you. You helped me, Michael—you made me see that everything happens because of God's will. Knowing that has given me peace.

I don't know if I will ever see you again. I can't put any trust in the future anymore, so I wanted to write to you now. There's so much more I want to say, but it would take too long. It probably doesn't matter.

I'm not sorry for what happened on our last evening together. I know it didn't end as you wanted, but it was still important to me. I want you to know that. I will never forget you.

I go back into the kitchen with the letter. The women are still crouching around the stove. They seem to be having trouble. Helena says the kindling is too damp. Somehow, it's gotten wet from last night's rain. I hand everything that was in my coat to Eugenie—the newspaper clipping, Gabriel and Lionel's letters, my old sermon notes . . . and Kitty's letter.

"Here," I say. "Try these."

I used to especially cherish Kitty's letter because of the tenderness I thought was in it. But now I only hear my words being used against me. Her unwillingness to accept blame. "What had to be done" is such a dishonest way to dance around the truth of what she did. I don't need this letter anymore. I don't want it. I don't want any of it.

Eugenie examines the papers.

"We're fine, Yuri. We should have enough kindling that's dry." She looks at Helena, who nods. "Besides, why would you give me these? Aren't these your old English papers? And this one?" She holds up Kitty's letter. "It looks important."

"They were all important to me. Not now, *diwchata*. I don't care about them. Or London. Please. Take them."

She doesn't argue. She shrugs and hands them to Helena, who quickly rips them up and stuffs them under several pieces of wood. She relights the fire, and it works this time. Then Eugenie turns to me.

"You haven't undressed yet. Go and undress and get in bed." She touches my wrist. "I'll bring you your tea soon."

I don't leave the kitchen right away.

"You wanted to know about my past. You've been worried about it. You shouldn't be. I did some terrible things, *diwchata*. I've been afraid to tell you. I know you want to know about that life, but it's hard for me to talk about it. It's not who I am anymore. I want you to believe me when I say there is no better life for me than what I have. With you. I spent all night thinking about it. I'm still unsure what I can say to convince you."

She smiles.

"Yuri, you already have." She looks at the stove. A bright orange flame is peeking through the iron grate. "I don't want to know anything. You don't have to tell me. If it doesn't matter to you anymore, it doesn't matter to me."

"I don't want you to have bad dreams anymore."

"I won't. Just go and change. Go to bed. Rest. Later you can tell me about the walk. Was everything OK?"

"It was. There were some things——" I recall the terrifying incident at Rudy's. "About your dream—you won't believe what happened."

IN OUR BEDROOM, I change into my nightshirt. The bed feels nice and soft as I climb in and pull the quilt over me. I've brought Lawrence's book with me, and I don't know why. I'm too tired to read. Or wait for Eugenie to bring my tea. I've hardly closed the book and put it aside before I'm drifting asleep. I cough and move over until I find the spot, still warm, where Eugenie slept last night.

I don't nod off right away. I lie there, listening to the sounds of the house. The women are talking now, laughing. I think the girls are teasing Eugenie about me, about what just happened. I hear her shoo the grandchildren out into the yard. The dogs bark and follow them, then rush past them, chasing each other through the clouds of dill closest to the house. I close my eyes. In my mind, I follow them past the summer kitchen and outhouse and back to the end of the property, way back—my little yard would make a cricket field seem small—to a streamlet, an offshoot of the Zimn, churning after last night's storm. I hear the faint voices of farmers talking in the fields beyond the stream. The jangling of the harnesses on their horses. The air is full of the bittersweet fragrance of wormwood and the honeyed scent of buckwheat and clover.

In my mind, I see the elderberry bushes, squatting at the forest's edge, with more fern flowers blooming under them. I must tell Justina about them. The count is probably going to need more than what Natalka has now. In the river, I see a head and shoulders bobbing in the current, long brown hair spreading out like seaweed, and then the figure turns and kicks under the surface.

Mist is rising from the forest floor like steam now. I follow the droplets of water as they fall from the trees and sink into the ground, seeping down to the powdered remains of ancient Slavic tribesmen, mingling with the roots of towering trees. A vast silence, disturbed only by the wind and the sounds of the farmers, hangs over the land. Solemn. Eternal. *Mine.* When I think of London, what do I feel now? What should I feel? Regret? I did. But I feel gratitude now. For what came of it. For what led me here. To this life. The ones I love most.

This, I think, is what Gabriel hoped I'd find.

Author's Note

THE UKRAINIAN VILLAGE and customs in this story are drawn from the experiences of my father, who grew up in a Galician village in the 1920s and 1930s. Though this story is a work of fiction, the night walk and the strange totem described in it are real. I'm sure the story contains some discrepancies or anachronisms that a scholar of Ukrainian history might point out, and that's fine. My goal here is to honor my father's memory and the many tales he told me.

For more about this proud people, whose identity and sovereignty are once again under assault, I recommend starting with the works of Anne Applebaum, Norman Davies, Robert Magocsi, Anna Reid, and Orest Subtelny, among many others.

Slava Ukraini.

Acknowledgements

THIS BOOK has gone through so many changes over the years (am I really done?), and many people have encouraged and helped me along the way.

I want to express my heartfelt thanks to Julie Ricks McClintic for believing in this story and wanting to share it with readers. Over the years Nicholas Delbanco has offered his mentorship, patience, and encouragement to me, and I'm grateful for this generosity.

I'm also grateful for the people who have generously provided guidance in various ways, including: Robin Blakely, Robert Bradford, Carmela Ciuraru, Jon Fasman, Andrew Frisardi, Philippa Gregory, Avedis Hadjian, Tom Johnson, David Kessler, Ross King, Maggie Kitch, Yi Shun Lai, Ellen Levine, Kai Maristed, Thane Rosenbaum, Jay Toffoli, Robert Weil, Zach Weismann, Richard Zimler, and my friends on Medium and WordPress.

Ezra Pound provided a gloss of the poetry of Propertius in Chapter 12 (thanks, Ez); a quote about the occult in Chapter 20 comes from *The Black Arts* by Richard Cavendish; a terrific resource for all things Victorian is victorianlondon.org, which was created by Lee Jackson.

Finally, I thank my sons Alex and Aidan for tolerating and supporting this work through many years (thanks bwuh-bwows), and my amazing bae, Coco, for her wisdom, love, guidance, fearlessness, energy, and joy (this list could easily go on for several pages). She has always reminded me—especially during life's harder moments—to never stop believing in myself.

RUBY VIOLET
PUBLISHERS

Learn More About
Ruby Violet Publishing
www.rubyviolet-publishers.com

Made in the USA
Monee, IL
01 February 2025

10469498R00163